The Whitstable Pearl Mystery

Julie Wassmer

Constable • London

CONSTABLE

First published in Great Britain in 2015 by Constable

This edition published in 2015 by Constable

A CIP catalogue record for this book is available from the British Library.

ISBN: 978-1-4721-1899-8

Typeset in Adobe Caslon Pro by SX Composing DTP, Rayleigh, Essex

Printed and bound in Great Britain by CPI Group (UK) Ltd, Croydon, CR0 4YY

Papers used by Constable are from well-managed forests and
other responsible sources

Constable
An imprint of
Little, Brown Book Group
Carmelite House
50 Victoria Embankment
London EC4Y 0DZ

An Hachette UK Company
www.hachette.co.uk

www.littlebrown.co.uk

Julie Wassmer is a professional television drama writer, working on various series including ITV's *London's Burning*, C5's *Family Affairs* and BBC's ....rked on for 20 years.

Her aut......... .... *dence*, was Mumsnet Book of the ......

For oyster fisherman Andy Riches
and Whitstable

'The poor Britons. There is some good
in them after all. They produce an oyster.'
Gaius Sallust to Julius Caesar 55bc

Chapter One

Pearl Nolan set an iced platter of Pacific rock oysters before a trio of bemused faces and wiped her wet hands on her apron. Her customers were a family, the parents in their late thirties, like Pearl herself, though she hoped she didn't look so defeated. The stroppy teenage daughter might have had something to do with that: the girl's skimpy top and nose piercing serving as clear acts of protest against a safe holiday away with Mum and Dad.

After only a few words Pearl had correctly placed their Gateshead accents, but had her customers remained silent she would still have known they were home-grown – the British had none of the brash confidence of the American tourists nor the cool sophistication of the French. The Germans and Scandinavians seemed to be always in a hurry. Either hiking or cycling, they usually ate on the hoof. But the Brits generally formed an altogether more insecure group, huddling together to investigate menus from the safety of the pavement before following the braver holidaymaker into 'The Whitstable Pearl' to sample Whitstable's most famous delicacy – the oyster. The Gateshead family, however, remained firmly unimpressed, staring down at their bivalves with a stunned distaste until the daughter offered a view with which even her own parents might agree. 'They look like snot.'

As the parents recoiled with embarrassment, Pearl sympathised: she was struggling lately to accept that her own child was finally growing up and away from her but at least Charlie was past all that adolescent rebellion. She moved closer to the table, about to point out the usual accompaniments – the lemon wedges and mignonette sauce which always served to make 'snot' more palatable – when a voice suddenly rang out behind her. 'She has a point.'

Heads turned to see Dolly approaching from the kitchen. Wearing a waxed apron emblazoned with a colourful Leaning Tower of Pisa, Pearl's mother glided across before pausing, oyster shell in hand, as though for dramatic effect. 'But then looks can be deceiving.' With a deft flick of the wrist, she tipped the shell's contents into her mouth, gave a sudden wet crunch and swallowed. 'Dee-licious.'

The family looked on, jaws dropping open, enthralled, or perhaps vaguely horrified by what they'd just witnessed, while Pearl recognised it was time to cut short her mother's performance. 'Enjoy,' she smiled, before steering Dolly, with a firm hold, towards the kitchen.

Looking back from the doorway, both women watched as 'Dad' summoned sufficient resolve to select a 'Pacific' from the platter. He downed it and Dolly struggled for saliva, admitting,

'God, how I hate oysters,' to which Pearl offered her usual reply: 'Don't I know it.'

A ring tone sounded a soulless 'Für Elise' and summoned Pearl to the kitchen. There, she searched for her mobile beneath cloth bags containing fresh shrimp and mussels while Dolly entered behind her, glancing down at the stack of prawn sandwiches she had just prepared, feeling confident she was able to resist them. Thanks to a liquid-only diet, Dolly now weighed the same as her daughter – nine stone and thirteen pounds precisely – though it had taken a month of sickening milkshakes to get her there. Turning sixty years of age might have proved a terrifying event if she hadn't used the opportunity to take herself in hand, celebrating her triumph over mortality with a bold set of magenta highlights and some newfangled corsetry in the form of high-waist Spandex knickers, which kept stray flesh miraculously in check.

Watching Pearl giving full attention to her mobile phone Dolly considered, not for the first time, how little she herself resembled her only child. Pearl was standing near the window, a shaft of summer sun falling upon her like a spotlight, emphasising the contrast between the lilac vintage dress she wore and her suntanned face and limbs. On most days she tied up her long dark hair and seldom wore jewellery, certainly no rings on her fingers that could become lost in restaurant dishes during their preparation; only a small silver locket lay flat against her bare throat. The restaurant was often used as an excuse for Pearl's simple style but Dolly sensed that her daughter's modest wardrobe of clothes – bought, for the most part, for comfort and practicality – represented a personal rejection of Dolly's own flamboyance.

The truth lay somewhere in between, since Pearl looked striking whatever she wore and whatever she did to herself. With gypsy-black hair and grey eyes the colour of moonstone, some said she had the look of the 'black Irish' – descendants of the Spanish Armada sailors who had escaped death on the beaches of the west coast of Ireland to serve under rebel chiefs such as Sorley Boy MacDonnell and Hugh O'Neill, Earl of Tyrone. Although Dolly was from Whitstable stock her late husband, Tommy, always a rebel at heart, had been able to trace his own roots back to Galway. Certainly Pearl had inherited her mother's spirit and her father's dark good looks. Being tall and willowy, it was clear she wouldn't be needing miracle knickers herself any time soon.

'No, the agency's open,' Pearl was explaining on her mobile. 'I just had to step out for a moment.' She checked her watch and slipped off her apron. 'Give me two minutes and I'll be right there.' Ending the call, she saw Dolly's raised eyebrows and said, 'Looks like I finally have a customer.'

'Don't you mean client?' queried Dolly. 'Your "customers" get seafood . . .'

'Yes – served by my favourite waitress.' Pearl gave a smile as she picked up a canvas shoulder bag but Dolly's face instantly set.

'Oh no, you don't,' she objected.

'I'll be as quick as I can.' Pearl moved swiftly to the door, where she dropped her mobile into her bag.

'But it's my day off,' hissed Dolly. 'I only agreed to make some sandwiches.'

'And no one makes them quite like you.'

Pearl's charming smile remained in place as she selected a triangle from the plate and took a bite. Dolly's face softened with anticipation. Unlike her daughter, she had always been a sloppy cook with the sort of disregard for ingredients that had once allowed her to substitute peanuts on a *truite aux amandes*. Now as she watched Pearl savouring the slightly tart lemon mayonnaise surrounding a layer of fresh prawn, she waited for more approval – but it failed to come.

Pearl took advantage of the moment to escape from the kitchen back into the restaurant and Dolly pursued her, protesting, 'But I've got the window to dress for the festival and a changeover at the B & B.'

'I know – but I'll be back, I promise. Until then, just remember . . .' she plucked an oyster from the counter and pressed it into her mother's hand . . . 'dee-licious.'

Three strides later and Pearl was gone. Dolly, mouth agape, watched the restaurant doors swing shut. After a moment they opened again, but this time she saw only tourists wearing hiking shorts, backpacks and red faces. She glanced down at the pale mucus nestled in the shell in her hand and, as if on cue, switched on her famous smile.

The heat hit Pearl as soon as she set foot in the street, reminding her of the last time she'd stepped off a holiday flight, although she hadn't done that for some time. Living in Whitstable with its pebbled beach, harbour and varied demographic of locals and newcomers always made Pearl question the point of paying for a summer break elsewhere. A few years ago, she'd splashed out on a package to Sorrento, where it had stormed virtually every day for a fortnight. Having found herself irresistible bait to mosquitoes she'd returned, pockmarked, and with a stinking cold, to hear that the weather on the North Kent coast had been perfect.

Since then, she'd stayed put, not least because she didn't like leaving the business in summer, especially to Dolly whose attitude to work had always been decidedly hippy. Taking off when the season was nearly over usually meant tipping up somewhere in Europe just as other restaurateurs wanted nothing more than to get away on their own annual breaks – in Whitstable. The quirky little fishing town had become not only increasingly popular, but more cosmopolitan than it had ever been, and 'The Whitstable Pearl' was taking full advantage of it – together with the recessionary 'staycation'.

After years of struggling to survive, Whitstable now benefited from an almost year-long season, with visitors arriving in February, braving even the coldest winter in thirty years to spend Valentine's breaks in one of the town's numerous B & Bs. Dolly's Attic was a favourite, a Bohemian little flatlet situated above the shop, Dolly's Pots, from which Pearl's mother sold her 'shabby chic' ceramics. For years Pearl had served oysters from Dolly's distinctive plates, but now they too were being snapped up by tourists as fast as the oysters themselves.

Whitstable, along with most of its business people, was thriving, but its newfound popularity had come at a price, because the nature of the town was changing. On most summer days, Pearl found herself pushing against a tide of tourists heading towards the gift and coffee shops in Harbour Street, and today was no exception. The sightseers always had time on their hands; they gawped and dawdled, ambling in and out of the many new boutiques and art galleries while the locals moved at an altogether brisker tempo, negotiating kids and shopping while weaving an efficient slalom route around the tourists who, today, seemed to be mostly DFLs

– the town's acronym for 'Down From Londoners'. Pearl gave up fighting against the flow and peeled off instead towards Squeeze Gut Alley.

Tourists rarely used the network of ancient alleyways, most of which had been constructed to create access to the town's main business place – the sea. A few centuries ago, these alleys had also formed escape routes for smugglers, but now locals simply relied on them to cut short their journeys around town. Squeeze Gut, as the name suggested, sliced a quick and narrow route through to a row of dwellings on a stretch of road known as Island Wall. With quaint, unpretentious clapboard facades, the charm of each seaside cottage could be found at the rear where gardens lay separated from the beach by just a low sea wall and a concrete promenade. Here, on the 'prom', all of Whitstable came to saunter and swagger, drawn to a sea view of such clear Northern light that its skies and sunsets had been described by the painter Turner as 'some of the loveliest in Europe.'

As Pearl hurried along, a bunch of noisy French teenagers scattered on the prom, offering her a view of the man standing outside her own cottage. Short, stout and suited, he was also clearly hot and bothered, fanning a panama hat before his face with one hand, while patting a sweating brow with the other. As Pearl grew nearer, she could hear him panting like an old dog.

'Mr Stroud?'

At the sound of her voice, the man instantly turned. From a distance he had seemed to be well into middle age but his heavy frame was ageing, and as Pearl drew closer she decided that his fortieth birthday wasn't too far behind him. He said nothing but merely offered a clammy hand which made Pearl instantly think of starfish. She opened a wooden gate to the garden of Seaspray Cottage and led the way to the small shed she now called an office. Once upon a time it had been a beach hut, but with a new extension and a few more windows added, she was sure it would now serve its new purpose.

As she fiddled with a stiff lock, Pearl could tell that Stroud, behind her, was becoming impatient, his damp little fingers tapping nervously against the doorframe. Finally, the door opened.

Pearl pointed to a wooden chair and instantly wished she owned something larger. 'Make yourself comfortable,' she said politely, knowing already that this would be impossible. The timber office was oppressively hot and her prospective client appeared to be melting.

Stroud tried to seat himself, shuffling his considerable weight like a circus elephant perched on a tiny stool, while Pearl moved to a window and opened it. A warm breeze stole into the room as she asked, 'How can I help?'

Still fanning himself with his panama hat, Stroud now stopped as though summoning reserves of energy he'd been saving for this very moment. 'You could start by telling me when he's back,' he said in a brisk Yorkshire accent.

'He?'

'Mr Pearl, of course.' He threw an irritated look around the room. 'Where is he? Still at lunch?'

Pearl looked down at a stack of newly printed business cards on her desk. She had delegated the task of designing them to her son, Charlie, and he had done a good job, apart from choosing the palest of fonts for the line beginning *Proprietor*. She looked up and explained. 'There is no Mr Pearl – only Ms Nolan.'

At this, Stroud's mouth fell ajar as if waiting for a suitable response to fill it.

'This is my agency,' she continued. 'Call me Pearl.'

Stroud sat, visibly struggling to absorb this. It was clear he was having a bad day, and this meeting was doing nothing to improve it. His mouth snapped shut as he came to a decision.

'This isn't going to work.'

'I'm sorry?'

'The job I want doing.' He glanced for a moment towards the door as though contemplating escape.

'Look, why don't you tell me what the job is?' Pearl asked calmly.

Stroud took a crumpled handkerchief from his breast pocket and began dabbing at his sweating brow again. 'I'm owed money,' he sighed. 'An outstanding loan. And I need it sorted.'

'You mean you need a debt collector and—'

'No, no,' broke in Stroud testily. 'What I need is information.' As he fixed his gaze on Pearl, his tiny brown eyes looked like two currants pressed into a potato head. Pearl's silence provided the cue for him to offload more concerns. 'It's been five years and I should've had a return by now, but there's been nothing. Not a penny.' He jabbed a stubby finger on the surface of the desk. 'Not even a gesture of goodwill.'

An understanding nod from Pearl seemed to calm him for a moment. She offered him a box of tissues from her desk and Stroud helped himself to one, shaking it open before blowing his nose like a small bugle.

'I'd be quite within my rights to bring pressure to bear, but I don't want the bloke scared off – not until I know he can pay,' he told her.

'And that's what you want me to find out?' As she met his gaze, Stroud's eyes squashed tighter.

'I want some checks run, a bit of digging around,' he continued. 'I need to know if this fellow is holding out on me.'

As though relieved of a heavy burden, Stroud then took a deep breath and turned his face towards the source of the breeze, but a ringing phone shattered his brief sense of peace. Checking the caller ID, Pearl offered an apologetic smile before picking up the receiver.

Dolly's voice barked down the line. 'No lemon!'

'In the fridge.'

'None there.'

'Then try the pantry.'

Stroud was shuffling uncomfortably in his inadequate seat as Pearl whispered urgently into the receiver, 'Can't this wait? I'm busy right now.'

Dolly failed to take the hint. 'So am I,' she replied. 'I've taken four more bookings for tomorrow.'

'Great.'

'Not if we run out.'

'Of lemons?'

'Oysters.'

'Don't worry. I've got plenty more on order.'

Stroud checked his watch, looking increasingly impatient.

'Pacifics and Irish too.'

At this, Stroud looked up and before Dolly had a chance to reply, Pearl set down the receiver, her hand remaining clamped on it as if to silence her mother. 'Sorry about that.' She summoned a tight smile. 'The Oyster Festival starts tomorrow.'

Stroud stared with some suspicion at the telephone. 'And what's that got to do with you?'

Pearl decided that if she couldn't have Stroud as a client, she might just tempt him as a customer. 'I own a seafood bar,' she admitted, 'just around the corner on the High Street.' Stroud said nothing but his frown put her on the defensive. 'It doesn't interfere with my work here. Usually.'

Still Stroud continued to eye her and Pearl decided to come clean. 'Look, the agency's new but I'm local and a good investigator. I used to be in the police force, and if you need a reference, my last clients will vouch for me.'

Pearl decided against explaining that Mr and Mrs Phillip Caffery were, in fact, her only clients so far and that the £1,000 reward she'd received from them for tracing a cherished Wheaten terrier had actually provided the capital for her to set up trading in a more professional way. The money had been used to redesign her office, invest in some advertising and specialist software, convincing her that the skills she had always possessed as a 'people person' could finally be put to use beyond the confines of her restaurant. The Caffery case had come along at just the right time and though Pearl wasn't overly superstitious, neither was she beyond ignoring life's small synchronicities, especially when they were nudging her in a direction she'd always wanted to take.

In some parallel universe, Pearl was convinced her doppelgänger was climbing the ranks to Detective Chief Superintendent. It should have been Pearl herself, except for the fact that she had made one tiny error in becoming pregnant at just nineteen. That had put paid to her police training, though Pearl knew, more than anything, that having Charlie had been no mistake.

'So you know about oysters?' the fat man enquired.

Pearl smiled. 'Oh yes. I know a good one from a bad one – and the best way to serve them.'

Stroud considered this for a moment, coming up with a revised view. 'Then maybe you can help, after all.' He pocketed his handkerchief and lowered his voice. 'Did you know that someone's been working the beds independently?'

'Someone?'

Stroud looked back at her, unimpressed. 'A fisherman by the name of Vincent Rowe. He came to me a while back. Had a plan to work some of the free waters east of that Tankerton sandbank . . .' He broke off, floundering for a moment.

'The Street,' said Pearl, rescuing him.

Stroud gave a quick nod before resuming his story. 'Said if I supplied the capital, he could re-lay some of the native oysters and be making a nice fat profit for us quicker than any other investment. I'd have expected a return by now but I've not seen a single penny – and if he can't cough up, I want to know why.'

'Why don't you ask him?' Pearl was well aware of the complicated division of foreshore fishing rights, not least because her own father had spent a lifetime dredging for oysters – a life misspent, some would say, since Tommy Nolan had been, at heart, a true poet. As a young man he had charmed the seafront bars with his verses set to music, wistful lines employing metaphors about life, love and the fishing of oysters, before marrying Dolly who hated them.

'He's been giving me the runaround,' Stroud complained. And I don't like being taken for a ride.' He plucked a smart leather wallet from his jacket. 'I'll pay a good cash retainer for you to nose around, check out his finances and tell me what he's worth. If he's holding out on me, I want to know.'

Pearl looked out of the window. A crimson kite sailed effortlessly past on the breeze and she wished she was on the end of it. Stroud's voice cut sharply into her thoughts.

'Well?'

Pearl looked back to see the thick wallet lying open in Stroud's sweaty palm. The offer was tempting, not just for the money but because the possibility of satisfying a bona fide client for her newly created business would go some way to justifying a long-held dream. She considered very carefully before giving her reply. 'I think you're right, Mr Stroud. I'm not the man for the job.'

Stroud didn't look entirely surprised, merely quietly satisfied that his initial instincts had been correct. He put away his wallet and rose clumsily to his feet. As he did so, he lost hold of his panama hat, which tumbled to the floor and rolled beneath Pearl's desk. This single event seemed to be the last straw for Stroud and his face turned puce as he reached down to retrieve it, causing Pearl to quickly intervene. She picked up the hat and while doing so noticed it was a fine specimen, with a pretty silk label stitched inside showing the image of a cathedral and the maker's name, *Portells*. She handed the hat back to him, but Stroud failed to thank her as he set it firmly on his head. Once at the door, he paused only for a second, before grunting, 'Thanks – for nowt.'

The door swung shut and Pearl watched through her open window as her lost client beetled off in the direction of town, past a few elderly tourists who had gathered on the prom to admire Pearl's seafront garden.

Taking a deep breath of fresh sea air to replace the stale smell he had left behind, she dialled a stored number in her mobile phone and, after only a few rings, heard a voicemail message sound. At the beep, her tone was casual and careful not to cause alarm.

'Vinnie, it's me. Ring me as soon as you get this, will you?'

Chapter Two

'You did what?'

'I turned him down.'

Locking the front door to the restaurant, Dolly asked, 'Well, what did he ask you to do? Spy on his wife?'

Pearl hesitated, wondering for a moment what kind of woman might marry a man like Stroud. 'Something like that.' She added nothing more, knowing all too well her mother's opinion of the agency.

More than twenty years ago, Dolly had been shocked to the core by Pearl's decision to join the police force, mainly because she had feared for her daughter's safety but also because Dolly was no fan of the police. Having been anti-establishment all her life, the image conjured in her fertile imagination, of Pearl, armed with a truncheon, confronting some innocent protester, was anathema.

Dolly blamed herself for having allowed her girl to watch

too much *Cagney & Lacey* as a child, though Pearl's decision had in no way been influenced by the US cop show. A psychologist might have linked Pearl's love of order, her need to find solutions and tidy up all loose ends as counterbalance to a childhood which, for the most part, had been carefree and unrestrictive. It was certainly true that Pearl had thrived within the framework offered by her basic police training, but during her probationary period she had also demonstrated that she was someone who not only engaged well with the public, but also displayed an instinctive understanding of people in general. It was this skill, above all, that had singled her out as a potential candidate for criminal investigation, until a positive reading on a pregnancy test had prompted her resignation, leaving Dolly to quietly celebrate, infinitely more comfortable with the idea of her daughter as a single mum than a lackey of the state.

'Sometimes dreams are best left as that,' Dolly had said at the time, offering the same look she wore now as she dropped the keys of the restaurant into Pearl's hand. 'I said you'd be attracting all sorts of weirdos.'

'And you'd know all about that,' teased Pearl, aware that her mother still harboured a few dreams herself.

The restaurant window had been newly dressed by Dolly for a competition which took place every year for Best Festival Display. Almost every business in town was inspired to compete for this highly prized accolade, but while most opted for a traditional style, Dolly rejected the ubiquitous fishermen's nets and treasure troves of oyster shells for something a little more abstract. This year, waves of blue taffeta flowed across a handful of scattered pearls.

'Well?' she asked tentatively.

'It's beautiful,' Pearl said honestly.

'But not very culinary,' Dolly finally decided. 'It needs something else or you'll be mistaken for a jeweller.'

'Fish?'

'Far too obvious, darling, but it could be a tad more aquatic.'

She continued to gaze at her artwork as Pearl leaned closer, suggesting, 'Haven't you got a rehearsal to get to?'

Her mother looked blank.

'Belly dancing?' Pearl reminded her.

Dolly's eyes instantly widened. 'Flamenco! How could you let me forget? Juana Pariente's class begins tonight.'

'Juana . . .?'

'The new course I signed up to – the teacher from Granada. I'll be late for my induction.' She set off, hurrying away up the High Street.

'Hold on!' yelled Pearl, but Dolly waved a dismissive hand before vanishing up Bonner Alley, leaving her daughter staring down at the keys in her hand then up at her name above the restaurant window which confirmed that, sometimes, dreams really could work out.

'The Whitstable Pearl' wasn't a grand place – the fancy restaurants were all situated down on the beach – but the small High Street eatery was full of character and, most importantly, it sold the best seafood in town. Apart from oysters, 'The Whitstable Pearl' offered a selection of signature dishes: squid encased in a light chilli tempura batter, fried scallop dotted with breadcrumbs, marinated *sashimi* of tuna, mackerel and wild salmon. Here were no grand culinary statements but a clear respect for simple dishes created with the best ingredients. Each course on the menu had been perfected over time but the simplicity of Pearl's dishes meant they could always be prepared or assembled in her absence. This provided two benefits: Pearl herself wasn't tied to the establishment, and secondly, the quality of her food was always reliable – unlike other local restaurants whose reputations soared and plummeted with a change of chef.

Charlie's drawings adorned the walls, and in spite of Dolly's grumblings, the restaurant remained a family-run business, one that had completely supported Pearl throughout her son's childhood while placing her firmly at the centre of the community, where a 'people person' should be. The only hitch was that the restaurant was no longer enough – for Pearl. For some time she had felt the need for a new challenge. Old ambitions had reawakened and Pearl sensed that if she didn't act on them now, she never would.

A void existed since Charlie had started at Kent University, not aching but troubling. The campus at Canterbury was just a fifteen-minute drive away, but it might as well have been on the other side of the world as Pearl had begun to realise the truth of what Dolly had always asserted: that she had put her life on hold for her son, eschewing many of its opportunities, even for romance. Pearl hadn't given up on the idea of finding the right partner and there had been sparks over the years, but nothing to match the white heat of her first love for Charlie's father. Blind dates, set-ups from friends, even a few website forays had led, for the most part, to little more than a string of dull evenings spent wondering when it might be appropriate to make an early exit.

Charlie had often been used as an excuse – childhood tooth-aches, temperatures and tantrums providing suitable pretexts to escape – but no longer, for Charlie was all grown up and out in the world himself, studying for a degree in History of Art.

With ten months at Canterbury already behind him, he was showing a surprising amount of independence, although Pearl sensed that whenever she arrived on campus with a carload of shopping and a bag of fresh underpants he was still grateful – until, perhaps, her last unscheduled visit when Pearl had found him revising with a 'friend'.

Tiziana, from Tuscany, had amber eyes, honey-coloured limbs and spoke English better than Pearl herself through a gateway of perfect white teeth. When she smiled, which she did every time she looked at Charlie, it was breathtaking, not least because of the effect it had upon Pearl's son. Charlie had dated girls before but somehow they had always seemed to lurk in the background, bit players, waiting in the wings while he chatted with Pearl about where he was off to or what time he'd be back. Tiziana, however, remained firmly centre stage – appropriate, thought Pearl, for a student of Performing Arts. With mink-coloured hair pulled up into a thick, tumbling chaos, 'Tizzy' had displayed star quality even while standing over a hot cooker, stirring sage-tossed tortellini as Charlie had gazed on hungrily – for her.

Pearl had found that first encounter disconcerting, not least because Tiziana had been so friendly towards her. If she had been merely a cold personification of beauty, 'all style and no substance' as Dolly might have said, there would have been something for Pearl to dislike, but instead the girl had been warm and generous, offering a souvenir from her home in the form of a waxed apron emblazoned with the Leaning Tower of Pisa. Pearl had accepted the gift, though declined the offer of supper, watching Charlie helping with cutlery and wine in a way he had never done at home. Several minutes later, Pearl had found herself sitting in her car on the street, dazed by what she had just witnessed – her son besotted by another woman. She couldn't help feeling there would be more emotional somersaults ahead of her and hoped she would land on her feet.

Pearl was happy for her son, how could she not be? Nevertheless, something had prevented her from wearing the apron and she had been grateful when Dolly had quickly commandeered it. If that 'something' had been the slight creep of jealousy, it seemed to offer even more reason to throw her energies into the agency, which she had started up two weeks ago, never expecting for one moment that a first client would present her with such a problem.

Pearl took it to the place she took all problems – and headed down to the beach. Often, merely witnessing the ebb and flow of the tide would throw up a solution or the hope of one, but today, scanning the horizon, she sensed that might not be the case.

Vinnie hadn't responded to Pearl's call although his boat, *The Native*, was clearly visible at sea. It prompted her to move on towards the Street, the narrow spit of shingle that projected over half a mile from shore, and which would soon reappear as the tide lowered. Clambering across a shallow breakwater, she found a young couple seated on the upturned hull of her own wooden dinghy. No more than teenagers, with hands entwined and faces turned to catch the last of the evening sun, the couple remained so still and silent that their image seemed almost photographic. The lyrics of an old song, 'Stay' by Shakespeare's Sister, sailed across to Pearl on the air, reminding her of another summer night on the same stretch of beach more than twenty years ago. Marcella Detroit's soprano rang out for a few more moments until the volume on a radio was finally turned down.

A pebble shifted beneath Pearl's shoe and the 'photograph' came to life, hands parting as the couple saw her standing in front of them. The teenagers obediently rose to their feet, moving off to find another perch as Pearl tipped the small craft upright and dragged it down to the water's edge.

The tide was turning so there was no need of an outboard. Less than fifteen minutes would take Pearl out to Vinnie, and as she rowed, some cool air was welcome. Out to the east, bleached wind-farm sails turned slowly on the breeze, new neighbours for the Red Sands Army fort that had sat eight miles offshore since the Second World War. Consisting of seven steel towers, the old fort had once served as an anti-aircraft defence, housing weapons, munitions and more than two hundred soldiers in an attempt to block the passage of enemy planes on their way to London. In the 1960s, the structure had been commandeered by pirate radio stations, a group of local DJs spinning Mersey Beat singles in the same bleak quarters in which soldiers had once risked their lives. But now the towers merely rusted on their old steel supports, marked by a lone bell buoy which tolled their existence to any sailor who cared to orbit them.

During the day, the sea had been almost blue but in the fading light the estuary waters were returning to their more usual pewter. Pearl drifted for a moment, resting on her oars to take in the coastal view from the sea. Lights were blinking on at the beach. The Hotel Continental was busy, cars arriving outside its Deco façade, headlights fading in the car park. Gulls swooped overhead, skimming close to the water as they headed in to shore. Tomorrow the Oyster Festival would begin – two weeks of tradition and contemporary culture that would tempt crowds from London and from further beyond – but for now, all was quiet.

Pearl took up her oars again and rowed on towards *The Native*. She could see that the forty-foot craft was still at anchor but knew that with a lowering tide it would be heading back at any moment. Having fished so many times with her father, Pearl was well acquainted with the routine: the heavy dredge, lowered off the stern, dragging along the seabed to fetch up a catch from which unwanted intruders would be plucked. Crabs were capable of cracking open the shells of young oysters but starfish were the oysterman's enemy, innocent baby fingers clamping onto the oyster's shell to suck the life from it. As a child, Pearl had helped her father to wrench them from their prey, and she thought suddenly of Stroud's handshake and pulled a little harder on the oars.

There was no one on deck as Pearl drifted closer to the vessel, but faintly she heard voices from the small cabin behind the wheelhouse. As she came alongside to tie her pointer to *The Native*'s starboard cleat, she realised it was a radio she could hear. Tapping against the hull, her own voice faded into the dusk. 'Vinnie. It's me – Pearl.' The only response came from actors playing out a drama on the radio in Vinnie's saloon. Pearl climbed aboard.

At *The Native*'s stern, a catch of oysters, packed into baskets, marked a good day's work, but as Pearl neared the cabin, the radio now seemed deafeningly loud and discounted the possibility that Vinnie might be taking a nap. On the wheelhouse wall, a St Christopher was firmly secured while a saucepan, unfettered by fiddles in the tiny galley, moved back and forth idly on a hotplate. Tide tables and paperbacks lay spread out on the saloon table, but Vinnie was nowhere to be found. The boat seemed to have been deserted – like the *Marie Celeste*.

Studio laughter suddenly burst from the radio. Pearl's heart beat faster as she stepped back out on deck. Anxiety was beginning to gnaw. The sky was darkening but with no sign of Vinnie she now began to wonder if he had, for some reason, joined another boat. Someone might have needed help, another fisherman perhaps, or more likely a day-tripper. The loud drone of a jet ski passed by into the distance, leaving nothing behind but its wake and a tug of anchor chain beneath the boat. Pearl made a decision. She would radio ashore and take in *The Native* herself before low tide.

Returning to the wheelhouse, she started up Vinnie's diesel engine and cranked the boat back into life. Heading quickly to the bow to bring up anchor, Pearl could see that Vinnie's hold was open, revealing a few stinking fish boxes stacked among bunches of coiled rope. She tugged hard, pulling up anchor line, hand over hand, until the task became increasingly difficult. Holding the rope fast, Pearl secured it to a cleat before leaning across the rail to check her progress.

In the fading light, the waters were murky, but something pale had surged beneath the surface. A small sea creature, targeted by *The Native*'s green starboard light, pulsed its way out of a dark cavity. A gull screeched low overhead and Pearl stepped back on the deck, shocked not by the bird's raw cry, but on recognising that the creature in the water was in fact a tiny starfish, emerging from the gaping hole of a mouth.

Vinnie was staring straight up at Pearl, eyes wide open, torso upright like a diver striving for the surface, but his strong, bare arms were floating on the outgoing tide. A fathom of anchor chain was wrapped tightly around his ankle.

Chapter Three

It was just after 10 p.m. when the call came through. Detective Chief Inspector Mike McGuire had been making his way through the public car park in Canterbury's Pound Lane, having just learned that his online bet in a motor-racing championship had crashed out at the final chicane. The race had been virtual but his stake had been real and McGuire winced, not only at the thought of how much he had lost, but because his new shoes were pinching. He had bought them at the weekend and worn them only for the very first time today – a pair of casual brogues which had slipped on comfortably enough this morning but after a long hot day felt more like a form of Inquisitional torture.

McGuire took a size ten, but lately his footwear seemed to be mysteriously shrinking. Either that or, at just thirty-nine years old, his feet were suddenly getting larger. He was sure it wasn't usual for feet to continue growing, but perhaps they were following his waistline, which had slightly expanded over the past year. He blamed that on the move to Canterbury. In London he had been more active, with a couple of evenings every week spent on the squash court, but no longer, since he was now mainly desk-bound – his working days increasingly consumed by the tyranny of paperwork.

McGuire regretted his transfer to Canterbury and lately hankered after all the things he had once hated about working in London: the constant adrenalin rush of activity, the pressure of too much needing to be done in too little time, the bustle on the street, the tension of a dog-eat-dog battle for survival. Chiefly, he missed the anonymity of life in the capital. By comparison, Canterbury seemed too parochial and safe. A city only by virtue of its famous cathedral, it possessed history, culture and a variety of shops – but none of the danger to which he was used.

Increasingly, it was the danger he missed. And Donna. But the two were now inextricably linked because of the way she had been taken from him. Her absence in his life had changed everything, stunting not only his ambition, but for a time, his very sense of purpose. One random incident had destroyed her: two drugged-up kids, speeding through the streets of Peckham in a stolen car had mown her down like a target on a computer screen, and in that instant McGuire's perspective had shifted so violently that only chaos had been left behind.

Weeks of wallowing in anger and sorrow, coupled with the nightly panacea of bourbon, had eased nothing. Only a return to work had offered a suitable framework to cling to: the mediocrity of routine replacing the crippling sense of loss that had paralysed him for so long. A year on and he was managing to wake each morning and sleep each night as though his heart was still intact. But he alone knew that the CID work which so often brought him into contact with death had, ironically, given him a reason for living.

McGuire reached his car, listening carefully to the details of the Whitstable incident before signing off, 'I'm on my way.' Then he slipped the phone into his pocket and a few moments later stepped on the accelerator, the pain of constrictive shoes offering a sharp, if strangely comforting, reminder that he was alive.

During the call, McGuire had learned that the 'scene of crime' had been secured: a fishing boat was now moored in Whitstable's harbour and an ambulance had been sent to confirm that life was extinct. A forensics van was on its way from a nearby road-traffic accident, and McGuire was relieved that his presence wasn't required.

Whitstable was no more than a twenty-minute drive away, through the sixty-foot-high western gate of Canterbury's city wall, a route which, historically, had been used as a horseway for fisherwives to enter. These days, the road to Whitstable consisted of a clear run past the fields and bungalows of Blean village, straight up to the crest of Borstal Hill which provided a view of the grey mantle of estuary coastline lying at its feet.

McGuire didn't reckon much to Whitstable – nor of any small town, come to that. The old police station had long ago been converted into apartments and there was now just a High-Street 'cop shop' – distinguishable from other retailers only by the blue lantern hanging outside and the fact that its opening times were 10 a.m. to 3 p.m. – on weekdays only. This neatly confirmed the place to McGuire as a forgettable backwater for visiting tourists and the kind of small-minded locals who liked to live in each other's pockets. He imagined the scene at the harbour: police tape vying with fishermen's bunting advertising cut-price Dover sole, then he made directly for his own station in Canterbury and parked in the space reserved for him.

McGuire headed straight up to the custody suite and pushed open a heavy door, coming face to face with a young woman raising a dunked biscuit to her lips. WPC Jane Quinn was twenty-two years old but looked more like a teenager, which sometimes came in useful when dealing with errant kids but proved a liability in most other instances. At the sight of McGuire, she sprang to her feet and the biscuit plunged into her mug, splashing coffee onto her lapel. She dabbed ineffectually at the wet stain as McGuire looked elsewhere, shamed by her lack of professional gravitas.

'What have you got?' he asked.

'Pearl Nolan, sir.' She offered up a file. 'Inspectors Shetcliffe and Barnes have formally interviewed her and there's a first account taken by the local DS at the scene.'

McGuire nodded cursorily towards the closed door in front of them. 'How is she?'

'Not too bad, considering. She's been fully processed but declined a lawyer.'

McGuire's gaze shifted to the coffee mug in Quinn's hand. 'Get me another one of those, will you?'

The young PC moved off quickly, leaving McGuire staring down at the file in his hand. Taking the weight off his feet, he sat down, plucked two cassette tapes from the file and loaded them into a machine, as he prepared to study the statement.

On the other side of the door in the interview room, Pearl pushed away a chipped mug. The coffee it contained was cold and the room was stuffy, reeking of stale tobacco in spite of a *No Smoking* sign on the wall. She had been left alone for some time during a break in questioning to which she knew she was entitled. Since being brought to the station she had experienced the system working at impressive speed, having been booked in, notified of her rights, fingerprinted, photographed, swabbed for DNA and made to surrender her clothes for forensic analysis. Although she was sure she would soon be eliminated as a suspect, the experience of having to wear a scratchy white zip-up shell suit while giving an account of the evening's tragedy made her feel vulnerable.

Forty minutes had now passed since she had signed her statement at 10.14 p.m. Now, restless and impatient, she considered making a complaint. She got to her feet and made a move towards the door when it suddenly opened before her. A new officer stood within its frame. Offering a tight, efficient smile, McGuire stepped forward to introduce himself.

Pearl was momentarily taken off guard, not just by his stature but the fact there seemed little about McGuire to indicate his status as a DCI. He wore blue denim jeans, a casual linen shirt, open at the neck, and a lightweight jacket which he shrugged off and threw across the back of a chair. His blond hair was cropped short at the sides but left longer on top – stylish, thought Pearl – realising that if she had seen him in her restaurant she might easily have mistaken him for a Scandinavian tourist.

She sat down again and McGuire joined her at the table. Quinn followed in with a mug in her hand and carefully set it down in front of her. The young constable offered a smile but Pearl shook her head. 'I think I've had enough for one night.'

McGuire sensed that Pearl wasn't just referring to coffee. Her fatigue was clearly evident in the dark crescents beneath her tired, grey eyes, but nevertheless, she seemed wired by a certain nervous energy, stoked not by caffeine, but by what she had experienced this evening.

'I need to ask a few more questions,' he explained. 'But this shouldn't take long.'

Quinn cued a cassette tape, giving the date, time and names of the officers present while McGuire watched the tape roll beneath a plastic window, pausing for just a moment before commenting: 'Sounds like you've had quite a night of it.'

Pearl considered he had just chosen an unfortunate turn of phrase since it made the whole tragic episode sound like a celebration of some kind. She said nothing but watched McGuire pick up a biro from the table, noting as he toyed with it that there was no ring on his wedding finger. His next question quickly snapped her attention back into place.

'I understand you knew the deceased?'

'Yes, I knew Vinnie,' Pearl agreed, though it was hard to think of him as dead, even after the struggle she had put up to drag his lifeless body back onto the boat. She had failed to do so under her own strength, and had relied instead on *The Native*'s winch to lower the corpse into her own dinghy, watching all the while as small crabs fell into the sea from the fisherman's sodden clothes. She closed her eyes, but an after-image remained.

'And you got to the boat about sunset?'

'Shortly after.'

'Can I ask why?'

Pearl opened her eyes. The abstract nature of McGuire's question had seemed almost metaphysical. Sensing this, he offered some simplification. 'Why did you go out to Mr Rowe's boat?'

Pearl reached for the mug before her and took a sip of bitter coffee. 'I'd left a message for him to call me, but he didn't. Later I happened to see *The Native* from the beach and—' She broke off suddenly as she saw that McGuire was staring beneath the desk, distracted, it seemed, by his own feet.

'Look, I told all this to the other detectives,' she said crisply, 'so why do I have to go through it all again?'

McGuire met her gaze. 'It's just a few questions following on from your statement, that's all.'

Pearl's eyes shifted to the file sitting on the desk and wondered what conclusions had been drawn. 'Was it an accident?' When he failed to answer, she continued. 'Look, I've heard stories of sailors losing concentration, stepping into the bight of an anchor chain before it's thrown overboard, but . . .' She swallowed hard. 'Is that really what happened tonight?'

McGuire set the biro down on the table, leaned back in his chair and steepled his fingers against his chest. 'What do *you* think?'

Pearl shrugged helplessly. 'I don't know. In fact, I don't even understand why I'm still here.' She looked back at him. 'Am I being treated as a witness or a suspect?' She knew that in any murder investigation, the prime candidates for arrest were usually those who found the body or those who had last seen the victim alive. Pearl fitted the bill on both counts but she was also aware that it was often necessary for a detective to arrest a witness under caution before finally eliminating them from inquiries.

McGuire finally spoke. 'You've been taken into custody for questioning.'

'I've been arrested.'

'Informed of your rights.'

'But not charged with any crime.'

McGuire considered her. It was clear that in spite of everything she still had her wits about her. 'Have you changed your mind about wanting a lawyer?'

Pearl took stock of the question and then shook her head. WPC Quinn leaned forward to the recorder. 'For the benefit of the tape—'

'No,' Pearl interrupted firmly. 'I do *not* want a lawyer. For the benefit of the tape, I happened to find a body.' She stared directly at McGuire. 'That's all.'

The clock on the wall ticked into another minute. McGuire held Pearl's look. His silence was beginning to irritate her, conveying to Pearl a sense of superiority or perhaps just sheer conceit, but when he spoke again it was in a sympathetic and measured tone, which took her by surprise.

'Look, I understand what you've been through tonight and I appreciate your efforts to explain what happened. We could do this another time but in my experience, a witness account is always best taken when events are still fresh in the mind.' His features softened as he threw over the final decision to her.

Pearl took her time – and a deep breath – before explaining, 'I rowed out to talk to Vinnie.'

'Talk about what?'

'Oysters. He was my supplier.'

McGuire picked up the biro again and began to make a note. Glancing up at the clock, Pearl saw that it was almost eleven and she thought of Dolly, who by now would have been informed of events. Pearl knew exactly what her mother's

32

reaction would be, but hoped that amidst the drama, she would remember to bring Pearl a change of clothes.

'But you didn't get to talk?' prompted McGuire.

'It wouldn't have been much of a conversation, since he was already dead,' Pearl said tartly.

'And you're absolutely sure of that, are you?' he asked.

Pearl looked up. 'He wouldn't have stood much chance against a fathom of anchor chain.'

McGuire tried to decide whether the spark of her anger was borne of shock, grief or just plain irritation with his line of questioning. Curiously, as a witness she seemed toughened rather than defeated by what she had experienced, and though he knew that ratcheting up tension in an interrogation some-times prompted an interviewee to drop their defences, he couldn't be sure which way Pearl would go. He decided to try another tack.

'Why didn't you radio the coastguard?'

Pearl recognised it was a valid question since Channel 16 would have linked her straight to the Dover coastguard. Instead, she had chosen an alternative. 'I radioed local Harbour Control,' she explained. 'There was no reply.'

'Why not then try the coastguard?'

'Because I'd already decided to bring the boat in. Look, the tide had turned. If I hadn't, we'd have run aground . . .'

'We?'

'Me and Vinnie.' She sighed with frustration. 'I know what you're thinking: the lifeboat could have reached us – tractor and trailer over mud? But I wasn't going to leave him out there any longer.'

'He was already dead.'

'All the more reason!'

It was clear from McGuire's look that he failed to understand. Pearl tried to spell it out for him. 'This is a small community,' she said. 'I've known Vinnie's family all my life, but even if he'd been a stranger I would still have brought in his body.'

She watched as McGuire thought about this as he tapped the biro softly, but insistently, on the desk. Then: 'Why?'

It wasn't just his question that irked her. The man's assuredness, impatience – even his brand-new shoes – all spelled out that he was from the city. It was clear that, in some ways, he was a tourist, after all.

'You don't know much about the sea, do you?' she said bluntly. 'How long it takes for fish and crabs to start feeding?'

At this, McGuire stopped tapping his pen and set it down. He was aware that she was testing him, challenging his authority, and that he could demonstrate his power by holding her overnight to continue his questioning tomorrow – but experience told him he would be better served using a new day to talk to the family of the deceased. By morning he hoped for an exact cause and time of death, but Forensics would have to move fast due to the effects of the sea on the decomposition of the corpse.

He made a decision. Closing the file on the desk before him, he said, 'I'll get someone to drive you home.'

With his change of tone, Pearl realised that she had over-reacted. For an instant, she considered explaining about Stroud's visit, then just as quickly reconsidered. The minute hand of the clock had shifted to the hour, and she had no desire to be stranded in custody while the police searched for a stranger on the eve of the Oyster Festival.

WPC Quinn cued the end of the tape. 'Interview terminated at 11.01.'

McGuire got to his feet but before he could speak, other voices suddenly filled the room from outside. The door opened and Dolly burst in as a constable tried to restrain her. 'Sorry, sir, but she just barged straight past me.'

McGuire held up his hand, watching Dolly as she stood stock still before Pearl, registering the white suit her daughter wore.

'Good God. What is this – Guantánamo Bay?' She spun round to McGuire. 'If you've done anything to infringe my daughter's rights . . .'

'Your daughter is free to go,' McGuire said.

Dolly took hold of Pearl's arm and moved with her to the door, but before the two women had reached it, McGuire's voice sounded once more. 'We'll need to speak again.' He offered Pearl a small card on which was printed his name and contact details. 'If you remember anything else,' he told her, 'call me.'

Pearl hesitated before taking the card, her fingers momentarily brushing the detective's, unsure if it was suspicion she read in his narrowed, blue eyes or the vague shadow of a smile. Then she turned and in an instant was gone while WPC Quinn quickly followed, leaving McGuire finally alone. For a while he simply stared at the closed door until a throbbing pain returned to his feet. He considered taking off his ill-fitting shoes but suspected he would never get them on again, so instead, he picked up the file that was lying on the table and looked down at it to see he had made only one small note during the entire interview.

The single word *Oysters* stared back at McGuire from the page.

Chapter Four

The weekend closest to 25 July always signalled the start of Whitstable's annual Oyster Festival, the date marking the Feast of St James. It was said that while the Saint's body was being brought by sea to Spain, a knight fell overboard during a violent storm and was saved only by a miracle when his clothes became covered in clinging oysters, which the sailors used to claw him back on board. On the morning of Saturday, 24 July, just seven hours after leaving McGuire's interview room, Pearl woke with a vivid image in her mind of Vinnie's body, covered in small red spider crabs as she struggled to drag him aboard her dinghy. She gasped, but having realised a new day had dawned, she instantly reached for her mobile. Searching through its contacts, she soon found what she was looking for.

A few moments after dialling Stroud's number, his recorded voice gruffly commanded her to leave a message, but Pearl decided against doing so and instead ended the call. Almost immediately her phone rang.

'You okay, Mum?' Charlie's voice was concerned but thick with sleep.

Pearl sat upright, running a hand through her tangled curls. 'How did you hear?'

'Gran called a minute ago. And I'm glad she did – so don't go biting her head off.' He paused for a moment. 'Poor old Vinnie. And you.'

Charlie was never a great talker on the phone, preferring to send texts studded with lols and :-)s. But he now began to broach something, awkwardly. 'Look, I – I was thinking I could come over . . .' He broke off as another voice sounded in the background. 'Can you hold on for a second?' Charlie disappeared from the line but after a muffled exchange, he returned. 'Mum?'

'Yes?'

He said sheepishly, 'The thing is, I'd like to come over but I can't. I've got some books to pick up this morning for that project I have to finish.'

'It's fine,' Pearl told him. 'I'll be busy enough as it is with the festival, so why don't I come to you at the end of the day?'

'Great.'

'Charlie?'

'Yeah?'

Pearl paused. 'Say hi to Tizzy for me.'

The line went dead in her hand and Pearl checked her watch, registering that it was 6.15 a.m. and that her fingertips were still stained with police ink.

*

An hour later, even after taking a cool shower, Pearl felt that the day would turn out to be oppressively hot. She had an instinct for the weather and no need for tide tables, for on a summer's day with the tide far out, the air would be still and often stifling, before a soft breeze and an almost imperceptible change of temperature prefaced the sound of waves once more breaking upon the shore. There was no such relief this morning as she headed down to the office in her garden and found just two messages on her answer machine: one from a gas company touting for business, the other a curt reminder from Ronnie, her window cleaner, that some payment wouldn't go amiss.

For a few moments Pearl wished that Nathan was at home, a stone's throw away in the white clapboard cottage across the road. But instead, Pearl's neighbour and best friend was far away in his native Santa Cruz, California, having been summoned to attend an old boyfriend's funeral. Pearl missed Nathan, who was good at dispensing hot coffee and sensible advice – and she fought the urge to connect with him, if only by email, knowing this was hardly the time to send news of another death. Instead, she stared across her desk at the chair Stroud had occupied less than twenty-four hours ago. Reminded that she had yet to explain to McGuire about the meeting, she took his card from her pocket. It gave the detective's name, rank and two contact numbers. Pearl's hand reached out for her phone, then hovered in mid-air as she decided there was something else, more important, to be done first.

As she stepped from her garden gate and onto the promenade, Pearl saw a group of uniformed kids, swarming like bluebottles on the beach. It was the local Sea Scouts, rehearsing *The Landing of the Catch* – a symbolic re-enactment of the first dredge of the season during which a catch of oysters is brought ashore to be blessed by the local clergy. Today's ceremony, presided over by the Mayor and a few other dignitaries, was scheduled to begin at midday but the Scouts had started early, no doubt keen to avoid a fiasco like that of last summer, when the launching of a pyrotechnic display from their training boat had failed spectacularly. A hatch had been left open, causing the Scouts' vessel to sink in full view of a massed crowd of locals and tourists. All the fireworks had been consigned to the deep and then, as if to compound the disaster, the rescuing tractor had become mired in the mud, leading to red faces all around. 'Accidents happen at sea,' was offered up by a spokesman, and that thought stuck with Pearl as she glanced towards the rising morning tide before heading briskly off towards town.

Moments later, she was standing outside a half-timbered cottage on Middle Wall, its front garden littered with plastic toys. Vinnie had already turned fifty years of age when his twin daughters, Becky and Louise, were born. At the time he had said, 'No man should become a father until he's old enough to become a grandfather,' making it clear that he harboured some guilt about the parenting of his first child.

Pearl cast her mind back to playing in this same front garden with Vinnie's son, Shane. A few years older than the boy, she had always taken advantage of the fact by bossing Shane mercilessly, whether they had been crabbing on the beach or swimming off the shingled Street. For a second or two, childhood voices echoed in her mind, singing handclapping rhymes while Vinnie upbraided them for being noisy on a Sunday afternoon. Pearl allowed herself to stay with that moment, knowing that all too quickly the memory of Vinnie's voice would fade, as the voices of the dead always do.

Then, bracing herself, she rang the doorbell. Footsteps could be heard approaching from inside before the mother of Vinnie's two daughters appeared on the threshold, fair hair scraped back from her pretty face, eyes puffy and raw with grief. Pearl's voice broke a painful silence.

'Connie, I'm so sorry,' she whispered. 'I should have called first, but . . .'

'No,' Connie said, quickly. 'Please – come in.' She opened the door wider for Pearl to enter, and once it was closed Pearl recognised how unnaturally quiet the house seemed.

'I got Mum to take the girls out,' Connie explained. 'I – I didn't know what else to do.' She cast an awkward glance down the hall. 'Come through and I'll make some tea.'

Grateful for a ritual to rely upon, the two women entered the small kitchen where sunlight streamed through a window to fall upon a bowed shelf stacked with knick-knacks and framed photos. On the other side of the garden door Vinnie's small terrier, Trixie, whimpered, her claws scratching at a glass panel before she gave up and skulked away to a kennel at the bottom of the garden. Connie filled a kettle, flicked a switch and sat down at the table with Pearl.

'When the doorbell rang last night,' she said, 'I actually thought it was Vinnie.' The ghost of a smile appeared on her lips. 'He's always forgetting his keys, but . . .' Her smile set into a grimace. 'Instead, there was a young copper there, and . . . when he said my name, all I could think was that I must've blocked someone's driveway with the car.' Fingers pressed hard into the flesh of her hands as if to stem a tide of emotion. 'Stupid.'

'No,' said Pearl, reproaching herself. 'I should have called you.'

Connie looked up. 'How could you? They said you were giving a statement.' She frowned, as if trying to collect the shattered fragments of her thoughts. 'They told me I had to go straight to the station to make an identification. But when I got there, I kept thinking they'd made a mistake. I couldn't believe something like this could have happened, even after I saw him.' She stared helplessly at Pearl. 'He was . . . just lying there. His hair was still wet, and he looked so peaceful, as if he'd just stepped right out of the shower and had fallen asleep.'

For a moment there was only silence as the two women contemplated this final image.

'Thank God you found him,' said Connie softly. 'Thank God he wasn't left out there all night.' The kettle suddenly erupted with steam and she got up quickly to deal with it.

'Have the police been back?' Pearl asked.

Connie wiped her eyes. 'Yes. A Family Liaison Officer and two detectives asking questions.'

'About?'

'They wanted to know when I last saw Vinnie but I . . . couldn't think clearly.'

'Anything else?'

Connie frowned for a moment. 'One of them – the detective . . .'

'McGuire?' prompted Pearl.

'Yes. He asked how Vinnie had seemed lately, and whether there was anything on his mind that could've affected his concentration.'

Pearl paused before asking, 'And was there?'

Connie took a deep breath. 'I s'pose it won't be long before the whole town knows.' She looked at Pearl, admitting, 'We're in debt.'

'I know,' said Pearl gently. And when Connie gaped at her, she went on: 'Someone came to see me yesterday. They were asking about Vinnie.'

'Who?' Connie asked immediately.

'A man called Stroud. He said he'd loaned Vinnie some money.'

Connie seemed to lose interest. 'He won't be the only one,' she said dully. 'Vinnie borrowed off the bank and from anyone else he could persuade. He never got straight after Tina ran out on him.' She said sadly, 'I kept asking if he could really afford to leave the company. We hadn't even recovered from paying for the IVF but we'd have done that, in time, if he'd only stayed put.'

'With Frank Matheson?'

'Yes – why not? Frank had always paid for half the running costs of the boat, but suddenly there was money going out everywhere. I tried, Pearl, but there was no way we could make it work.' She got to her feet, but then realised she had nowhere to go and sat back down. 'Working for Matheson meant good steady work and no responsibility, but that wasn't enough for Vinnie.'

'He wanted to work for himself, Connie, but he was doing this for all of you.'

'Was he?' asked Connie starkly. 'And where has it got him?' A sudden flare of raw anger dissolved quickly into despair. 'Of all people, my Vinnie should've been more careful.'

Connie was staring through her tears to the shelf on the wall and Pearl's gaze followed, seeking out, beyond the tiny figurines of pottery cats and dogs, a photograph taken of Vinnie's son Shane Rowe on his twentieth birthday. The boy was posed proudly beside a powerful motorbike that only months later had been responsible for his death, although a coroner was to conclude that two Ecstasy tablets and a moderate amount of alcohol had also been to blame.

'What happened to Shane was an accident,' Pearl said. 'But Vinnie didn't take risks. He was always careful.'

'About some things, maybe,' Connie agreed, blinded by tears.

'What do you mean?' asked Pearl quickly.

A sudden blast of reggae music invaded the room from the radio of a car passing by outside. As the song receded, Connie hung her head and remained silent. 'Does it even matter any more?' she said helplessly. 'Vinnie's gone.'

Stepping out onto the street again a short time later, Pearl found that the sun still shone, in spite of everything, but a bass drum pounding from somewhere near the beach seemed an echo of her own heavy heart. It was too early for tourists but the festival flag-sellers were already taking up positions on the pavement, sorting out carnival whistles and fabric snakes on sticks.

As Pearl made her way down to the harbour she saw that the fishing fleet was already out on the rising tide. Only *The Native* remained behind, sealed off by police tape and chained to the South Quay near the Harbour Office. Of all days it seemed bitterly ironic that Vinnie should be absent for the start of this festival, even more so because in spite of Pearl's efforts to bring his body home, Vinnie's boat still lay moored in an area known as Dead Man's Corner – so named because all that fell into the sea locally was said to wash up here, including bodies.

Some years ago, the city council had reached an agreement with a local Trust to improve this stretch of harbour. A talented landscape architect had designed a large deck with a timber seating area on which people could relax and watch harbour life go by. It was hoped that the development might help to change the area's name to something less macabre, but the construction of a decorative gabion wall only served to make it more fitting since it consisted of a large wire-mesh cage with a tideline face filled with driftwood and other flotsam and jetsam.

Pearl noted that several arrangements of flowers had been left overnight in a pile on the quay. Beside them were a few small toys: a tiny bear with a tartan ribbon around its neck and a plastic boat that had once entertained a child's bathtime. The harbour air was sticky, and laden with the odour from shells dumped outside some black-timbered whelk cabins. Pearl's mind wandered to the members of the white-suited forensic team who had clambered over Vinnie's boat last night, rifling through his possessions for clues to his death, perhaps even ripping the St Christopher from his wheelhouse wall. Vinnie had no need of it now.

Turning her back on Dead Man's Corner, Pearl slid open the heavy door to a corrugated iron hangar on the South Quay. Inside, the building was refreshingly cool, with the gentle sound of water trickling as if from a thousand small fountains. Pearl drew near to its source: a filter system bathing a column of trays stacked with live oysters. She reached out and inspected a grey, crusty shell. On it were twelve rings – one for each year of the oyster's life. Pearl knew how very little these creatures needed to survive: just the perfect shallow mix of salt and freshwater which the estuary coastline provided. Since Roman times, Whitstable had proven itself to be a perfect environment for oysters. In the 'glory years' at the start of the twentieth century, more than a hundred boats had been involved in dredging, and oysters had been so plentiful that they had been considered not the delicacy, but the mere padding of a steak and oyster pie. But a combination of harsh winters, disease and pollution had brought hard times for oyster-growers. Only with the introduction of new varieties had the area's stocks survived, and Pearl considered now how pampered they were, lying here, fattening on the day of the festival that honoured them.

'That you, Pearl?'

Pearl turned around to greet the elderly man who now shuffled towards her. Billy Crouch had long retired from the sea but his cheeks were as ruddy as if they were still facing a Force-9 gale. He was short and stocky, and in his clean white apron looked much like a cartoon penguin.

Pearl rummaged in her bag. 'I need an order, Billy.' She handed him a business cheque, then asked quietly: 'You've heard what happened?'

At this, Billy nodded sagely, as the trickling of water upon trays replaced all conversation.

'It's a terrible thing,' he said finally.

'Had you seen him lately?'

Billy Crouch shook his head. 'I'd been down at Seasalter all week,' he said. Pearl was aware that the old fisherman made good use of a static caravan park, just east of Whitstable, to escape from his wife, Sadie.

'Vinnie came to see me one night a few weeks ago. Helped me get some bait in at low tide. I hadn't seen him for a while so I was glad he made it down. Even more so now.' He offered up a sad smile. 'It ain't right, Pearl. A young fella like that with his whole life still ahead of him.' He sighed. 'Is it true it was the anchor?'

Pearl nodded, realising that with almost twenty years' age difference between the two men, Vinnie had always been 'the youngster' to Billy and now would forever remain so. 'How did Matheson take it?'

The old man shrugged. 'There's only one thing keeps *him* awake at night.' Billy rubbed his thumb and forefinger together. 'As long as there's plenty of this, Matheson's happy – with or without Vinnie.' He handed Pearl a receipt for her order, saying, 'But the time'll come, you mark my words, when there won't be a single native oyster left in these waters.'

'You've been saying that for years, Billy.'

'And it's never been truer than it is today,' he insisted. 'A good fisherman goes out – and what does he come back with? A couple of hundred if he's lucky. I'm telling you – them Pacifics have got to be got rid of. I've tried to tell Matheson, they're like grey squirrels taking over.'

'Which is why Vinnie was working the free waters,' said Pearl, 'laying new seed.'

'Wasting his time.'

It wasn't Billy's voice but another which had cut in. An imposing figure stood in the doorway. Frank Matheson paused for a moment then closed the hangar door behind him. In his mid-forties he looked much older due to a greying hairline which was receding like the tide on a shore. At more than six-feet tall he towered over most and Pearl knew it was difficult not to feel cowed in his presence.

'I warned him,' Matheson continued.

'Warned?' repeated Pearl.

'Said he'd come unstuck. Told him to reconsider. He had a family to think of.'

'I doubt he needed reminding of *that*,' said Pearl in Vinnie's defence.

Matheson eyed her. 'Then how did he think he was going to look after them?' He gestured towards an empire of oyster trays. 'I've stocks here from Colchester, France, Ireland – that's how we've survived. But Vinnie was on a hiding to nothing.'

'And you once said the same to me,' Pearl reminded him, remembering only too well the opposition her own business had suffered in its early days. One good fish restaurant was said to be all that the town required, but she had gone on to prove everyone wrong – including Matheson.

He plucked the order from Billy's hand and looked at it cursorily, together with Pearl's cheque. 'Vinnie was small fry,' he said, dropping the cheque into his till and slamming its drawer shut, meeting Pearl's gaze with a look that announced that all conversation was over.

Pearl picked up her bag and walked to the door where she glanced back to see Matheson disappearing into his office. Only Billy remained at the counter, stroking the grey stubble on his chin, looking uneasy as he registered where his priorities lay. Offering up a shrug to Pearl, he quickly followed after his boss.

Stepping out onto the quay again, Pearl took a deep breath but it failed to calm her anger and she strode off in the direction of the busy Horsebridge. The area was so-called because it had once served as an approach route for horses to unload at sea. In time, Europe's first passenger and freight steam railway, the Crab and Winkle Line, had taken over transportation and for years the site had remained ramshackle, even more so after a bomb had dropped in the vicinity during the last war. Few people these days remembered the nearby disused bus garage which had been taken over and run by local artists. Johnny's Art House had served as a space for exhibitions and various events. Dolly had once rehearsed there with an eccentric group of women dancers known as the Fish Slappers. However, the council had inevitably torn down the old building to make way for a new development, and the Horsebridge Centre was now the town's cultural hub. Shaped like the upturned hull of a ship, the new building staged art exhibitions, concerts and classes ranging from yoga to flamenco. It overlooked a fine old pub and a spacious beachfront restaurant which had gained a good reputation with the London press.

Matheson's words still echoed for Pearl and she knew that he was right: in relation to the burgeoning town, Vinnie had indeed been small fry – but then so was Pearl, which was why, perhaps, she alone had understood Vinnie's need to strike out on his own. Had it been so wrong for a fisherman to want to fish free waters? Or for Pearl to try to be what she had always felt herself to be: the one to make sense out of chaos, the one to make everything right? Vinnie's death appeared to be a senseless loss – an accident pure and simple – and yet something was urging Pearl on to search for further answers.

Rounding the corner back on to the High Street, she found herself swamped by a surge of festival tourists. For a moment, they obscured Dolly, who was busily chalking a special menu on a board outside the restaurant but, sensing Pearl's presence, she looked up and took time to assess her daughter's mood. Pearl was staring directly at the restaurant window, noting the slight alterations Dolly had made to her festival display. A sea horse had appeared, and another creature now lurked beneath the blue taffeta: a small starfish that could not fail to remind Pearl of the events of last night.

Dolly read her daughter's thoughts but before she had time to comment, Pearl herself spoke. 'I didn't get to ask,' she began. 'How was the flamenco last night?'

Dolly saw through Pearl's bravado and offered up a small shrug. 'It'll play havoc with my knees,' she reflected, 'but on the "up" side, Juana turned out to be a Juan, and he said I have a nice pair of castanets.'

Against all odds, a smile now played upon Pearl's lips. 'Come on,' she said, as she slipped her arm through her mother's. 'You and I have work to do'.

Together they stepped into the oyster bar and prepared for business.

Chapter Five

By noon on that first day of the Oyster Festival, every table in Pearl's small restaurant was taken – apart from one. A group of DFLs were at the seafood bar: stylish girls with expensive tans and even more expensive handbags perched on stools to sip champagne as their partners tipped oysters down their throats like tequila slammers.

Pearl stood at the kitchen door staring back into the restaurant, curious about a booking that had been taken yesterday during her meeting with Stroud. Considering all that had happened since then, the appointment now seemed a lifetime ago. Although she had made several more attempts to contact Stroud, he was still failing to respond to her calls and Pearl knew it was only a matter of time before she would need to confess all to McGuire. She realised that McGuire would suspect her motives for not having done so. If shock and fatigue proved to be sufficient reasons for not coming clean last night, the detective would surely question why she hadn't called him this morning but had chosen, instead, to visit Connie in search of more answers.

The pressure of running a seafood restaurant on the town's busiest day of the year offered a suitable excuse for the time being. With Ahmed, her part-time commis chef, busy in the kitchen and Dolly working front of house, Pearl gave her attention to a young waitress who stood biting a fingernail as she hovered by the microwave.

'Everything all right?'

Ruby quickly nodded as she saw her boss approaching but Pearl sensed the girl's anxiety. A pretty seventeen-year-old, Ruby could sometimes look pale and under nourished. In the morning sunlight her skin seemed almost translucent, allowing tiny blue veins to shine through it like threads, her pallor only emphasised by the fact that she had recently lightened her hair.

'It'll be hectic,' warned Pearl, 'but over in no time. Just remember all I've told you, and you can't go wrong. Write everything down, and if you're going to drop something . . .'

'Don't do it over the customer,' Ruby finished, and smiled.

Pearl returned the smile. 'Good girl.'

The microwave gave a sudden 'ping' which acted like a punctuation mark to the exchange and Ruby turned and took out a dish of steaming broccoli. She slid it efficiently onto a tray then headed speedily out of the kitchen.

'Surprised you're here.' Pearl's greengrocer, Marty Smith, was standing at the door, dressed in a signature green T-shirt that matched the colour of his eyes. He slipped his baseball cap from his head to wipe it across his hot brow. 'Must have been one hell of a shock for you.'

Marty came forward but Pearl neatly sidestepped him, moving across to the stack of cardboard boxes he had just set down at the open door. Marty was tall and good-looking, and though he paid good money to three efficient delivery boys, he always made Pearl's deliveries in person.

'Everything here?' Pearl checked through the boxes as Marty nodded.

'I threw in some Spanish rocket free of charge,' he said. 'And some artichokes.' He smiled and handed her a receipt book. As Pearl signed, she could feel his eyes upon her. 'You should've called me,' he said, lowering his voice as Ahmed walked by. 'I'd have come straight away if I knew you were in trouble.'

'I know you would,' replied Pearl. 'But there was nothing you could have done, Marty. I was with the police until almost midnight.'

'Police?'

'Giving a statement. Answering questions.' She handed back the receipt book and wiped a strand of hair from her face.

Marty gave a wistful smile, wishing he could have done it for her. 'No wonder you look dead beat.'

'Thanks a bunch,' Pearl grinned. She went to unpack her delivery but Marty was quicker and picked up one of the boxes himself.

'No, I didn't mean . . .'

'I know what you meant.' Pearl looked back at Marty and straight away wished that she hadn't, but the sight of his sad green eyes only served to toughen her resolve. 'I'm fine. Really I am.' She gave an efficient nod towards the crate in Marty's arms and he was forced to relinquish it.

He trailed after Pearl as she headed to the cold store. 'Well, why don't we do something when you've finished up here? We could go down to the beach.'

Pearl's heart sank for she knew what was coming. In a symbolic move, Marty had traded in his old, one-man canoe for a two-person kayak and was desperate for someone else to fill it.

'Might take your mind off things?' he suggested.

'I'm driving over to see Charlie,' she explained.

Marty made a quick computation. 'I could meet you there,' he said. 'Take you to that new Italian restaurant on the precinct.'

With one shake of her head, Pearl dashed Marty's dreams. 'It's really not a good time.'

Marty recognised the look he was used to – the one that closed down all further opportunity. He nodded slowly and drew his cap back onto his head before trying one last time. 'There's a traders' meeting in the Conti' this week. If you make it down, I could at least buy you a drink?'

A small ray of hope still shone for Marty Smith. Pearl found it hard to extinguish.

'I'll try,' she told him.

Marty gave a satisfied smile and turned now for the door. As he left, Pearl heaved a sigh, watching his baseball cap bobbing along the upper section of the kitchen window. Pearl's greengrocer was only a few years younger than herself: a kind and honest man who rose early and worked late, having single-handedly transformed his father's greengrocer's shop, once modestly known as 'Granny Smith's', to the upmarket organic store 'Cornucopia'. Marty owned a large house in Tankerton and drove a convertible sports car which turned heads when it sped through the High Street. By most people's standards, he was an eligible bachelor although Love had seemed to elude him.

A few years ago, Pearl had accepted a casual date, an exploratory mission of sorts, to investigate why Marty Smith still remained romantically unattached. Girlfriends had come and gone, but no relationship had ever blossomed for him and, in that sense, Pearl felt an affinity, allowing herself to wonder if she and her greengrocer might have even more in common than a taste for Spanish rocket.

One sultry summer's evening, Marty had arrived at the door of Seaspray Cottage looking fit and handsome, wearing a smart suit and crisp white shirt in place of his usual jeans and T-shirt. The evening had seemed promising until a cloud of pungent aftershave accompanied him into the living room. After a quick drink and a thirty-minute drive to Broadstairs in Marty's open-top convertible, the aftershave was still there, catching the back of Pearl's throat as a waiter had shown them to their table. Marty had booked a good restaurant overlooking the sea – a nice gesture if he hadn't been trying too hard. He had opened doors, pulled out chairs and popped up like a Jack in the Box from his own seat every time Pearl disappeared to the loo. There was champagne instead of wine, but this, at least, had put Pearl's date more at ease.

In the warmth of her company, Marty had begun finally to relax, sharing his dreams and speaking animatedly of plans for an organic juice bar on the High Street. He had admitted that sometimes he found it hard to talk to women, although he had always felt Pearl to be a kindred spirit, someone who had earned his respect for the passionate way she ran her own business. As he continued, it had become achingly clear to Pearl why

Marty was still without a partner. He described a future filled not with people but expanding stock, of persimmons replacing plums, of Swiss chard substituting sprouts. That evening, over a candle-lit dinner, Pearl knew for sure that Marty Smith would never light her fire and if Marty knew it too, he still clung to a hope of changing her mind – one day.

Pearl ruefully glanced down at the complimentary Spanish rocket he had left for her. Plucking a few leaves, she tasted it and found it strong, pleasant and slightly nutty – like Marty himself. Only then did she notice that her mother was at the kitchen door. Dolly, lips puckered, issued a fierce whisper. '"Whinge" is here.'

Dolly disappeared back into the restaurant and Pearl headed swiftly after her, to see that Ruby was now seating several customers. Harcourt was the name Pearl had noticed in the Reservations book after returning from her meeting with Stroud. The telephone code for the village of Merry Wives Lees had confirmed to Pearl that the booking was for established customers: Robert Harcourt and his wife, Phoebe, who had been dubbed 'Whinge' by Dolly.

Harcourt was a respected architect, the designer of several prestigious London developments as well as the impressive barn conversion which the couple now called home. A sprawling design statement, the house could be seen from miles away, totally at odds, Pearl thought, with the fact that just a few hundred metres down a narrow country lane, an oak-fringed village green still existed on which villagers erected a Maypole each spring and played cricket every summer. Tradition was everything in a small place like Merry Wives Lees, and yet within just a couple of years, the Harcourts had managed to insinuate themselves into the social fabric of the area, achieving a standing that seemed almost historical. Both were bourgeois, middle-aged Londoners seemingly unaware of any irony as they had taken up new roles as unofficial Lord and Lady of the Manor. It was similar to the phenomenon Pearl was witnessing among some of the wealthier incomers to Whitstable: proud owners of newly gentrified homes forsaking their city roots to display in the windows of their new 'coastguard cottages' a fine model yacht or other sailing vessel as evidence of their assimilation. The Harcourts, however, had no need for the nautical, embracing instead the usual props and features of country life: dried hops in the kitchen and a newly built walled herb garden, designed to look as though it might have been there for centuries.

Although essentially a coastal town, Whitstable was adjoined by plenty of countryside to its south which offered cherry fields, orchards and boating opportunities along the Great Stour River, but the smarter villages were always apt to look down on the little fishing town as somewhere not to live but to visit. Whitstable, in turn, lorded it over its coastal neighbours, principally the larger resorts of Broadstairs, Margate and Ramsgate, which stood on a peninsula that, at one time, had been entirely separate from the mainland. While inhabitants of those towns still spoke of Whitstable as being 'off island', some Whitstable locals used a pejorative term for all parts east of itself as 'Planet Thanet'.

Today, it appeared that the Harcourts were in tourist-guide mode, having quitted their rural haven to introduce new guests to the festival. Not everyone, however, seemed happy with their seating arrangements.

'Do we have to be so close to the window?' whinged Phoebe, in a voice that cut like a knife.

'You don't *have* to be anywhere,' her husband replied. 'I simply thought Leo and Sarah might like to be able to see the Parade.'

'Absolutely,' smiled Sarah, who was tall, elegant and dressed completely in taupe. Pearl noted that she wore a simple linen trouser suit and a stylish pair of sculptural silver earrings which complemented the geometric cut of impossibly glossy, shoulder-length fair hair. Silver bracelets jangled at her delicate wrists and a matching necklace lay against her sunkissed throat. Sarah was in her late forties but looked to be the kind of woman who would remain chic and beautiful all her life – thanks to money.

'How about you, Alex?' Robert turned to the young man in his early twenties, who stood sandwiched uncomfortably between his parents.

'I'm easy,' the boy replied, wiping a lick of blond hair from his tanned forehead. Like his mother, Alex was tall, with ice-blue eyes and an athletic build. Pearl saw Ruby blush as he smiled at her. Meanwhile, ferret-featured Phoebe Harcourt fanned a menu before her face.

'I'm sorry, but I'm finding it so frightfully hot in here,' she complained. 'Aren't you, Leo?'

The man beside her was distinguished, thickset with greying hair; he wore a heavy diver's watch that became visible as he pulled up his shirtsleeves. 'It was forty degrees in Cape Town,' he announced. 'So we're acclimatised to heat.'

Phoebe accepted this with lips pursed tight like a knitted buttonhole.

'I still think we could have booked somewhere a little more al fresco.' She gave her husband a challenging look while Ruby glanced helplessly across at Pearl.

'Is everything all right?' Pearl asked, coming forward to the rescue.

'It will be,' replied Robert, though his wife failed to take his hint.

'No air conditioning yet, I suppose?' Phoebe whinged.

'Afraid not,' Pearl said smoothly. 'Perhaps you'd be happier in the shade?'

'That'll be the day,' murmured Robert. Phoebe gave her husband a sharp look while Pearl took the opportunity to pull out a few chairs from under the table. 'Who'd like a street view?'

'Done,' said Leo, indicating seats for his wife and son.

Robert Harcourt chose his own place, looking sidelong at Phoebe. It was clear 'Whinge' remained unhappy with the arrangement but she dropped her menu onto the table in a clear admission of defeat. 'Pinot grigio and a dozen oysters to start,' he ordered.

Ruby scribbled down the order and hurried off to the kitchen.

'Oh, and some of those delicious herrings marinated in madeira!' he called after her.

Pearl left the party and returned to the seafood bar. The DFLs had left, to be replaced by new customers – and to Pearl's surprise, she saw that McGuire was among them. He was sitting on a stool at the bar, idly thumbing through a programme for the Oyster Festival, and though he was dressed casually in a loose white T-shirt, black jeans and trainers, Pearl suspected he was here on business.

'It's not a good time for questions,' she warned him, on her way towards the kitchen.

'How about oysters? Is it a good time for them?'

Pearl saw McGuire smile before he tossed the festival programme down onto the counter. She picked up a menu and handed it to him, before leaning closer to point out a sheet of paper inside. 'Festival Specials,' she explained. 'Oyster Fritters, Oysters Rockefeller, Asian . . .'

'Asian?' asked McGuire. Looking straight at Pearl, he managed to put her off her stride.

With her finger still hovering over the menu, she had to look away from him to explain: 'Served with rice wine, vinegar and ginger. But if you're not that adventurous, there's always lemon and mignonette sauce.'

McGuire said nothing but continued to study Pearl, in preference to the menu.

'That's the classic option,' she continued. 'Chopped shallot, white peppercorns, wine and . . .' She broke off, realising that McGuire wasn't paying much attention. Instead his eyes were scanning Pearl's face as though he might need a detailed description for further use. She found herself unable to recall her final ingredient.

'And?' prompted McGuire.

'Sherry vinegar,' she suddenly remembered.

McGuire offered a smile, remembering that only twelve hours ago and beneath the stark lighting of a police questioning room, Pearl had looked drained and vulnerable. Now, in her own environment with sunlight streaming through the windows, she was vital, her skin tanned, high cheekbones beginning to flush – perhaps with some impatience. 'So what's it to be?' she asked finally.

McGuire's gaze shifted to the stack of grey shells on the counter.

'How about I just try one of those?'

Pearl recognised that McGuire was wasting her time but nevertheless she picked up a shucking knife and shoved its blade between the hinge of a large rock oyster. Holding McGuire's look, she gave a sudden sharp twist, forcing open the strong adductor muscle from the shell; sliding the blade beneath the oyster itself, she added a quartered lemon and presented the plate to the detective. He looked down, casting a cool eye across it.

'So that's it? The famous Whitstable oyster?'

At that moment, Ruby passed by from the kitchen, carrying a platter destined for the Harcourts' table. Pearl waited for her waitress to pass before taking a seat beside the detective. Leaning close, she lowered her voice to a whisper. 'The native can only be served when there's an r in the month.'

Pearl read McGuire's look as he glanced over to the Harcourts' table where Ruby's platter was being met with some enthusiasm.

'I know,' said Pearl. 'Ironic when the festival's in July.' She picked up the festival programme, about to explain more when Phoebe Harcourt's voice rang out from across the room. 'You – we need more lemon!'

Ruby smiled nervously at her customer as she hurried back to the counter. Pearl quartered two more lemons and handed them to her, saying in an undertone: 'Sorry, I should've warned you.'

'No problem,' Ruby whispered before hurrying back to the Harcourts.

McGuire carefully noted Pearl's reaction. 'Difficult customers?'

'Oh, the Harcourts like to give us a run for our money.'

'The guy by the window?' McGuire said. 'That's Leo

Berthold – the businessman who's just bought the Hyde in Canterbury.'

Pearl frowned at this. 'You mean the old Hyde Hotel?'

'The new one,' McGuire told her. 'At least it will be, once the renovation is finished.'

Pearl experienced a sinking feeling. With its fine old paintings hung against ancient Anaglypta wallpaper, and cobwebs dangling from original chandeliers, the Hyde had always resembled a kitsch film set rather than a prestigious city hotel. She recalled that it was only last winter when a friend of Charlie's had been hired to play a New Year's Eve session on the old baby grand piano in the bar. It had been a memorable if embarrassing night, during which a well-oiled Dolly had performed 'I Will Survive' and some cheesy classics by Abba. Now, thought Pearl, even the piano would no doubt disappear, swept away like everything else to be replaced by the predictable features of yet another 'boutique' hotel: a riot of etched glass at odds with the ancient buildings of West Gate. She viewed, with fresh eyes, the man sitting by the window with his stylish wife and handsome young son as they raised their glasses with the Harcourts.

McGuire, in turn, observed Pearl before he remarked, 'They say he's keen to invest in the area.'

'In Canterbury, you mean?'

'Maybe Whitstable too.'

Pearl continued to study the scene at the window table where young Alex Berthold toyed with the shells on his plate while Phoebe, buoyed by pinot grigio, trilled an anecdote to Sarah at her side. Robert Harcourt was holding Berthold's attention, perhaps angling, thought Pearl, to design a new hotel for his friend. 'Taking over like grey squirrels,' she murmured to herself, remembering Billy Crouch's words.

As McGuire looked at her, Pearl directed her attention to his plate. 'What you have there is a completely different variety to the native. Pacific rock oysters were only introduced relatively recently, but a shortage of fishermen means they've been allowed to grow too big. There are some on the beds out there right now that weigh more than two kilos.' She smiled. 'How would you fancy getting through half a dozen of those?'

The single oyster on McGuire's plate had remained untouched. Pearl guessed the reason why. 'It's no secret there have been other problems.' She paused for a moment. 'Sixty per cent of young oysters are actually killed off by herpes.' Seeing McGuire's expression, she went on reassuringly, 'No need to worry, unless you're an oyster. What's really needed here is some proper investment to re-lay native seeds.'

'Seeds?'

'A young oyster starts off as a larva and becomes a spat after it's found a suitable place to grow. It's a seed once it's large enough to survive predators.' She fixed her gaze on McGuire. 'That's what Vinnie Rowe was trying to do.'

'Survive predators?'

'Re-lay native seeds.' She waited a moment. 'But he was in debt. I spoke to his partner Connie this morning. He'd been trying to compete with the bigger companies, but—'

'Not managing to do so if he owed money.'

Pearl saw that McGuire was unimpressed with her line of thinking. It was time to come clean about Stroud.

'I had a visitor yesterday at my agency.'

McGuire stopped toying with the oyster on his plate. 'Your what?'

'I recently started up a small detective agency.' McGuire began to smile. 'You find that amusing?'

The policeman shrugged. 'I thought your business was oysters.'

'My business is people. As is yours.' She sighed with frustration. 'Since we've at least that much in common, why don't you tell me what you've discovered so far?'

McGuire was taken aback, not just by Pearl's question but by her tone. He smiled, enigmatically this time, his silence serving only to increase Pearl's impatience. 'Look,' she said, 'I presume you've had forensic reports back to confirm Vinnie's death was an accident, or . . .'

'Or what?'

'Or you'd be out making proper inquiries instead of sitting here pretending you've got a taste for oysters.'

She had expected a suitable defence from McGuire, but instead he was just noticing that her eyes were the same colour as the sea that morning – pale grey shifting to blue with just the slightest change of sunlight. Finally he gave voice to the single question in his mind. 'Are you kept very busy in a town like this?'

Pearl frowned. 'What d'you mean?'

'With this agency of yours.'

She hesitated. 'I told you – it's new.'

'Then I wish you luck.' McGuire was sure she would need it, since Whitstable was the kind of innocuous place where local newspapers carried such dramatic headlines as CHILD LOSES SHOE, SHOCK AS SHOP SHUTS and ARCHBISHOP NOT COMING TO TOWN.

Pearl opened her mouth to protest, but a sudden loud drum roll outside put a stop to all further conversation. Customers and staff were looking towards the door where Dolly stood, beckoning urgently to her daughter. Pearl quickly got to her feet. 'I'll be back,' she announced, deserting the detective as she went to join her mother. Customers began to follow.

At the Harcourts' table, Leo Berthold pressed a white napkin to his lips. 'This is it?' he asked.

'This is it,' confirmed Robert, ushering his guests from the restaurant.

Outside, a sticky heat rose from the pavement and the sound of triangles and trumpets from the Sea Scouts' band segued clumsily into a burst of loud samba, heralding the arrival of the festival parade which was winding its way from the harbour onto the High Street. Hundreds of locals, young and old, were following a papier mâché figure which towered, some four metres tall, above the parade.

Leo Berthold was forced to shout across the music as he turned to Robert Harcourt to ask, 'What the hell's that supposed to be?'

'Sam the Giant,' explained Harcourt. 'He was put together by some local artists, I believe. He's meant to reflect the town's association with the sea, which is why he's wearing that coat covered in oyster shells.'

Swathed in fishing nets, the figure now revolved, gliding its way towards the restaurant. Two carnival 'Big Heads' flanked Sam; one was known as Dollar Dan, named after a Victorian deep-sea diver who was said to have lived on Dollar Row, while the other was his companion – a fabled seahorse called Bobbin. Following on behind snaked the samba band. Pearl recognised most of its members. Local musicians, more usually seen performing in pubs and clubs, had joined force with some enthusiastic DFLs who were shaking maracas and blowing carnival whistles to the persistent beat of a steel drum. Students from the local circus school brought up the rear, jugglers and costumed harlequins on stilts, but with an eccentric twist on the usual horse-drawn dray, a group of Newfoundland dogs could be seen heading in their direction, harnessed to a miniature carriage loaded with oyster baskets. The dogs came to a halt at Pearl's feet, slobbering foam in the heat.

'Tradition,' continued Robert to the Bertholds. 'All symbolic, of course. The "catch" comes ashore and gets delivered to various restaurants and cafés. This place is on the list for obvious reasons.'

A stout woman in her sixties, dressed in Victorian costume, bustled towards Pearl. Although she looked as if she might have stepped straight out of the pages of *David Copperfield* she was, in fact, Billy Crouch's wife, Sadie. Pearl accepted the basket she offered, while Sadie leaned in to her, looking increasingly peeved.

'I could murder whoever it was decided on bonnets,' she hissed, tipping her despised headwear back from her forehead before she glanced about at the excited faces surrounding her. 'If you ask me, it's a disgrace this has been allowed to continue today. We should be mourning, not celebrating.'

'I know,' said Pearl, 'but what can we do?'

Sadie Crouch gave a defeated shrug. 'Nothing,' she agreed, 'except smile for the cameras. As usual.' As the procession wound on, Sadie picked up her skirts and flounced back to the Newfoundlands, one of which was now peeing up its cart.

Pearl noticed that in a moment of bad timing, Sarah Berthold was actually holding up her mobile phone to take a photo. After checking the image she had captured, she turned to her son. 'How wonderfully bizarre,' she said serenely. 'Like a mini Rio. I can't for one moment think we'll be bored here, can you?'

She re-entered the restaurant and her son smiled after her, but Pearl sensed it was only a valiant effort on the boy's part. Overall, he seemed jaded and vaguely troubled, and as Ruby passed close by, Alex moved towards her, as if jostled by the crowd. They shared a look, but the girl broke away as she noticed her boss staring across and said, 'I'll take that for you, Pearl.' She headed off to the kitchen with the oyster basket.

Just then, Leo Berthold called to his son. 'Alex?'

The boy looked back to see his father indicating a single empty seat at the table. Alex dutifully took his place while Pearl moved directly on to the seafood counter. She had been expecting to rejoin McGuire but was brought up short as she found only an empty stool and an uneaten oyster – evidence that the inspector had slipped her net.

At closing time a few hours later, Pearl watched Ruby bagging up some rubbish before setting it outside the back door. 'You did well today,' she told her.

'Cool,' beamed Ruby. 'I'd rather be busy than clock-watching all day. That Saturday job I had at the sweet shop was lethal. I was wishing my life away.'

'Never do that,' Pearl advised. 'It goes fast enough as it is.'

The young waitress looked down at her grubby hands and went to the sink to rinse them. Wisp-thin, Ruby seemed to be always on the go, as though never wanting time to think. It wasn't surprising, Pearl thought. She sensed the reason why. At seven years old, the girl had arrived from London to take up residence with her grandmother in Whitstable's only tower block. Windsor House, overlooking the cricket ground on one side and the Labour Club's beer garden on the other, had become Ruby's new home after her young mother had died from an overdose that some said had been suicide. Mary Hill had risen to the challenge of taking care of her only granddaughter, finding a place for Ruby in the same primary school as Charlie, and after a while the girl had begun to find her feet, fitting into the life of the town as though she had known nothing else. But the truth was, Ruby had indeed known another life before arriving in Whitstable and Pearl was sure that memories of it still haunted her.

When the girl wasn't occupied, she seemed vague, almost otherworldly, as if her mind was drifting elsewhere against her will. In time, that was to become true for Ruby's grandmother too, as Mary's absentmindedness began slowly to progress into dementia. Less than a month ago, Mary Hill had been settled into a Canterbury care home, and after some concern from Social Services as to how Ruby might manage without her, officials had finally agreed that the teenager could stay on alone at her grandmother's flat. Since leaving school in the summer, Ruby had been working hard at 'The Whitstable Pearl' to maintain not only an income but also her independence.

Pearl now handed a small brown envelope to Ruby, who tore it open like a child with a Christmas present. Inside, she found loose change and a few five-pound notes.

'All those tips are for me?' she asked, incredulous.

Pearl nodded, guessing that the money left by Robert Harcourt had been more of an ostentatious display for his guest than a sign of appreciation for their waitress's service, but she kept her silence and watched Ruby proudly slip the envelope into her pocket.

'Good-looking, wasn't he?' Pearl ventured.

Ruby looked up.

'The boy, Alex,' continued Pearl, 'at the Harcourts' table. Didn't I see him smiling at you?'

Ruby caught the mischief in Pearl's eyes. 'I don't think so. I'm well out of his league.' She started for the door, then paused and asked, 'By the way, how's Charlie getting on at uni?'

'Just fine.'

Ruby nodded. 'Good. Say hi from me when you next see him, will you?'

'I'll do that, Ruby,' Pearl said kindly.

After locking up the restaurant, Pearl got into her car and took the back route to Canterbury along the old tree-lined Wat Tyler Way. The route allowed her to avoid festival traffic and gave her some time to unwind. It was still a warm evening but less humid away from the sea, and in just over twenty minutes she was pressing the doorbell to her son's student flat.

Charlie's voice sounded back from an intercom. 'That you, Mum?'

Pearl stepped back on the pavement and peered up at the window. The front door opened gently beneath her hand and a single flight of stairs took her up to Charlie's landing. Charlie had spent two terms sharing digs on campus before surprising his mother by finding a suitable place to rent at a very reasonable price. However, his plan had gone awry when his prospective flatmate had dropped out of college just as Charlie had moved in. Pearl had helped out with a deposit, and the first month's rent, but knew there would have to be further discussion if Charlie continued to stall about finding another flatmate.

The block was no more than a decade old and well maintained with a clean stair carpet and newly painted walls, but sometimes Pearl would be met in the hallway by evidence of student life in the form of empty beer bottles on their way to the recycling centre. Most of the residents had now left for the summer holidays. Only Charlie remained.

Pearl found her son standing at his open flat door and offered the smile she reserved only for him. Charlie held her close and for longer than his usual embrace, warm but also protective. 'How was the traffic?'

'I escaped most of it,' Pearl said, 'though I might not be so lucky going home.'

Charlie ushered his mother inside.

The first thing Pearl noticed was that the flat was unusually tidy. Charlie didn't exactly fit the description of a student slob but a 'frogs and snails' element was always evident in his territories, although it seemed to have been supplanted now by a touch of 'sugar and spice'. Fat candles sat on glass saucers around the fireplace, soft cushions lay plumped on a satin throw upon the sofa and a large bowl containing pretty seashells had replaced the usual drink cans on the coffee table.

'Go straight through to the kitchen,' Charlie said. 'I've got some wine opened.'

Once there, he poured her a glass of rioja while Pearl unpacked the carrier bag she had brought with her. 'How was your day?' he asked.

'Hectic,' Pearl replied. 'Which is why there aren't too many leftovers.' She took several items from the bag, lifting foil covers from two dishes to reveal a coral-coloured quiche made of sweet potatoes and fresh salmon, and some tiny white-bodied anchovies, glistening in olive oil.

'Lemons,' Pearl remembered. 'Why do I always forget them?'

'No problem.' Charlie opened the fridge door with a

flourish. Pearl noted immediately how clean and orderly its interior had become – triangles of Parmesan and balls of mozzarella stacked in plastic containers alongside green and black olives marinating in garlic and oil. He handed Pearl a fat lemon. 'Tizzy says she can't live without them,' he announced.

Pearl calculated it had taken precisely three minutes for Charlie's new girlfriend to enter the conversation. 'By the way,' he continued, 'she said to say hi. In fact, when I told her what had happened last night she was really concerned about you.'

'Nice of her,' said Pearl, looking around as if for a distraction. 'Shall we take all this into the other room?'

Pearl ferried the tray of food into the living room and set it down on a glass table while Charlie followed in behind.

'You sure you're okay?' he asked. 'I mean, you might be suffering from delayed shock.' He handed Pearl the glass of wine and sat down with her at the table.

'I'm fine – really,' she told him.

'But Gran said you got arrested.'

'Taken in for questioning.' Pearl squeezed lemon juice across the anchovies as Charlie watched her. 'The police had forensic evidence to collect, and anything I said, without being properly cautioned, would have been inadmissible in court.'

He thought about this. 'So . . . how come you went out to Vinnie's boat in the first place?' He picked up his fork and began breaking into the thick slice of quiche on his plate. 'Did you happen to see something?'

'Like what?'

'I dunno,' he shrugged. 'But Gran said Vinnie was already dead when you found him. So, was it just coincidence you happened to be there, or did you already know that something wasn't right?'

For a moment, Pearl was reminded of being questioned by McGuire, the stuffy interview room where the hands of a clock had turned far too slowly. In spite of the warm room she gave a sudden shiver. 'Can we drop it please, Charlie?'

'Sure. Sorry, Mum.'

Pearl watched her son eating, pleased as always to see him tucking into her food. 'The quiche is good,' he mumbled with a full mouth.

'It's always good,' smiled Pearl, relieved that her cooking had created a suitable distraction.

'Did I tell you Tizzy makes a great risotto?'

Pearl felt her smile tightening. 'You have now.'

'I'll get her to give you the recipe.'

Pearl looked up and Charlie recognised his mistake. 'Sorry. That came out all wrong. You make a great risotto.'

'And I *never* use recipes.'

'Course you don't. I told her how you like to cook – a glass of wine . . .'

'Or two.'

'A bit of this . . .'

'A bit of that . . .'

'And suddenly,' Charlie clicked his fingers and indicated the food on the table, 'it's all there like magic.'

Pearl took a sip of wine, but her curiosity had been piqued. 'And what did Tizzy say when you told her that?'

'Tizzy's Italian. She just laughed.'

'*Laughed?*'

'Said it sounded very English. Very . . . hit and miss.'

Pearl frowned. 'Hit and miss?'

'She's right. You always wing it.'

'I improvise.'

'Same thing.'

'I never miss,' Pearl insisted.

'Not often anyway.'

Pearl caught Charlie's teasing tone and relaxed as she returned it. Setting down her glass she leaned back in her chair, feeling it was time to broach something that was on her mind. Waiting for Charlie to finish the last of the anchovies, she decided to bite the bullet. 'D'you think you might come home soon?'

Charlie took another olive. 'To help with the restaurant?'

'To visit.'

At this, Charlie looked up.

'Properly, I mean. I know you've been busy, but now that the holidays are here . . .' She stopped, noting her son's guilty look. It had, in fact, been several weeks since he had been back in Whitstable. Each time Pearl had invited him he had found a suitable excuse, usually citing the pressure of his studies, though last summer had been a different story. Then, he had moved straight back home as soon as term had ended, keen to catch up with his Whitstable 'posse'. This year, time and a little distance seemed to be driving a wedge between Charlie and his old schoolfriends. Pearl was anxious it didn't do the same for her and her son.

Charlie wiped his hands on a serviette and hesitated, as though framing a difficult explanation. 'Look, Mum, I . . .'

Pearl felt the need to stop him before he said something she didn't want to hear, but a ringing phone brought a halt to any further conversation and Charlie got to his feet to answer it. As he picked up his mobile, Pearl noted how tall he seemed to have grown, standing away from her, looking increasingly like the father he had never met. Pearl had to concede that perhaps Dolly was right: Charlie had come to replace all the love she had lost one summer many years ago.

'Ciao.' Charlie was listening carefully to his caller before offering a casual reply. 'No, I'm here with Mum.' He glanced back and winked at Pearl, but the intimate tone he was using on the phone made her feel uncomfortable, like an intruder. She pushed her plate away and headed off to the bathroom, but even after closing the door behind her she could still hear Charlie's voice from the other room. 'No, she seems okay,' he was explaining to the caller. 'She's a tough old bird. Gran'll look after her.'

Pearl moved to the sink. Turning on the tap she found the sound of running water silenced Charlie's voice so she let it run, watching for some time as it swirled around the sink. When she looked up again, her gaze shifted to some pretty bottles of Italian cologne sitting on sparkling glass shelves. These were the shelves that were usually splattered with toothpaste or ringed by the bottom of coffee mugs, but now a new pink electric toothbrush stood on display beside Charlie's, clear evidence for Pearl of why her son hadn't rushed home as soon as term had ended – and why he needed no flatmate.

Pearl saw her reflection in the bathroom mirror. She looked glum – defeated, even – but made a conscious effort to summon a cheerful expression before she went back into the living room.

Charlie was just slipping his mobile phone into his pocket as Pearl rejoined him.

'Tizzy?' she guessed brightly.

He nodded. 'She says she's been thinking about you.'

Pearl gave a stiff smile. 'Thanks.' She moved to the table

and, for want of something to do, began clearing away empty plates. 'I'll make us some coffee.'

But as she started for the kitchen, Charlie said, 'Not for me, thanks, Mum.'

As Pearl turned, he explained, somewhat guiltily, 'I have to go and pick Tizzy up.' He came forward to take the tray from Pearl's hands. 'Don't worry about all this. I'll take care of it all when I get back.'

Charlie moved on into the kitchen and set down the tray while Pearl followed quickly after him, asking, 'Is anything wrong?'

'No,' he said. 'Tizzy just needs to get to a rehearsal quickly. Did I mention that she sings?'

Before Pearl could comment, Charlie continued animatedly, 'She's got some great gigs lined up. In fact, she's playing on the last night of the Oyster Festival at Dead Man's Corner.' He waited for his mother's reaction but Pearl felt slightly dazed by the news, having forgotten that the culmination of festivities this year was due to take place on the harbour's new stage.

'You'll come, won't you?' her son asked, unnerved by her silence. 'Bring Gran too.' He mustered an expectant smile and Pearl found herself giving in to it.

'Of course,' she promised.

Satisfied now, Charlie picked up Pearl's bag and pressed it on to her. 'Thanks for coming, Mum.' For a brief moment his soft lips brushed lightly against Pearl's cheek before he broke away, saying, 'Wait until you see Tizzy perform. She's absolutely amazing.'

'I bet,' Pearl murmured.

Once out on the street, she went over to her car, glancing back up at Charlie's window, expecting to see him wave as he always did – except this time he wasn't there. She got in and was about to set her key in the ignition when she caught sight, in her rearview mirror, of Charlie leaving the apartment block. For an instant Pearl thought he might be coming across to her, but instead he walked in the opposite direction, to where his old Piaggio scooter was parked on the street. A car drove by at speed, obscuring Pearl's view. Once it had passed, she saw Charlie was still there, having mounted the scooter and slipped on his crash helmet. He kicked the scooter into life and the loud buzz of its engine sounded like an annoying insect before it began to recede into the distance – taking Charlie with it.

Pearl started up her own engine, noting with dismay that the fuel gauge showed the tank was on reserve – one more thing to add to today's list of grievances. She switched off the engine, took the key from the ignition and her mobile phone from her pocket before reaching for something in her glove compartment. Staring down at the business card in her hand she finally dialled a number, and when the call connected, asked one simple question.

'Could you please put me through to Detective Chief Inspector McGuire?'

Chapter Six

'Why didn't you mention any of this last night?' McGuire's impatience was clear but Pearl remained calm as she continued to fill her petrol tank, eyes firmly fixed upon the gauge.

'I told you,' she said flatly. 'I wasn't thinking clearly.'

'How about now?' asked McGuire. 'Any other information you're withholding?'

Pearl slipped her credit card into the payment machine. 'You would have found out sooner if you hadn't done the disappearing act in my restaurant.'

Having summoned him with her call, she now made him wait while she punched her PIN number onto the machine's key pad. Taking her receipt, she opened the driver's door, but as soon as she was back behind the wheel, McGuire got in and sat down beside her. He had half a mind to re-arrest her and take her straight back to the station for more questioning.

Legally, he could hold her in custody for twenty-four hours and, if nothing else, use the time to impress upon her that his investigation was no game. However, following up the lead she had just given him seemed a more productive option. He held out his open palm. 'Give me Stroud's details.'

Pearl considered his request for a moment then took her mobile from her pocket. Selecting Stroud's number, she passed the phone to McGuire and watched as he made a quick note of it. 'I tried again only this morning to contact him,' she said, 'but it seems to be on permanent voicemail. I think he may have gone back to where he came from.'

'And where's that?' asked McGuire, still busy with the phone.

'My guess would be the Balearics.' At this McGuire looked up but Pearl shrugged. 'Everything about him screamed ex-pat, you see. Especially his hat.'

'His what?'

She saw McGuire was frowning. 'A folding panama,' Pearl revealed. 'Made abroad. I noticed the label. The maker, *Sastre . . .*'

Pearl reached out to stop the detective from writing it down. 'No. *Sastre* is Spanish for tailor. The name beside that was *Portells* and I'm pretty sure that's Catalan.' She realised that her hand still rested on McGuire's and as she withdrew it, he resumed writing.

'Then there was the cathedral,' she continued.

'Canterbury?'

'No – Palma. A picture of it was on the label. Very distinctive.'

'The hat?'

'The cathedral. If you'd ever been there, you wouldn't forget it.'

McGuire looked up slowly now, unsure if she was toying with him.

'Majorca,' she explained finally. 'We used to go there on holiday every year. That's where my mum fell in love with flamenco.' She waited, expecting some kind of a response that failed to come. 'Look, I could be wrong, but the more I think about it, the more likely it seems that Stroud is an ex-pat. He had that look – you know, bothered by heat and bored by too much sun?'

McGuire's continued silence began to rankle. 'What happened to you earlier?' she demanded. 'One minute you were there in the restaurant, and the next, you had vanished into thin air.'

'I got a call from Forensics.'

'And?'

McGuire stepped out of the car.

'Oh, come on,' Pearl protested. 'I found Vinnie's body. Don't I have a right to know?'

McGuire turned slowly and leaned an arm on the passenger door. He fixed her with a look. 'Don't get in the way of this investigation.'

'Ah, so you are at least investigating?'

McGuire ignored the remark.

'Look, I've told you everything I know about Stroud,' she insisted. 'If Forensics did find something . . .'

'Of course they found something,' snapped McGuire. 'Plenty of fingerprints and DNA.'

He glared at her accusingly and Pearl made a sudden realisation. 'Mine?' His look answered her question.

'All right,' she admitted, 'so I raised the anchor and disturbed the body, but at that point I didn't know Vinnie was dead.'

'You brought in the boat and contaminated the scene.'

'I wasn't thinking at the time!'

'That much is obvious.' McGuire's tone served as a full stop to the exchange. He began to move off, but having taken only a single step, Pearl spoke up again.

'About Stroud . . .'

McGuire stopped in his tracks and turned round.

'You could always try checking the flights from Manston? It's a small airport out on the Margate road.'

'I know where Manston airport is!' McGuire erupted. Pearl noticed a small blue vein pulsing at his temple.

'Then did you also know that they recently started flying cheap packages? From Madeira, Portugal, France and . . .' she paused, observing that the tiny vein was now pulsing ever faster '. . . the Balearics too.' She offered a small smile. 'Good luck, Inspector.'

Turning the key in her ignition, Pearl drove down the crossover from the petrol station as McGuire continued to stare after her. He saw her glance back at him just once before her driver's window closed, and when the vehicle had finally been assimilated into the heavy stream of traffic, he became aware that he had been grinding his teeth. He released the tension in his jaw and was beginning to move towards his own parked car when he looked down and saw what he had just trodden in. The sign on the lamp-post in front of him warned of a fifty-pound fine for dog fouling. Someone had patently ignored it.

When Pearl reached the roundabout at Borstal Hill less than an hour later, she took a route through Tankerton to avoid the busy festival traffic. Although many old photographs and postcards depicted Whitstable's neighbouring town as a slightly more upmarket residential area, the two areas had elided over the years so that little now stood between them other than the landmark of a faux castle. The 'castle' at Tankerton was in fact an old manor house, built in the late eighteenth century as a summer home for a wealthy Londoner and sold a few hundred years later to the local council for the princely sum of £10,000. Some of the grounds had been taken over for use as a bowling green while the building itself had become the location for private parties and civic events like the annual May Day festivities and council members' meetings.

If Whitstable's key natural feature was its working harbour, Tankerton had its Slopes: a long stretch of grassy banks which led from the coastal road of Marine Parade straight down to the promenade and sea.

It was yet another beautiful evening as Pearl parked her car and sauntered along the top of Tankerton Slopes which overlooked a long swathe of coastline. At the eastern end, a skateboard park had been built in an attempt to contain the teenagers who, for some time, had used the prom as a practise place for their moves. A few years ago, Charlie would have been among them, rehearsing spins and kickbacks throughout the long hot summer days while in winter he had tobogganed down the snowy Slopes on estate agents' *For Sale* boards plucked from neighbouring front gardens. Now, thought Pearl, a beautiful young woman called Tizzy was the object of a new passion, and another generation had taken Charlie's place on the Slopes in the form of a few scrawny boys wearing baseball caps and baggy jeans, who were monitoring an older boy's flips.

Pearl took the opposite direction, casting her eye over a colony of beach huts whose brightly painted decks and porches pointed straight out to sea. The huts were laid out in three well-defined rows, separated at intervals by paths leading down to the promenade. Although they were no bigger than eight feet by ten, in recent years the huts had become sought after by Londoners as daytrip boltholes, their value driven up tenfold in as many years. Most had been lovingly restored but others lay in disrepair. Many had been personalised, bearing names like *Lazy Daze* or *Funky Mermaid*, but all seemed to be unoccupied at this point in time as the Oyster Festival in town proved to be the main attraction. In a week's time, thought Pearl, the smell of barbecued fish would again be hanging in the air, wine corks popping as hut owners re-positioned themselves following the festival.

Pearl stood at the top of the western Slopes where, for the price of a twenty-pence coin, an ancient telescope offered a view out to sea. But today there were no takers, nor was there the usual army of kids clambering over two impressive replica cannons that stood guard on the crest of the Slopes. A 'pitch pot' beacon stood between them, comprising an iron basket on top of a tall pole. All Whitstable children learned that throughout centuries, such coastal beacons had been set alight to signal any approaching danger. Used as warnings of the Armada and throughout the Napoleonic Wars, today only a warm breeze blew in across the sea as Pearl took a path down the Slopes to the beach.

She saw how clumps of yellow horned poppy had somehow taken root amidst the harsh shingle. Sea holly and sandwort had moved in to keep them company. While seagulls brawled over scraps amongst the long grass, only an elderly couple, walking a miniature poodle with a ball in its mouth, crossed Pearl's path as she stared out towards the Street. No one knew for sure how the mysterious spit of shingle had sprung into existence: some believed it to be the remains of a Roman road built on land that had subsequently been surrendered to the sea, while others said it had originated as an ancient landing stage for vessels, but Pearl knew that for Vinnie this would have served as a clear marker for the free fishing waters and that, in spite of all his hard work, the oysters he had tended would remain unharvested.

McGuire was right: Pearl *had* contaminated the forensic evidence, unaware that while she was searching the empty boat, Vinnie's body had been lying weighed down beneath her in the cold estuary mud. She reproached herself: how could she not have known? And considering all her training, how could she have failed to make some record of the scene using the camera on her mobile phone? The police forensics team would certainly have photographed everything on their arrival and Pearl knew there was hardly a chance of McGuire allowing her to see the results. Could there be something on those shots, she wondered, some small and seemingly insignificant detail that might offer a clue as to what had actually happened?

She closed her eyes and cast her mind back, allowing it to become a lens through which she might focus on all that she had seen that night. Slowly she began to form a mental image of Vinnie's boat lying east of the Street as the tide lowered. Twenty minutes had taken her from shore to the boat and she had observed nothing else at sea during that time – other than the rusting towers of the fort. Dusk was just falling once more when she saw, in her mind's eye, her own hand tying a pointer to Vinnie's starboard cleat, winding it into a firm figure of eight. But what else had she witnessed on climbing aboard? Or rather, what might she now remember?

Glancing aft and stern, she had been seeking only Vinnie when her gaze had settled on something else, taking in, perhaps only subliminally, something meaningless at the time but which now began to assume more significance. What was it? And what could it be that now prevented her from fast-forwarding the scene replaying in her memory?

The drone of an engine began breaking into her thoughts, becoming louder, and finally so intrusive that she was forced to open her eyes as if waking from a dream. A vivid memory had just come to her, a single image plucked from the many events of that night. Simultaneously, her mobile rang and she grabbed it from her pocket, barely registering the caller ID, as she finally put words to her thoughts. 'The culling table.'

McGuire's confused voice sounded on the other end of the line. 'What?'

'At the stern of the boat,' Pearl went on. 'It's where the oysters are sorted once they come aboard. Vinnie's catch was packed into baskets, so he would have already used the culling table.'

'So?'

'So he must have weighed anchor safely in order to have sorted his catch.'

A pause followed at the end of the line. 'Maybe the accident happened when he tried to re-anchor?'

'Why would he have needed to do so?' Pearl asked. 'There was little chance of the anchor dragging. There was only a light breeze and the boat was in shallow water with plenty of chain on the bed. No,' she argued, 'Vinnie would have gone out at high water, fished and weighed anchor to sort his catch before heading back before the tide turned.'

McGuire considered this. 'Then maybe something stopped him heading back?'

'Or someone?' suggested Pearl.

'Stroud,' said McGuire. 'He had a flight booked to Majorca this morning.'

'From Manston?'

'Yes.'

'Then I was right.'

'Not entirely.' McGuire cleared his throat. 'He didn't take it.'

'What did you say?' Pearl was struggling to hear over a new noise that persisted in the background. Looking up, she registered that it was the engine of a jet ski.

'Stroud didn't take the flight,' McGuire repeated.

The racket was suddenly silenced as the jet-ski rider brought the machine up onto a ramp on the shore. Wearing a black wetsuit and pushing back a damp fringe from his forehead, Alex Berthold approached the steps leading to an elegant property that faced straight out to sea from the foot of the Slopes.

'I'll need to talk to Stroud,' McGuire was saying. 'Find out exactly what he did after leaving your office.'

'But it doesn't make sense that he would have gone out to the boat.' Pearl was now on her feet, watching Alex climb the steps to the lilac-timbered veranda of an elegant building called Beacon House, which overlooked the Street.

'Why not?' asked McGuire.

'Because he didn't want Vinnie to know he was around. That's why he was trying to hire me.'

Alex entered the house while Pearl moved to the side of a beach hut, using it as cover. From there she sighted Sarah Berthold picking up a tray of empty glasses from a table in the garden. Husband Leo paced as he spoke into a mobile phone.

'You turned the job down,' McGuire went on, 'so maybe Stroud decided to deal with things himself.'

Pearl observed Leo Berthold finishing his call, going back into the house after his wife, leaving nothing more to see. But a sound seemed strangely to persist in the air, like the faintest echo of Alex's jet ski.

'In any case, I'll know for sure once he's picked up,' said McGuire, becoming suddenly aware of silence at the end of the line. 'Are you still there?'

Pearl did not hear him, for she was easing herself towards the source of the noise: a dilapidated beach hut which stood miserably among its smarter neighbours in the back row. A heavy bar was shoved through two metal loops against its closed doors. Pearl noted that the padlock was missing. Slipping her mobile into her pocket, she climbed onto the hut's rickety timber porch, aware that the noise was becoming louder: a steady humming. She tugged hard on the metal bar, managing to slide it out through the loops, but the wooden doors, having swollen in the sun, remained firmly closed. Pearl heaved them open.

Instantly a cloud of winged insects flew up into her face.

She raised her arms instinctively, trying to shield herself from what she first assumed to be a swarm of wasps or bees, but as the insects began to settle, Pearl saw that they were, in fact, blowflies – fat bluebottles covering every surface of the hut. The smell coming from inside was so vile, it caused her to retch. Her eyes adjusted to the darkness, locking onto something lying at her feet. She held her breath, bending down to what she thought to be a large bundle of clothes covered in grains of cooked rice. Then she noticed that the grains were writhing. Bloated white maggots were tumbling blindly between the cracks in the floorboards while a thick stain of blood had crept from beneath the clothes to form a dark map on the floor.

'Pearl?' McGuire's voice still sounded as Pearl retreated into the fresh air and took the mobile phone from her pocket.

'I'm here,' she replied weakly, bracing herself before returning into the hut to inspect the body. As she turned it over, the face looking back at her wore an expression not of irritation but of clear surprise, perhaps in response to the shattered section of floorboard which was wedged through the body's diaphragm. A man's hand fell forward like a small bloated starfish floating on the surface of a sticky pool of blood. Pearl stared at it for some time before remembering the phone in her hand.

'So is Stroud.'

Chapter Seven

The next day brought another fine morning, cotton buds of white cloud scudding across the sky on a warm breeze. Pearl sat at her breakfast table outside the Hotel Continental, a large cappuccino in front of her as she looked across at the hotel's car park. Amongst the many tourists' cars, the racy convertibles and family estates, there were several police vehicles and Pearl recognised McGuire's among them. The hotel was just a stone's throw from a gate which led from the pavement to the promenade. A uniformed constable had been posted there since the previous evening to prevent any dog walkers or rubber-neckers milling around. Nevertheless, below a colourful banner advertising a children's festival crabbing competition to take place later in the day, a small crowd had gathered on the beach to stare up at a single, dilapidated beach hut, sealed in police tape, with an inflatable forensic tent at its porch.

Pearl dropped another sugar cube into her coffee and checked her watch. It had just gone eight and she would have to get back soon to the restaurant to prepare for a busy day. A few seconds later she saw what she had been waiting for: McGuire stepped through the gate to the car park, pausing as he caught sight of her. He glanced towards his car and back again at Pearl – as though torn. Finally, he made his way towards her.

As he sat down, a waitress hurried across but McGuire shook his head, making it clear he wasn't planning on staying. Pearl stirred her coffee, noting that his Viking blond hair was damp with sweat. He had failed to shave and a pale shadow of beard was visible at his jaw. She offered a smile. 'I take it you didn't get much sleep.'

But McGuire had other things on his mind, no time for pleasantries. 'I've been briefing the press,' he announced, knowing that, at long last, the local papers would finally have a headline of note: BODY FOUND IN BEACH HUT, although a police surgeon's report had been rather more prosaic. 'The cause of death was a heart attack.'

'You don't expect me to believe that,' said Pearl.

'It seems Stroud had an existing heart condition. We found medication at the scene.' From his pocket McGuire took a clear plastic evidence bag which contained a small bottle of pills. As Pearl tried to focus on the label, he slipped the bag quickly back into his pocket.

'Have you contacted his doctor?' she asked.

McGuire remained silent, prepared only to divulge information which was, or soon would be, in the public domain.

'Of course you have,' she answered herself. 'So you must now have an address for Stroud.' She waited expectantly.

McGuire sighed, then gave in. 'He was from Yorkshire originally,' he conceded, 'but was based in Menorca. So yes, you were half right.'

A slow smile spread across Pearl's face. She had guessed the wrong Balearic island, but with only twenty miles between them she felt she hadn't done too badly. 'What about the blood?'

'What about it?'

'You saw for yourself how much he had lost.'

'Looks like he collapsed and fell forward onto the broken floorboard.'

'But you haven't established that for certain?'

McGuire failed to comment but glanced back towards his car, where he saw WPC Hearne was now standing.

'Whatever happens, you'll still be making house-to-house inquiries for witnesses?' Pearl persisted.

McGuire suddenly realised how much she was sounding like Welch, his Canterbury superintendent, who relished throwing questions at him, like small darts, at every opportunity.

'I told you in my statement last night,' Pearl went on, 'that Beacon House is usually hired out for photo shoots and weddings because of its perfect view of the Street, but I managed to speak to the owner this morning.' This made McGuire look back at her. 'Marion spends most of her time in London but happens to be a member of our book club . . .'

McGuire suddenly cut in. 'The Bertholds are renting the house for the summer.' Having silenced Pearl, he said stiffly, 'I've taken full statements and I'll be launching an appeal for anyone who might have known Stroud.'

Pearl picked up her coffee cup and considered him. 'A bit testy this morning, aren't we? I'm only trying to be helpful,

Inspector. I wouldn't want you to think I might be . . . withholding information.' She smiled but McGuire ignored her, got to his feet and turned to leave. Pearl piped up again. 'Have you thought any more about the catch?'

'What about it?' he said flatly.

'I told you last night,' she reminded him. 'Vinnie had finished work for the day. His boat would have been at anchor while he sorted the catch at the culling table. He was ready to head home, so it makes no sense at all that he would have been trying to re-anchor at low tide.'

McGuire gazed out to sea, as he reflected on this. 'Maybe he knew that Stroud was in town and decided to stay at sea.'

Pearl shook her head slowly. 'I told you, it was a lowering tide. And how would Vinnie have found out that Stroud was—'

'I don't know,' interrupted McGuire. 'Perhaps Stroud called him.'

It was clear the policeman was keen to bring an end to a speculative exchange but Pearl pressed on regardless. 'Did he?'

Viewing Stroud's mobile-phone records was yet another item on a very long list of things to do. As much as McGuire would have liked to have the last word, escape seemed an attractive option at this point. He took a step away.

'Inspector?'

McGuire reluctantly stopped again.

'Someone closed the doors of that beach hut with Stroud's body inside. The doors were barred when I got there, remember?' She held his look but the detective merely carried on across the street to join WPC Hearne, who was still waiting for him. Pearl watched McGuire get into his car. No sooner had the engine started up than his brakes squealed as the vehicle rounded the corner into Beach Walk. Pearl took her time, picked up her cup and drained the last of her cappuccino.

'Where the hell have you been?' Charlie demanded as soon as Pearl entered the kitchen.

'Having breakfast at the beach – why? What are you so upset about?'

'He's been trying to call you.' Dolly was standing close to Charlie, as though offering a united front.

Pearl slipped out of her jacket. 'I'm sorry, I left my phone on charge.' She pinned back her hair, ready for work.

Charlie, frustrated, turned his attention to Dolly. 'And what's *your* excuse?'

'For what?' asked Dolly innocently

'For not telling me any of this last night.'

Dolly opened her mouth to speak but Pearl was quicker. 'I told your gran not to. I was with the police.'

'Again,' said Dolly balefully. 'Though I s'pose he's not bad-looking for a Flat Foot.'

Charlie said crossly, 'Is *anyone* going to tell me what's going on?'

Pearl paused. 'I found another body.'

'I know,' Charlie told her. 'But only because I happened to hear about it on the radio.' He gave his mother a reproachful look which made Pearl feel suitably guilty.

'Look, I didn't want to worry you,' she began contritely.

'Worry me? My mother happens to stumble across two bodies in as many days, and I'm not to be told in case it *worries* me?'

'The new man had a heart attack.'

'Are you sure about that?' frowned Dolly.

'McGuire's already briefed the papers.'

'McWho?' asked Charlie.

'Detective Chief Inspector McGuire,' Pearl replied.

'The Flat Foot,' added Dolly.

Charlie put a hand to his brow as though collecting his scattered thoughts.

'Okay. Whatever's been going on here, I want you both to come to me tonight.'

'Why?' Pearl asked. 'Because I found a body?'

'Two bodies,' corrected Dolly.

'Because you've given me something to think about,' Charlie replied. 'Or maybe this has. What you said yesterday. You were right. I should have been back to visit but I've . . .' he petered out, looking guilty.

Pearl offered a suggestion. 'Had other things on your mind?'

Charlie's expression softened. 'I'd really like you both to meet Tizzy. Properly. Over supper. What do you say?' He waited anxiously for a response.

A pause followed, during which Pearl and Dolly exchanged a look.

'We can be there by eight?' suggested Pearl.

Charlie gave a relieved smile.

For Pearl, the second day of the Oyster Festival was always less hectic than the first. The parade brought tourists to the High Street but it was at the harbour that the rest of the week's events were centred – a schedule that included kite-flying, a tug of war on the mudflats, children's activities and the annual Oyster Challenge. This took place at Dead Man's Corner on the final day and consisted of swallowing half a dozen oysters with a half pint of Pilsner, as fast as humanly possible.

Pearl's presence at the restaurant was only essential on the evenings when the restaurant was booked as the venue for a private celebration – a birthday or family get-together. She had even hosted the odd wake and knew, as she looked around 'The Whitstable Pearl' at the end of another busy day, that she would no doubt be called upon to host Vinnie's. She was just upending the last of her chairs onto a table when her phone rang. The woman's voice on the line was faint and overlaid with the sound of children squealing in the background. Nevertheless it was instantly recognisable.

Pearl listened carefully before giving her reply. 'I'll be right there.'

Setting off down the High Street, she headed for the harbour where it appeared the whole town had congregated. The smell of a Whitstable summer hung in the air: the aroma of sweet candy floss and barbecued fish. A young fiddler offered a soundtrack with an updated rendition of an old folk song, his bow dancing across electric strings. Tipsy tourists milled around stalls that offered not just oysters on the half shell but cockles, whelks, prawns and calamari. At the quay, an old barge had been taken over by a children's theatre company. On its deck, two young actors performed a duel, thrusting rapiers before an audience of children who watched, either rapt in attention, or lost to fatigue. Throughout all, Vinnie's boat remained chained to the quay, surrounded by flowers, as tourists continued to celebrate.

Finding a route through the crowds, Pearl made her way towards Reeves Beach, where Vinnie's terrier scampered across to roll at her feet. Pearl stroked the dog but her eyes had already sought out Connie, perched on a breakwater, watching a group of children swarming at the tide's edge. Becca and

Louise were among them, queuing to collect oyster shells from a pile left near the shore. Pearl sat down next to Connie.

'They wanted to come down and build a grotter,' Connie told her. 'They made one here with Vinnie last year.' Pearl knew, as did every Whitstable resident, that the hollow structures made from sand and oyster shells had been constructed for a hundred years or more by the generations of local children who had begged 'a penny for the grotter' just as kids now begged money for a 'guy' on 5 November. On the beach, with another festival, the tradition continued.

'I'm trying to keep them occupied,' Connie said quietly. 'Or maybe it's me who needs to keep busy.' She looked at Pearl, seeming strangely calm.

'You've heard about Stroud?' Pearl asked.

Connie nodded slowly. 'The police told me.' She shifted her gaze back to her girls, falling silent as she watched them picking up shells.

Pearl laid her hand upon Connie's. 'Look . . .'

'No. It's over, Pearl,' Connie said quickly. 'I don't know this man and I don't really care. And if that seems hard, I can't help it. All I know is my Vinnie's gone. Me and the girls have to come to terms with that, and move on as best we can.'

'And you will,' said Pearl gently. 'But right now there's a lot to consider. If Vinnie's finances were as bad as you say . . .'

Connie's eyes flashed. 'You think I'm lying?'

'Of course not,' countered Pearl. 'I'm just concerned, that's all.'

'Then don't be,' snapped Connie. 'The insurance money'll take care of us.' She looked away, guilty for her outburst.

'Insurance?'

Connie nodded. 'Vinnie took out a policy, long before he

ever went to work for Matheson. I was worried he might have let it lapse, but . . .' she frowned, confused. 'When I notified the company today, they told me he'd made every payment. Whatever else he let slide, Vinnie'd made sure we were taken care of.'

'So he wasn't careless,' said Pearl.

Connie looked ashamed. 'Look, I – I didn't know what I was saying yesterday. I needed to blame someone. Anyone.'

'Even Vinnie?'

Connie glanced away again to her daughters arranging oyster shells on the beach. 'Now I know how he must've felt when Shane died.'

'Angry?'

'Yes.'

A sudden thought came to Pearl. 'The insurance company is bound to make inquiries, so be careful. If you say anything that might lead them to suspect . . .'

'Suspect what?' Connie read the look in Pearl's eyes and began to shake her head. 'Oh no. *No.* If you're suggesting for one minute . . .'

'All I'm saying is . . .'

'Vinnie would *never* have taken his own life. You *know* that! Whatever mess he was in for money there's no way he would've done that.'

Thinking it over, Pearl accepted that Connie was right. He would never have left his family, whom he loved. 'Then why are you so angry with him?' she asked.

For a few moments Connie was torn, as if struggling to make the right decision. Finally, she got to her feet and gazed out to sea as the words began to flow like the waves on the shore.

'I went out on the boat a couple of weeks ago. It was a lovely Sunday afternoon and the girls were off with Mum so I said I'd help Vinnie clear up. The saloon was a mess and I got cracking on it while Vinnie stayed up on deck. But while I was sweeping I found *this* lying under the table.' Connie reached into her handbag, unzipped a section and took something from inside. 'At first I thought it was just a piece of fishing line, then I realised . . .'

She stopped and opened her hand, offering to Pearl the delicate earring she held in her palm. Pearl turned it over, inspecting the long dart of silver with a single flash of blue at its centre. 'What did Vinnie say?'

Connie bit her lip. 'Nothing. I haven't told a soul – until now.'

'There has to be an explanation,' Pearl said sensibly.

'There is,' Connie replied. 'Vinnie was an open book, so if this was innocent – why didn't he tell me?' Her eyes scanned Pearl's for an answer but a child's presence suddenly interrupted them. Becca stood between them, reaching up for her mother's hand to tug Connie away to the beach.

'Wait,' said Pearl, but Connie shook her head.

'It's over,' she said softly. 'I don't want to talk about this ever again.' She then turned and moved off with her daughter, leaving Pearl staring down at the earring in her hand.

Just before eight that evening, Dolly was eyeing the road ahead intently, as if it was she, and not Pearl, who was driving.

'Vinnie with another woman?' Dolly spluttered. 'I've never heard anything so damn ridiculous.'

'Why?'

'Because he's not the type, that's why.' Dolly, like Pearl, was having difficulty speaking of Vinnie in the past tense. 'Too fast,' she added, pointing at the speedometer.

Pearl eased off the accelerator. Dolly was a terrible back-seat driver especially when sitting in the front, where she was apt to slap the windscreen like an instructor demanding an emergency stop.

'Vinnie would never have got mixed up with someone else,' Dolly continued.

'He got mixed up with Connie.'

'He got close to her,' Dolly qualified. 'But that was different.'

'Why?'

'Because his marriage was over.'

'He and Tina weren't divorced.'

'But they might just as well have been.' Dolly heaved a sigh. 'Look, Tina Rowe could have worked at her marriage but she chose the bottle over Vinnie and ran off with his money instead.'

'*Their* money,' corrected Pearl.

Dolly glowered. 'She took Vinnie's share as well as her own, and if you ask me that was robbery. She was lucky he didn't set the police on her.'

Pearl secretly agreed with everything Dolly had just said, but felt the need to play devil's advocate. It was true that Vinnie's marriage had been in difficulty long before Connie had ever come on the scene. The couple had spent more than twenty years together until the loss of their son had finally torn them apart. For Tina, refuge had come in alcohol while Vinnie's escape had been in his work.

'In any case,' huffed Dolly, 'what's one cheap little earring meant to prove?'

'Not so cheap – or so little,' said Pearl, producing it from her pocket. Dolly took a look at it before giving a dismissive sniff.

'There has to be another reason for it being on the boat,' she insisted. 'What kind of woman canoodles on an oyster dredger?'

'You did.'

Dolly gave her daughter a knowing look. 'But never in jewellery, darling.'

Pearl managed to squeeze her Fiat into the only parking space available outside Charlie's block. As she killed the engine, Dolly waved through the passenger window up at Charlie's window. 'There he is,' she smiled. 'My favourite grandson.'

A few moments later, Dolly's only grandson was ushering them inside the flat as the strong, sweet smell of cinnamon escaped into the hallway. Once inside the sitting room the source became instantly visible: an arrangement of scented tea lights filled almost every surface.

'Are we having a séance?' asked Dolly.

'Tizzy likes candles,' Charlie explained in a whisper. 'She says they give a room atmosphere.'

'A fair bit of heat too,' said Dolly as she slipped a shawl from her shoulders. It was an elaborate item, red silk with a huge embroidered flower on the back.

'Wow, where d'you get this?' asked Charlie, as he took it from her.

'Jumble sale, darling, almost twenty years ago. But I knew it would come in handy one day.'

'Flamenco,' Pearl informed him. 'She's just started classes.'

'I thought you were doing ballet dancing?' Charlie said.

'Belly dancing,' corrected Pearl.

'But it didn't do my back any favours,' Dolly explained. 'Flamenco suits my temperament.'

'You mean it's difficult?' Pearl teased.

'Passionate,' replied Dolly. She gave a sudden flourish of her wrist before taking an apple from Charlie's fruit bowl and raising it above her head. '*Cojelo, comelo y tiralo!*' She drew down her arm as though plucking the apple from a tree. 'Take it – eat it – throw it away!' But with one dramatic movement the apple escaped from her grasp and landed on the floor beside a pair of elegant gold leather sandals. All eyes rose to see Tizzy inhabiting the footwear. Charlie quickly picked up the apple but at the sight of his grandmother's teeth marks decided against putting it back into the bowl. Dolly smiled. 'Sorry. It slipped right out of my hand.'

Everyone seemed to be waiting for Tizzy's reaction but in what seemed to be a perfectly timed moment, the girl's face suddenly set in a smile that was like sunshine after rain. 'You must be Dolly. I'm so pleased you could come.' She came forward to plant small kisses on either of Dolly's flushed cheeks.

'You too, Pearl.' She turned to give Pearl her full attention, offering a warm embrace before asking, 'Would you like to pour some drinks, Charlie?'

Charlie traipsed off obediently, to return with an open bottle and some glasses. 'Prosecco okay for you, Gran?'

Dolly eagerly took a glass from him. 'They don't call me the Great White Wino for nothing.' She watched as Charlie poured. 'Half measures for your mother. She's driving.'

Pearl gave Dolly a sidelong glance but before she could comment, Tizzy had raised her own glass. '*Salute*,' she said warmly.

Pearl sipped her prosecco and noted Tizzy's outfit. Wearing a black bodice and leggings, the girl's slim build seemed to belie some form of inner strength, giving her the appearance not of a pretty, stick-thin model but of a physique that was far more powerful: compressed and intense like a dancer or gymnast honed for a disciplined routine.

Tizzy gestured to the table. 'Shall we sit down?'

'I was going to bring some oysters,' remembered Pearl.

'I'm glad you didn't.' Tizzy smiled.

Dolly raised her glass. 'A girl after my own heart!'

'No, please don't misunderstand. I love oysters but tonight we have other seafood on the menu.' She said politely, 'Will you excuse me?' Setting down her glass, she moved off quickly to the kitchen.

Charlie stared after her. 'Need some help?'

Tizzy's voice sang back from the kitchen. '*Grazie, tesoruccio,* but I'm fine.'

Dolly and Pearl eyed Charlie, who seemed slightly embarrassed. 'She's been busy since this morning – shopping and chopping.'

Dolly leaned into her grandson. 'And where did you find a stunning girl like that?'

'The theatre,' he replied. 'A friend dragged me along to see a student play. I wasn't really up for it but Tizzy was in the cast. She did this amazing monologue and totally stole the show. I couldn't take my eyes off her.'

'I can believe that,' said Pearl, picking up her glass.

'It wasn't just her looks, Mum. It was the whole thing, her whole performance. All the time I was watching her it was like . . . well, like she had me under a spell.'

Dolly and Pearl exchanged a look but Charlie failed to

notice. 'Anyway, I plucked up the courage to buy her a drink and . . . here we are.' He raised his glass.

'Yes,' Pearl said affectionately. 'Here we are.'

Tizzy entered briskly from the kitchen carrying a tray in her hands.

'Okay, everyone. *Mangiamo!*'

Charlie sprang to his feet and helped to set the hot tray on the table. He laughed. 'The first time Tizzy said that, I thought it was the name of the dish.'

'You've never been too hot on languages,' Pearl agreed.

'Oh, but he's getting better,' said Tizzy. 'I made him practise his French when we were in Belgium.'

Pearl's smile slowly faded. 'Belgium?'

Tizzy looked up at Charlie. 'We made a weekend trip to Bruges to visit the Groeninge Museum. You had some work to do on that project.'

'The Flemish Masters,' Charlie nodded.

'But I . . . thought you went to Bruges alone,' said Pearl.

'Did you?' asked Charlie innocently.

A silence fell for a moment, broken by Tizzy. 'Well, we certainly had a wonderful time, didn't we?'

'Sure,' Charlie replied, returning her smile.

Tizzy turned her attention back to the meal. 'Come, let's eat. I wanted to cook you something really special from my home. *Cee alla Pisana.*'

'Something from Pisa?' guessed Dolly.

'Exactly! *Cee* is the name we use for baby eels caught in the River Arno.'

Dolly's smile instantly faded and Pearl knew the reason why: her mother was as fond of eels as she was of oysters, but Tizzy, unsuspecting, continued brightly: 'We sauté them in garlic and olive oil, with a little sage and *parmigiano*, but there's only one problem.' She paused. 'They really have to be Italian eels.'

'Oh what a shame,' lied Dolly, taking a swig from her glass to celebrate.

'So instead, I've made another dish – also from Tuscany.' Tizzy leaned forward to raise the lid from the casserole, immediately releasing a fierce aroma of fish, garlic and herbs. A tomato-red broth bubbled like lava before them. '*Caccuccio di Livorno*,' she announced, picking up a ladle to stir the broth gently. 'In Italy we Tuscans are called *mangiafagioli* – bean-eaters – but we love fish too. This dish has octopus, squid, crayfish, mullet, prawns, ray fish . . .'

'Skate,' corrected Charlie.

'But no eels,' said Pearl for Dolly's benefit, noting how efficiently Tizzy rubbed garlic against the toasted bread she was setting into bowls.

'My father always said this recipe came from the fishermen in Livorno. At the end of the day they would make it using the smallest fish from the catch. *Kukuk* is an Arabic word meaning small.' The girl ladled seafood over the crusty bread. 'But there's also another story,' she went on, 'about a poor fisherman's family who lost everything in a storm.' She took a saucer of chopped parsley, sprinkling it across each bowl. 'After three days of going hungry, the children went begging to the other fishermen in the port, asking only for one fish. When they finally returned home with their little catch, the mother found what she could – some herbs and tomatoes from the garden, a little oil, some lemon – and with these things she prepared a sauce for the fish. Soon, the delicious smell of the mother's cooking reached the neighbours, and everyone in the town came along to ask for the recipe.'

Charlie gave Pearl a knowing look. Tizzy caught it. 'Ah, but Charlie tells me that you don't like recipes, Pearl?'

Pearl gave a small shrug. 'I prefer to find my own way with a dish.'

'She's like that with everything,' commented Dolly. 'Always has to work things out for herself.'

'Is that true?' Tizzy held Pearl's look.

'Perhaps,' Pearl conceded. 'Or maybe I'm just like the mother who made this stew for the very first time.'

'Agreed,' said Dolly quickly. 'Loaves and fishes. Pearl can make something out of nothing.'

Tizzy considered this before raising her glass. 'Then here's to fishermen. And their families.'

After a moment's respectful silence, Dolly took a sip of wine and tucked into her food. 'Delicious,' she decided, but Pearl remained silent as she stared down at her bowl.

'You okay?' asked Charlie. Pearl nodded and picked up her spoon.

Tizzy observed her before suggesting softly, 'You've been through a lot, Pearl. Finding two dead bodies, as you did, is almost unbelievable.'

'Yes,' said Pearl. 'I'm sure that's how McGuire feels.'

'McGuire?' Tizzy echoed.

'The officer in charge of the investigation.'

Charlie frowned at his mother. 'So what's to investigate? You said the guy in the beach hut died of a heart attack.'

'And the fisherman's death was an accident,' said Tizzy.

'So they say.'

Tizzy noted Pearl's expression. 'But you don't agree.'

Pearl took a moment to consider. 'It's hard to believe Vinnie could have made such a mistake.'

'But if he didn't, what could have happened?' Charlie shrugged, baffled.

Dolly reached for her glass. 'I think what your mother means is that it's hard to accept that Vinnie's gone. It's often that way with a sudden death. But the funeral will make it real.'

'Do you want me to come?' Charlie asked.

'Thanks,' said Pearl, 'but it may not be for a while. The police have yet to release Vinnie's body and they'll probably want to hold an inquest. In that case, the cause of death will be decided by the Coroner.'

Silence settled. Tizzy turned to Pearl. 'I'm sorry for your loss,' she said softly. 'Accidents happen at sea, even to those who feel most at home there.' She selected a crayfish claw from her bowl, inspecting it cursorily before reaching for a chrome shellfish cracker. 'My father used to have a sail boat. He had sailed since he was a very young boy and had never come to any harm until . . . one day, when we were out on the sea together, he lost concentration, for just one moment.' She closed the cracker on the crayfish claw.

'What d'you mean?' asked Dolly bluntly.

Tizzy's grip relaxed on the cracker for a moment as she took up her story. 'We were talking, laughing. I can still see him, resting his arm through the spokes of the helm.' Her expression clouded. 'But we were in shallow water, and suddenly there was a terrible scraping sound on the keel. We hit some rocks. . . . the helm spun.' A loud crack sounded and Tizzy stared down, confused for a moment, until she dropped the shattered crayfish claw from the cracker into her bowl.

'What happened?' asked Pearl.

The question seemed to bring Tizzy back to her senses. 'I managed to sail the boat back, but my father was in agony. His arm was so badly broken.' She looked down at the table. 'He never sailed again.'

Pearl's instinct was to comfort the girl but Charlie was quicker. His hand reached instantly for Tizzy's. The look that passed between them was enough to melt Pearl's own heart.

'*Mangiamo*,' said Tizzy once more.

Pearl picked up her spoon and tasted the *caccuccio*, having to admit, even to herself, that it really was truly exceptional.

Just before 10 p.m., Dolly was struggling with her seat belt, complaining, 'Has this thing got smaller?'

'It's caught in the door,' Pearl said stiffly. Dolly re-opened the passenger door and closed it again, this time managing to secure the belt as Pearl started up the Fiat. The roads were almost empty and Pearl was sober while Dolly, by contrast, reeked of wine. Apart from the prosecco, she'd also drunk quite a bit of grappa. Pearl had realised that her mother was plastered when Dolly had broken off during a rambling anecdote about her time in the Fish Slappers to tell Tizzy that her hair looked like spun gold.

'What a girl,' said Dolly now. 'As if all that fish stew wasn't enough, there was the excellent chicken too. What did she say she'd stuffed it with?'

'Asparagus and shrimp.'

'Ashparagush 'n shrimp,' slurred Dolly. But she was yawning now, and running out of steam as Pearl's car joined the main road. Settling into the fast lane, Pearl switched off her indicator, realising that Dolly wasn't worrying any more about speed.

'Did you notice how her hands trembled?' asked Pearl, as the car sped through Blean.

'Mmmm?' Dolly was both sloshed and sleepy.

'She shook like a leaf and hardly ate a thing.'

'I'm not surprised. I'd be nervous as hell with you as a prospective mother-in-law.' Dolly gave Pearl a sidelong glance and a sloppy smile before her head lolled back on the rest.

'Don't be silly,' said Pearl, as her eyes returned to the road. 'They've only just met.' But her words fell on deaf ears as she heard Dolly's distinctive snore.

Pearl's car pulled up in Harbour Street outside Dolly's home. With her pottery shop on the lower floor and the upper rooms rented out to her bed-and-breakfast guests, Dolly now occupied only the small extension that took up most of her tiny garden. Pearl always thought of it as less of a home and more of a museum, housing as it did an eclectic collection of *objets trouvés,* shelves full of perfume bottles, driftwood and pieces of sculpture bought from other artists in an effort to encourage them. Pearl was never able to relax in her mother's house, always feeling the urge to tidy up while Dolly was more than happy with things just the way they were.

'Coming in for a nightcap?' Dolly pulled her flamenco shawl tightly around her shoulders as she felt the stiff breeze blowing in off the sea.

Pearl shook her head. 'I'll wait until I get home.'

Dolly kissed her daughter and held Pearl close. 'Don't go finding any more dead bodies, will you?' She touched Pearl's cheek and set off still worse for wear down the alley which led to her garden gate. Pearl waved a goodbye and watched until the gate closed after her, then she got back into the car. She'd been sitting at the wheel only for a moment before she remembered something. Getting out again, she locked the Fiat and took a short cut to the beach through Terrys Lane. There, she found herself confronted by a trio of young men. Unsteady from alcohol, they scattered clumsily to allow her to pass then headed towards the Duke of Cumberland pub from which a trumpet solo grew louder as they went inside then faded as the pub door closed after them.

Pearl moved on towards Reeves Beach and halted as she saw what she had anticipated: scores of tiny flames glowing in the darkness – festival grotter candles that had been lit at dusk – although the stiffening breeze was causing some to gutter and die. Walking amongst them, Pearl noted how each little structure was quite distinct, some bearing flags like sandcastles while others had been decorated with colourful sweets or small toys. It didn't take long to find the grotter Vinnie's daughters had begun that afternoon. Crouching down to inspect it, Pearl found that its candle had long been extinguished but an abandoned box of matches lay close by and in spite of the damp, she managed to strike a light. Pearl was brought up short as she saw how the arrangement of shells at the grotter's door spelled the single word *Dad*.

For a moment, Pearl allowed herself to wonder how much of Vinnie might be remembered by his two daughters. It would fall to their mother to keep his memory alive, like a small flame struggling to survive on a beach. Pearl thought of her own son who had also grown up fatherless. Although Charlie never spoke about his absent father, Pearl had kept a story alive in her son's heart – one of a summer filled with love and loss, though how much of that unchallenged story was real or imagined was now arguable, for the years had a way of moulding the truth to fit, like a comfortable pair of shoes . . .

For some reason that image made her think again of McGuire. Three days ago he had been a stranger, but now she felt linked to him in a search for the truth behind the death not only of Vinnie, but of Stroud too – the irascible Yorkshireman who had sat so uncomfortably in her office one hot afternoon and who now lay, perhaps even alongside the fisherman, in a chilled body drawer at the police morgue.

Pearl looked out to sea to where the navigation lights from a few freighters twinkled like a marcasite necklace strung across the dark horizon. Jazz still sounded faintly from the Duke of Cumberland pub, but the beach was now deserted. The breeze was continuing to stiffen so she took the short cut home through the car park at Keam's Yard. It wasn't long before she sensed that something was wrong.

At first, it seemed to Pearl that she was hearing the echo of her own footfall, but when she stopped in her tracks, the footsteps continued, so she ducked quickly into the darkness of Starboard Light Alley where, at the side of her own cottage, an old oyster yawl sat permanently moored. The *Favourite* had been painstakingly restored by a bunch of local enthusiasts and its hull now offered a perfect hiding place.

For a few breathless moments, Pearl heard only silence, until the tinkle of a small bell signalled the presence of a familiar soul: Nathan's ginger tomcat, Biggy, was mewing at her feet. In her neighbour's absence Pearl had been feeding the animal, who was keen to show his appreciation. Biggy wound his fat body around Pearl's feet and she dropped her guard to stroke him.

Just at that moment, a man appeared behind her. Pearl turned instinctively but saw that he had approached, not from the beach, but from a parked car on the street. He was in his early thirties, fair and bespectacled, staring at her, confused. 'Can you tell me where the High Street is, please?' he asked.

Pearl looked beyond him to a car in which a young woman was peering at a road map. 'Straight on,' she said finally. 'You can't go wrong.' The young man nodded and went back to his car. After a few moments, he drove past as his companion waved her thanks from the open passenger window.

At the door to Seaspray Cottage, Pearl scolded herself for becoming hostage to her own imagination. Slipping her key into the lock, she stepped into the living room and shrugged one arm from her jacket while fumbling for the light switch with the other. It was at that moment that she realised she wasn't alone.

An empty wine bottle stood on the table, a glass perched in the intruder's hand. Looking older and jaded but no less attractive than she had been nearly a decade ago, Tina Rowe turned to face Pearl. Her eyes were swollen with sadness but Pearl saw no tears. Instead, Vinnie's widow summoned a cold smile.

'I've been waiting for you, Pearl.'

Chapter Eight

Tina Rowe took something from her pocket and set it down on the table. 'You should know better than to leave keys under flowerpots.'

Pearl leaned forward and picked up the key, knowing as she put it into her bag that Tina was quite right.

In the harsh glow of the overhead light Pearl became acutely aware of the years that had passed since she had last set eyes on Vinnie's estranged wife. Tina Rowe was now approaching fifty, and though she looked much younger, the network of deep wrinkles around her mouth and eyes seemed not so much expression lines as evidence of a decade of pain etched into her being. The clothes she wore were stylish and expensive: a fuchsia-pink linen tunic and tailored trousers over a trim figure, but a matching crumpled jacket lay tossed carelessly over the back of her chair and the tips of her manicured fingernails had lost some of their pale pink varnish.

As the sound of a festival firework cracked and whistled up into the sky from the beach, Tina glanced edgily towards the empty wine bottle on the table. 'Is there anything else to drink?'

Pearl moved to a cupboard and opened it to reveal some alcoholic detritus: whisky left over from Christmas, ouzo bought for a Greek supper party and various technicolor liqueurs.

'Scotch'll do fine,' said Tina quickly, shifting her weight from one awkward foot to another. Pearl poured out a hefty measure and handed it to her uninvited guest. Tina hesitated. 'Aren't you going to join me?' Pearl shook her head and Tina quickly gulped down some whisky, grimacing like a child taking necessary medicine. For a moment she seemed strangely healed.

'You've heard about Vinnie,' said Pearl.

Tina looked up from her glass and nodded slowly as though reminded of something she was trying to forget. 'Was it really . . . an accident?'

As Tina waited for a response, an image sprang to Pearl's mind, not of Vinnie's body shackled to an anchor chain, but a grotter flame struggling to survive on the beach. She thought of Vinnie's new family and knew there was no useful purpose to be served in sharing her doubts with Tina. 'Apparently,' she replied.

At this, Tina turned to slump on the sofa and stared deep into the amber liquid in her glass. Pearl moved to sit beside her. 'I'm sorry,' she began.

'I didn't ask for sympathy, did I?' Tina's voice was like a sharp instrument puncturing all compassion. 'I know what you think of me, what the whole town thinks of me for running out on him.' She looked up. 'Vinnie could do no wrong so how could I ever do right?' Her eyes begged for an answer but Pearl knew better than to give it. There weren't many in Whitstable who had either time or sympathy for Tina Rowe.

'Maybe all that matters now is that you and Vinnie once loved one other.'

Clearly not the reply she had been expecting, Tina's face seemed suddenly to cloud with confusion. 'How come we couldn't make it work?' she asked. 'How come just being together only reminded us of what we'd lost?'

'Because,' said Pearl, 'you lost a lot.'

At this, Tina forced her eyes shut tight, as though holding back a weight of grief. When she opened them again, Pearl saw that there were still no tears.

'It's not the way it's meant to be, is it? Having to bury your own son?' As soon as Tina spat out the words, she realised something. 'Your boy must be the same age now as my Shane was when he . . .'

Pearl looked away, unable to comprehend that Tina might possibly balance the loss of one child against the existence of another.

'What's Charlie up to these days?' Tina asked, her tone suddenly and shockingly bright. Pearl said nothing but Tina pressed for an answer. 'Oh, come on. He must be doing something.'

'He's studying.'

'At university?'

Pearl nodded.

'Where?'

'Canterbury.'

'Not too far away then.'

'No.'

'Has he got a girlfriend?'

'Yes.'

'Pretty?'

Pearl nodded and this time, Tina raised her glass. 'Well, good for Charlie! He's always had his head screwed on and so, for that matter, have you.' She took another sip of Scotch and winced again, but this time her expression failed to soften and instead she was overcome with pain. 'Why was it my boy and not yours?'

Pearl reached out to comfort her but Tina sprang quickly to her feet and began pacing as her speech rattled off like gunfire. 'You knew my Shane. Everyone knew him. He had everything – looks, mates, plenty of girls – so why would he need to go and ruin it all by taking drugs?' She turned to face Pearl. 'You were here that summer, Pearl. You were here for the festival, you must remember,' she said desperately.

'I do,' said Pearl immediately. 'But I wasn't at the concert. I was out on the beach that night. I . . . I didn't find out until the next day.'

Tina stared searchingly at Pearl before she finally turned away. 'You know that Vinnie blamed me,' she said flatly. 'Like mother, like son. He said if I hadn't liked to drink, if I'd set a better example . . .' She was unable to finish, then burst out: 'I know I drink too much but it only got out of hand after we lost Shane. That bitch started going after Vinnie, and what else did I have but this?' She held up the glass which shook in her trembling hand.

'You had Vinnie,' offered Pearl softly.

'No,' said Tina. 'I lost him the day I lost my boy.' She crumpled suddenly, shoulders collapsing in as though she had been punched. 'What am I going to do, Pearl?'

'You'll get through this.'

'You don't understand. I'm weak.'

'You're human.'

Tina whispered, lost, 'Am I?' Setting down her empty glass, she stared at her shaking hands. Pearl gripped them with her own.

'You've been away for nearly ten years, Tina,' she said. 'And you've survived.'

'Yes.' Tina began to nod slowly, her expression set as though she might be acknowledging this for the very first time. 'But that's all I have done. Survived.' She then freed her hands, bracing herself as though summoning the courage to make a difficult confession.

'When I left here I was determined I was gone for good. That's why I cleared out the account. But I couldn't do it, Pearl. I couldn't leave things like that, so it wasn't long before I got back in touch.'

'The postcard, you mean? The one you sent Vinnie?'

Tina waved a dismissive hand. 'That was just out of spite. I'm talking about later.' Her fingers pressed hard against the empty glass in her hand. 'I used to phone him. Not all the time, just when I needed to hear his voice.' She smiled fleetingly. '"Drunken dialling", he used to call it. And I knew he didn't want to talk to me because he kept on saying how we had to move on. Often he wouldn't even answer but . . .' she frowned, recalling something. 'He picked up one night. Three years ago – on the anniversary of our Shane's death.' She sighed. 'That's when he told me all about it.'

'About what?'

'The big plan. To get free of Matheson and go to work for himself and for his . . .' she fought to get out the word she found so hard to say: '. . . *family*.' She paused to take a deep breath. 'He said he was looking for an investor, someone to help him get started. And because I felt guilty for cleaning him out – for everything – I put someone in touch with him.'

'Who?'

'A guy called Doug Stroud.' Recognising that Pearl had registered the name, Tina rose to her feet and refilled her glass.

'I was out in Menorca when I met Doug,' she went on. 'He was from Bradford originally but he'd lived in Spain for a while and owned a bar on the main square in Mahon. I was there one night with a friend and he came across and bought us a few drinks.' She offered a weak smile. 'You could say me and Doug had an understanding. He wanted more trade for his bar and I wanted . . .'

'Security?'

'Protection.'

'From what?'

'Isn't it obvious?' Tina pointedly raised her whisky glass before setting it down on the table. 'Doug didn't know much about fishing but I backed up everything Vinnie had said. "Give it three years and you'll be part of something special", I told him – and I honestly believed that. But the three years came and went and Dougie started getting impatient. That's when he found out.' She gave another sigh.

'Found out what?'

'That me and Vinnie were still married.'

Pearl was incredulous. 'You hadn't told him?'

'Why should I? It was hardly as though we were living as man and wife. All the same, I reckoned Doug was less likely to cough up the money if he knew.' She said tiredly, 'But after a while he hired a private detective and found out anyway.'

Pearl summoned up a memory of Stroud – a cranky little fat man in an expensive panama hat.

'Doug was always hiring detectives,' Tina continued. 'He was paranoid, insecure, especially about his women so . . . it wasn't long before he started to think I'd set him up.' She picked up her glass. 'I tried to put him straight but he wouldn't have it. Said he wanted his money back. All of it.' She sipped her drink. 'I wouldn't mind but we weren't talking that much – a few grand, that's all. I'd seen him lose more in a casino.' She turned to face Pearl. 'If it had been anyone other than Vinnie, he would have kissed it all goodbye. But he was never going to do that.' She fell silent, brooding over the past.

'So what happened?'

Tina shrugged. 'Nothing. For a while I honestly thought he'd let it go, but then a few weeks ago I took a call for him from a travel agent and realised he was planning on coming here.'

'To Whitstable?'

'Yes. I tried to warn Vinnie, but he'd always told me never to phone him at home. He wouldn't return any of my calls on his mobile, so I followed Doug over.'

'Without him knowing?'

'I could hardly tell him. I wasn't sure what he was planning, you see. He had a temper – not like me and Vinnie, we were like firecrackers together – but Doug . . . he was slow-burning and could be vindictive, sneaky. But I never, for one moment, thought he would harm Vinnie.'

'So what *did* you think?'

'That something was going to happen, and whatever it was would all be my fault because I'd put the two of them together.' She set down her glass. 'If I'm really honest, Pearl, it was all just an excuse to see Vinnie again. So I flew over on Friday afternoon and booked into the Walpole Bay Hotel up at Cliftonville. I've got a friend, Shirley, who works there. I didn't mean to, but we tied one on that night, then yesterday, just as I was getting dressed, I heard the reporter on the local telly news saying something about a fishing accident. I looked up at the screen, and when I saw *The Native* there on the quay . . . I knew it was Vinnie.' She reached for her glass with a trembling hand. 'I threw up. I was in shock. Hungover. I tried Doug's mobile but he didn't answer. I called and I called, right through to Saturday evening, but his phone was always off. I didn't know what to do. I could hardly go round to Connie and offer my condolences.' She forced back tears. 'And now Doug is dead too.' She paused. 'Do they know what happened?'

Pearl considered this for a moment. 'The police say he had a heart attack.'

'Police?' Tina said sharply.

'Two sudden deaths, linked like this? They have to investigate.'

Tina looked down at her hands and frowned as though trying to make sense of this. 'Yes,' she said at last. 'Yes, of course, you're right. Doug had got himself all worked up before he flew out. His heart wasn't good and his doctor told him he needed to rest but he never listened.' She appealed to Pearl. 'What should I do?'

'Talk to the investigating officer. He's asking for people to come forward and it's best you do that as soon as possible.' Pearl reached into her bag and took McGuire's card from her purse. She handed it to Tina who looked dazed, her eyes bloodshot but her complexion wax-like and drained of all colour.

'But right now,' Pearl went on, 'you could do with some sleep. I'll get the spare room ready.'

'No,' Tina protested. 'I'll be fine. Right here – like this.' She grasped a soft tartan blanket from the back of the sofa and pulled it close to her like a child seeking comfort.

'Are you sure?'

Tina nodded. Pearl was too tired to argue. Instead, she headed straight for the door. Once there, she turned to say good night and saw that Tina was taking off her earrings. As she set them down on the coffee table, Tina sensed Pearl watching and felt that something was wrong. 'What is it?' she asked.

Pearl's gaze had shifted to the small silver studs lying on the table beside a now empty glass. 'Nothing,' she replied quietly. 'Get some rest and I'll see you in the morning.'

Moving off to the kitchen, Pearl listened for a moment for any further sounds from the living room. Hearing nothing, she headed upstairs. In her bedroom she crossed creaking floorboards to the old latticed window and opened it before securing the latch. As she did so, the soft, almost imperceptible wingbeat of a tiny bat disappeared up into a cloud of stars, but something else quickly drew her attention. The sea breeze was pushing gently at her curtains, allowing Pearl to glimpse, with their rise and fall, a figure stepping out of the shadows on Island Wall. For a moment she thought it was Marty who was standing beneath the streetlamp that illuminated the old yawl lying alongside Pearl's cottage, but its sodium bulb now cast a jaundiced glow on McGuire.

Pearl wondered what he might say in mitigation if she tackled him for following her home through Keam's Yard. Those footsteps must certainly have been his. Some excuse would surely come to mind – though she was sure she wouldn't believe it. He stood motionless, staring directly up at her window, but after a few moments he left, walking towards the lights of town while Pearl lay down on the coverlet of her bed and allowed the darkness to wash over her, like the tide washing over the seashore.

Chapter Nine

The radio was sounding the eight o'clock morning news as Pearl stared down at her sofa. On it lay only a neatly folded tartan blanket. A cushion showed a slight indentation and an empty glass sat on the coffee table, but other than that, there was no evidence of Tina Rowe's presence. 'I'm telling you,' Pearl insisted, 'I left her right there.'

Dolly picked up the glass and sniffed it before giving a small shrug. 'Well, maybe she sobered up and thought twice about being here.' As she set down the glass, Dolly added, 'Think it could have been Tina's earring that Connie found on the boat?'

'No. She said she flew in only two days ago.'

'Tina Rowe says a lot of things,' said Dolly. 'But it's usually the drink talking.'

Pearl eyed her mother. 'Pot, kettle . . . *prosecco*?'

Dolly winced. 'I've got a migraine coming on.' Her hand moved to her brow and Pearl sympathised.

'Sit down, Mum,' she said. 'I'll get you some tea.'

'No time,' warned Dolly, reaching for her bag. 'I've left Ruby at the restaurant and I've B & Bers to sort out before my shift.' She started for the door, then suddenly remembered something. 'I nearly forgot this.' She plucked from her pocket an old bus ticket, some fluff and a half-eaten tube of mints before finding the crumpled piece of paper which she pushed onto Pearl. 'I took the message from the machine this morning. Someone wants a party catered.' Dolly mustered a brief smile, hooked the straps of her handbag over her shoulder and said, 'Right, I'm off.'

Once Dolly had gone, Pearl stared for a moment at the conundrum of her empty sofa. She considered calling the Walpole Bay Hotel, then reconsidered and unravelled Dolly's message instead. With some difficulty she made sense of the local phone number scribbled in her mother's eccentric handwriting. The name beside it was much easier to decipher. Sarah Berthold.

Beacon House had looked out over the Street for more than a hundred years, having got its name from a signal which had once stood in the garden as a low-water warning to sailors. Although there were grander, more expensive seaside homes – especially along the western coast of Seasalter, where a millionaire's row of 'new builds' jostled for the title of best design statement – Beacon House boasted a more distinctive style and, arguably, the best sea view in Whitstable. The house was of a New England style, with wooden frontage and wraparound decking, and could be approached from Marine

Parade above it or via a small secluded piece of woodland into its rear terraced garden. There was also a more direct route from the Hotel Continental car park – one that Pearl had taken this morning.

The gate to the prom, she noticed, was no longer manned by a police constable. Holidaymakers now populated the beach, swimming, sunbathing and playing frisbee as though unaware of the macabre finding she had made only two days ago. The old beach hut, which stood just twenty yards from the garden fence of the house, was no longer sealed by police tape but secured by metal chains.

Pearl climbed the wooden steps to the lilac veranda, thinking about the short phone conversation she had just had with Sarah Berthold. During the call, the woman had sounded friendly enough, though a little stressed, as she suggested a meeting as soon as possible to discuss the proposition she had in mind. With Dolly and Ruby in place at the restaurant, Pearl had agreed to come straight away, keen to cast an eye over the Bertholds' summer abode.

It was another fine morning but the first thing Pearl noticed when she arrived was that all doors and windows were firmly closed. At the side of the house, near a fence that separated it from the beach huts, sat a long, narrow boat-house, ramshackle, but painted a fashionable indigo like the sea in a Dufy painting. A trailer was parked outside, close to a ramp which led down to the beach. Bistro tables and stylish canvas loungers studded the deck area while a riot of multi-coloured paper lanterns hung from the rafters, in keeping with the festival atmosphere.

Standing on the veranda, Pearl turned to stare back at the sea, fully understanding how a house like this, with its unique view of the Street, was in demand not only as subject matter for style magazines but as a holiday home for wealthy people like the Bertholds. A voice startled her.

'Sorry. Did you ring the bell?'

Pearl turned to find Sarah standing behind her at the French doors. 'Not yet,' she replied. 'I was just taking in the view.'

'Wonderful, isn't it?' Sarah said brightly. 'But the Army fort is a bit of an eyesore and I can't quite make up my mind about the wind farm.' She beckoned. 'Come on through.'

Opening the doors wider for Pearl to enter, Sarah closed them again afterwards. 'We've had our fair share of gawpers,' she explained, ushering Pearl through an imposing sitting room into an altogether more casual farmhouse kitchen. 'But I suppose that's to be expected with a location straight off the promenade. Coffee?'

Pearl nodded. 'Please.' Sitting at a bleached pine table, she saw that the garden doors leading out onto the rear deck area were open. Sparrows fluttered down onto the painted fencing then took off again, chattering in the sunlight.

'Do you live locally?' asked Sarah as she poured hot water into a cafetière.

'A cottage on Island Wall.'

'Ah, so you'll know what I mean about a lack of privacy.'

Pearl smiled. 'You do get used to living in a goldfish bowl after a while.'

'Not sure I'd like to,' replied Sarah, picking up a tray. She indicated the garden doors.

The two women moved out onto the rear deck where a table was dressed with a blue and white gingham cloth. A small vase of anemones sat beside a document folder.

'Don't get me wrong,' Sarah continued, 'I do love this house, it's so . . .' she struggled for the right word. 'Quirky,' she decided. 'So I was concerned when it seemed we might have to move.' She threw a glance towards the garden fence. 'The body in the beach hut. Sounds like the title of a detective novel, doesn't it? It's a great tragedy, of course,' she added, aware that she had been too flippant. 'But, well, we thought there might be a health risk with the beach hut being so close. The police, however, explained that we were quite safe.'

Sarah glanced again towards the garden fence beyond which some beach hut roofs were clearly visible.

'Strange how so many people milled around afterwards,' she said, pouring out the coffee. 'Mawkish. They actually came fully prepared, with beach chairs and sandwiches, staring up at the hut all day as if something equally ghastly might happen again. I couldn't help thinking of Madame Defarge, knitting beside the guillotine while heads rolled.' She offered a small smile then gave her attention to the folder on the table. 'On to brighter things,' she continued. 'As I mentioned on the phone, I'm planning to throw a little party here on Tuesday evening and I would love it if you could come up with a menu.'

Pearl took a notebook from her pocket. 'For how many guests?'

'No more than eight. Early evening, around seven, and the forecast's fine so I thought we might eat on the deck. This place has such an informal feel, I'd rather like the food to complement that. Something summery but substantial. Seafood only. That's why I thought of you. That was a wonderful lunch we had with the Harcourts in your place.'

'Thank you. Is it a special occasion?'

Sarah shook her head. 'Reciprocal hospitality for Robert

and Phoebe – but, as usual, my husband will be inviting some business associates.' She heaved a small sigh.

Pearl finished making some notes. 'Yes, I had heard about the development in Canterbury.'

'Oh, the hotel's only one of many projects. Leo never stops. He spends so much of his life just "protecting his investments" as he puts it. He really can't help himself. It's what motivates him.'

She had picked up the cafetière to refill their cups when a voice called, 'Ma? Where are you?'

'Out here,' Sarah called back.

A few moments later, Alex Berthold appeared in the door-frame. He was wearing loose Bermuda shorts but his tanned chest and feet were bare. His ice-blue eyes met Pearl's and he said, 'Sorry. I didn't realise there was anyone here.' He came forward. 'You're from the restaurant, right?'

'Right,' Pearl smiled.

Alex glanced at his mother, as if for more information.

'I've asked Pearl to cater for the party on Tuesday.'

Alex held Pearl's gaze for a moment as he assimilated this.

'Cool,' he finally decided, while Sarah seemed relieved by his response. She waved a hand towards the kitchen.

'You'll have to wait for breakfast, but there's coffee here.'

'No problem,' said Alex quickly. 'I'll get something while I'm out.'

He turned to leave but Sarah immediately asked, 'Where are you off to?'

'To meet a friend,' the boy replied with more than a hint of irritation. Then, as though regretting his reaction, he turned slowly back again and said politely to Pearl, 'See you on Tuesday.' He tossed his head back and beads of shower water dripped from his blond hair onto the hot deck. Almost as another afterthought, he leaned over and gave his mother a peck on the cheek. 'Bye, Ma.'

Sarah watched her son disappear into the house and said, 'Sorry about that. I know I shouldn't be so nosy, but I'm never sure what his plans are from one day to the next.'

'I know the feeling,' Pearl said ruefully. 'I've a son too.'

At this Sarah looked up inquisitively.

'Charlie's at university in Canterbury.'

'Alex is on a gap year,' Sarah told her.

'Not off travelling?'

The woman looked vaguely uneasy as she craned her head to see Alex slipping on surf shoes as he left the house. 'No,' she said eventually. 'My son had a few health problems last year so we thought it best to delay his studies.'

'Nothing serious, I hope?'

'Not at all,' said Sarah determinedly. 'It's all behind him now.'

Pearl turned to watch Alex heaving an expensive jet ski onto its trailer and was reminded just how long Charlie had had to wait for her to afford a new skateboard for him one summer.

Sarah continued, 'As you can see, he's thoroughly fit. He usually prefers snorkelling when we're on holiday. We have a home in Cape Town,' she added, 'but for years we've summered in Sardinia. I rarely saw Alex from June to September.' She frowned momentarily. 'But it's lovely that we've managed some proper time together this year. We even took a trip to Holland and Belgium at Easter.'

Her smile returned as the jet ski roared off into the distance, and she said to Pearl, 'Now where were we?'

'The menu,' said Pearl. 'I just had an idea. How about something Italian for the main course?'

'Pasta?'

'A recipe from Livorno. Seafood in its own broth.'

'Sounds wonderful. Can we confirm the details tomorrow?'

Before Pearl could respond, the doorbell sounded. 'Sorry, I'd better answer that.' Sarah headed directly back into the kitchen, and as Pearl followed slowly behind her, she paused to glance around the sitting room. A panelled staircase led to a galleried hall and the upper floor boasted several bedrooms, most of which must have stunning sea views – but still in Sarah Berthold's eyes, the house was merely 'quirky'. Pearl was just considering this as Sarah opened the front door.

'Inspector . . .'

Turning instantly, Pearl saw McGuire standing on the veranda. His eyes locked with hers before he gave his full attention to Sarah. 'You're busy, Mrs Berthold.'

'Always,' she told him with a charming smile. As if any confirmation was needed, the telephone suddenly rang and, flustered, Sarah put a hand to her brow. 'I'm sorry, Inspector. Will you excuse me?'

McGuire nodded and Sarah sped off to answer the phone. Once it had stopped ringing, McGuire addressed Pearl as he stepped across the threshold. 'What are *you* doing here?'

'Admiring the view.' She stared beyond him towards the sea. 'What about you?'

When he failed to reply, she smiled. 'Still playing your cards close to your chest, I see. Surely you've taken me off your list of suspects by now?'

'Maybe – maybe not.'

'Is that why you followed me home last night?'

McGuire said nothing but his look spoke volumes.

'I had an unexpected visit from Vinnie's wife,' she told him.

'I know,' said McGuire. 'I've just interviewed her.'

'Oh?'

'She turned up at the station this morning. Said you'd told her to do so.'

Pearl considered this for a moment. 'I thought she might have bolted.'

'Why would she do that?'

During the pause that followed, Sarah Berthold's voice could be faintly heard, talking on the phone in the other room. Pearl looked back at McGuire. 'Did you happen to check if Tina arrived in the country on Friday?'

McGuire repeated his question. 'Why would she have bolted?'

Pearl saw that a few days spent pursuing his inquiries in Whitstable seemed to be suiting McGuire. Pale spidery laughter lines still fanned from the corners of his eyes but the skin stretched taut across his cheekbones was now suntanned and his hair looked a shade lighter than when she had first observed him across a table in a dingy interrogation room. She smiled. 'Why don't I tell you over a drink, later?'

Pearl wasn't exactly sure if McGuire was tempted or frustrated by her suggestion but there wasn't any time to find out as Sarah Berthold could be heard saying goodbye to her caller before shouting out from the other room, 'Sorry, Inspector, I'll be right with you.'

McGuire called back, 'No problem.' But his eyes remained on Pearl. 'Where?'

'The Continental at six-thirty?' she suggested.

Before McGuire could reply, Sarah Berthold was suddenly

between them. 'And I didn't even get a chance to introduce you. Inspector McGuire, this is . . .'

'Miss Nolan and I have already met,' he said immediately. As he held her gaze, Pearl smiled.

A few moments later, having said goodbye to Sarah, Pearl looked back up at Beacon House from the promenade, wishing she could be party to the conversation going on with McGuire. She then glanced along the coastline. The tide was rising but there was no sign of Alex or his jet ski, only the sound of children's raised voices as a festival crabbing competition got under way on the seashore. Pearl's mobile gave a sudden bleep. She checked it to find the incoming text was from Sarah, who was giving her own mobile number as well as Alex's, in case she needed to be contacted urgently about Tuesday's supper. She had signed off positively: *Looking forward to it!*

Pearl stored both mobile numbers and then thought for a moment before she dialled another. The call went straight to voicemail. 'Hi, Charlie, it's me.' She braced herself. 'I need a favour.'

After the restaurant had closed that evening, Pearl sat in her garden with two glasses of mint tea set upon an old metal bistro table that she had recently picked up for a song. After a few coats of Rousseau Green spray paint, it now looked as though it might have come from one of the trendy shops on Harbour Street – especially with Tizzy sitting at it.

'Does this mean you've changed your mind about following recipes?' the girl asked.

'No,' replied Pearl. 'But I'm making an exception for yours.' She gestured at the few sheets of paper that Tizzy had just written out for her. Today, Charlie's girlfriend looked much like a 1950s starlet – a young Bardot, thought Pearl, with her long hair pulled up into a high ponytail that emphasised her fine cheekbones and a slender neck.

'I don't expect you to follow it exactly,' said Tizzy sweetly. 'Not after what you said about needing to find your own way.'

'That makes me sound difficult, doesn't it?' asked Pearl. 'But I'm not. It's just . . . for me cooking is all about instinct, and I have to trust mine.'

'In everything?'

'Most things.' Pearl found herself holding Tizzy's look for a second before waving a hand before her face. 'I think it's getting hotter. Shall we go inside?'

Picking up her glass of tea, Pearl followed Tizzy into the sitting room, feeling much like an old fox stalking a young gazelle. It suddenly occurred to her that it might simply be Tizzy's youth and beauty that made her feel so awkward, rather than the fact that she was Charlie's new love.

In the sitting room, Tizzy bent forward to inspect a collection of framed photographs on a side table – her lithe body forming a perfect right angle. '*Tesoruccio!*' she exclaimed. 'He looks so cute here.' She was smiling at a photo, taken on a beach, which showed Charlie as little more than a toddler.

'Another Oyster Festival,' Pearl remembered. 'We'd been crabbing off the Street and he won a prize. You see the flag he's holding?' She peered across Tizzy's shoulder at the familiar image. With Beacon House in the background and children congregated on the shoreline as they had done that very afternoon, time seemed somehow to have been arrested.

Tizzy read Pearl's thoughts. 'You haven't changed.'

'Oh yes, I have,' Pearl replied softly.

'But look,' the girl said. 'Even the clothes you're wearing – this could have been taken yesterday.'

Pearl considered this for a moment. 'That's one good thing about wearing vintage clothes – they never date. And I must admit I still have that lilac silk waistcoat, though I haven't worn it for years.'

'Beautiful,' said Tizzy, but the girl was no longer looking at the photograph; she was looking at Pearl instead. 'You and Charlie are very close,' she added softly.

'Yes,' agreed Pearl. 'We're a close family.' She set the photograph down on the table. 'And how about you? Do you have any brothers and sisters?'

Tizzy shrugged. 'Just my mother. Like Charlie,' she said, 'we are both alone.'

'Only children,' corrected Pearl. 'So your mother must miss you now that you're here.'

'She understands,' said Tizzy, 'that I've found something for myself here.' As she looked back at Pearl, she went on, as though recognising a need to lighten the mood, 'It's taken me quite a while to discover what it is I want to do.'

'Drama,' said Pearl.

Tizzy nodded. 'I wish I had begun studying sooner, but I took time out to travel and do other things. Now I know this is for me.' With her head tilted thoughtfully to one side, she added, 'I like to study people, don't you?'

'Study?' echoed Pearl.

'Discover how people reveal themselves. A look, an anecdote, the clues they leave behind. We all do it, don't we? We can't help it.' Tizzy set down her mint tea and Pearl felt suddenly exposed, wondering how much of herself she was revealing to Tizzy. She decided to move the conversation on.

'Charlie told me he saw you in a play. He was very impressed with your performance.'

'It was only a student production,' Tizzy shrugged, 'but I enjoyed it.'

'Which play?'

'Just . . . something we improvised. Maybe that's what made it special. Like cooking without a recipe?'

Pearl found herself returning Tizzy's smile and for a moment they found some accord, until Tizzy glanced at her watch and said, 'I really must go.'

'Can I give you a lift?' Pearl asked.

'Thank you, but I'm not going far – to a rehearsal, that's all. We're using the space at the old Coastguard's station.'

'In Whitstable?'

'Yes. Charlie suggested it. He's been so helpful – about everything.' The girl got to her feet. 'You are coming to the concert?'

'I wouldn't dream of missing it,' Pearl promised.

'Good.' Tizzy smiled and hoisted a canvas bag across her shoulder. 'Let me know how you get on with the recipe.' She kissed Pearl gently on both cheeks before hurrying to the garden door and out along the path to the promenade. Once there, she raised a hand and waved, but as Pearl waved back she found her arm lingering in the air for far longer than was necessary, since Tizzy had failed to look back.

Moving into the house, Pearl saw the recipe lying on the coffee table and read it through one more time, not registering the words themselves but reading beyond them to another message. The handwriting was neat, no errors or crossings out, just large curling letters confidently filling the page, but there seemed something curious about the script. After a few moments, Pearl realised what it was: the letters were leaning back instead of moving forward on the page. Pearl then made another discovery – she was squinting but assumed this was due to the bright sunlight reflecting off the paper in her hand, and so rejected, completely, the possibility that it might be time for glasses.

Chapter Ten

At 6.15 p.m. McGuire was seated on a comfy sofa in the bar at the Hotel Continental. His usual drink of choice was an amber Mexican Pilsner, but having learned that the hotel bar stocked plenty of choices to tempt a wide clientele, he considered trying a raspberry wheat beer before opting instead for something called oyster stout. McGuire was just pouring it into a tall glass when he noticed a little boy standing close by, observing him. McGuire glanced around the busy bar. There were plenty of families there, but none looking as though they were missing a small child. McGuire offered the boy a stilted smile, but seeming to suspect a lack of sentiment behind it, the child responded only with a loud sniff which left two thin trails of mucus in place beneath his nose.

McGuire set down his glass and was about to call a waitress when he saw Pearl hurrying across with a glass of wine in one hand. 'Sorry, I got tied up,' she said. The little boy looked up at her, offering another sniff. Instinctively, Pearl put down the wine, grabbed a serviette from the table and efficiently wiped the child's nose.

A woman suddenly appeared, flushed with sunburn, and grabbed the child's hand. 'There you are!' She looked at Pearl and said apologetically, 'Sorry about this but he likes to wander.' She picked up her young son, then hurried across to join a man who was struggling clumsily with a buggy at the door.

Pearl watched them, then turned to McGuire. 'I'm guessing you don't have any?'

'Any?'

'Kids.'

'Is it that obvious?'

'Just a little.' Pearl set down her bag and was about to take a seat when she spotted somebody entering the bar. It was Marty Smith. He glanced around, his features instantly softening as he saw Pearl. He made a beeline for her.

'You made it then?' Marty was out of his Cornucopia gear and wearing instead a black jacket, jeans and a winning smile. He registered Pearl's confusion. 'The tradesmens' meeting,' he said, the smile faltering. 'Shall we have a drink before it starts?'

At this, Pearl stared guiltily down at the glass in her hand, before explaining, 'I'm . . . actually here with Inspector McGuire.' Marty's gaze followed Pearl's to the man seated behind her. 'I'm helping him with his inquiries,' she continued.

'I see,' Marty said curtly. 'Well, don't let me interrupt you.' Looking wounded, he took a single step back then turned to march off to the bar.

Pearl sat down and picked up her wine while McGuire glanced after Marty. 'Boyfriend?'

Pearl glanced sidelong at the inspector. 'He happens to be my greengrocer.'

'He's got it bad,' said McGuire, noting that Marty was still staring across from the bar. 'But I guess you already know that.' Pearl opened her mouth to speak but McGuire was quicker. 'Why didn't you tell me?'

'Tell you what?'

'That you used to be in the force?'

The vague smile on Pearl's lips suddenly disappeared and she set her glass down. 'You really have been investigating.'

McGuire waited for an answer.

'It was a long time ago,' she said finally.

'All the same, I'm still curious.'

'Like you were about my agency?'

McGuire inspected his oyster stout. 'Anyone can start a detective agency, but not many private detectives have been in the force.'

'I left.'

'Why?'

For a moment, Pearl found herself trapped in McGuire's gaze. 'Personal reasons.' She sipped her drink. 'In any case, we're not here to talk about me.'

'So why are we here?' asked McGuire.

'Two dead bodies,' said Pearl starkly. 'One highly improbable accident at sea and the other . . . an unlikely death by natural causes.' She paused. 'Want me to continue?'

McGuire shrugged. 'Feel free.'

Pearl took some time to focus her thoughts. 'I'm guessing that by now you have forensic reports, exact causes and times of death, and evidence taken from the scenes of crime.'

McGuire raised a finger but Pearl quickly qualified, 'If,

indeed, any crime was actually committed.' She went on: 'I presume your Superintendent needs to satisfy himself that all possibilities regarding suspicious circumstances have been eliminated.' She offered McGuire a look. 'There's an established link between the two victims . . .'

'Deaths,' corrected McGuire.

'But you still have unanswered questions.'

McGuire took a mouthful of his oyster stout. 'Such as?'

'Firstly, an experienced fisherman is usually more careful than to step into the bight of his own anchor chain. Secondly, all the evidence we have shows that Vinnie would have been taking up anchor at the time of his death and not laying it.'

'The full oyster baskets . . .'

'And the clear culling table indicates that he would have been safely at anchor for some time. He'd finished fishing for the day.'

'What if the accident had taken place while he was taking up anchor?' McGuire asked.

Pearl shook her head. 'In that case, most of the anchor line would have been laid out at sea, together with the chain. It wouldn't have been on deck for Vinnie to step into.'

McGuire reflected on this. 'And the second body?'

'More straightforward. Stroud arrived in the country on that flight from Palma. I can say for sure that he was in Whitstable by 4.20 p.m. on the day of his death because that was the time he came to see me. He left my office at around four forty-five. You and I both know that within twenty-four hours after death a corpse will solidify due to rigor mortis. Shortly after that, it begins to rot.' She sipped her wine. 'Due to the rank condition of Stroud's body when I found him, I'd say he must have suffered his heart attack only a few hours after leaving me.' She looked to McGuire for confirmation.

'Roughly.'

'So the questions we need to ask are: how did he come to find his way to a deserted beach hut off Tankerton Slopes? And, more importantly, who was it that locked the door on his body?' She eyed McGuire. 'Even considering the remote possibility that the beach-hut door was barred by someone unaware that Stroud was inside – say, teenagers or a passer-by – it would still have taken a fair amount of effort to force the bar through those metal loops.'

'So?'

'So I would have expected there to have been fingerprints.'

'There were,' replied McGuire. 'Yours.'

'But I wasn't the one who barred the door. I merely opened it.'

McGuire drank some more of his stout. 'Okay, let's run with your version of events,' he said. 'If Vinnie Rowe's death isn't accidental and someone else is involved – who is it?'

Pearl smiled. 'Motive. Method, Opportunity. What do we already know? That Vinnie was in debt? I have that from Connie, but you can confirm it from his bank records which I'm sure, by now, you've had access to. It was a gamble for Vinnie to strike out on his own, but for what it's worth I think he would have succeeded. He was a good fisherman and knew what he was doing. Vinnie's only problem was staying afloat financially until those free-water stocks were ready to trade. This was the first year he'd have been able to sell Pacifics, but come September he'd have had fresh natives too. I was backing him with orders. I'm sure other restaurants would have done the same, in time.'

'Conjecture,' McGuire said curtly.

'You're running with my version, remember?' She reached for her glass and then froze.

'What is it?' asked McGuire, noting that Pearl's gaze was fixed on someone at the door.

'That's Vinnie's old boss, Frank Matheson.'

McGuire saw that Matheson was shrugging off his beige linen jacket at the bar.

'Have you talked to him yet?' asked Pearl.

'Why should I?'

'For one thing, he took it personally when Vinnie left. Sam Weller said that poverty and oysters always seem to go together, but Frank Matheson's the exception to that.'

'Sam who . . .?'

'Keep up. Haven't you ever read *Pickwick Papers*?'

McGuire's look answered her question.

'Everyone knows Matheson's made a few million from the oyster trade but I reckon he could have chosen anything to invest in and still he'd have made a success of it. He's a driven man. Without him, there probably wouldn't even *be* an oyster industry left in Whitstable – but his motivation is money. Nothing more.'

A maitre d' moved swiftly to greet Matheson, ushering his important customer up a few steps to a select table in the busy restaurant. McGuire observed Pearl. 'You don't like him.'

'Not much. Vinnie worked for him for over twenty years and Matheson could have been fairer to him, offered Vinnie a share of the profits – but he never did. He also failed to back him with this venture.'

'Maybe he thought it was a risk.'

Pearl shook her head. 'No. Matheson knew it would take

time for Vinnie to make a profit. I think he was just counting on Vinnie running out of money and having to beg for his job back.'

McGuire looked unimpressed. 'Man breaks free of his boss. Hardly a motive for murder.'

'Just checking my ingredients.'

When McGuire looked baffled, she clarified. 'Clues to a crime are like ingredients for a meal, don't you think? Put them together in the right way and the result can be very satisfying.'

'Is that right?' said McGuire flatly.

'Oh, come on. You get a taste from different foods, don't you? Well, I get the same from people. Some are sweet, some acidic . . .' she glanced towards the direction Matheson had taken '. . . some downright sour. But then some have a strange, almost indescribable quality to them. A bit like umami.'

'What?' McGuire frowned.

'That savoury kind of taste you get from fermented and cured food. Miso soup, black olives, tinned anchovies . . .'

'So what's your point?'

'Talking to Tina Rowe last night left me with an aftertaste, like quinine in tonic water. She's bitter and full of self-pity, although I'm sure I would be too in her position.'

Pearl told him the whole story. 'Look, she and Vinnie lost a son. They never got over it. Tina began drinking heavily and Vinnie got closer to Connie, who was working as a barmaid at the Duke of Cumberland. When Tina found out, she took off, but not before clearing out the joint bank account. A few weeks later she sent a postcard from the Costa del Sol. Vinnie was heartbroken and humiliated – but he did have Connie to console him.' Pearl looked knowingly at McGuire. 'Tina told me she flew in on Friday evening. It would be easy enough for me to find out if she was telling the truth, but easier still if you confirmed it for me now.'

McGuire paused. 'She wasn't lying.'

'Can you check if she was back in the country before then?'

'When?'

'Two or three weeks ago.'

'Why would you want to know?'

'Because it was around that time that Connie began to suspect Vinnie might be seeing someone else.'

'His ex-wife?'

Pearl corrected him. 'Vinnie and Tina never actually divorced, but if Tina was abroad at the time she couldn't possibly have been the other woman – that's if Vinnie ever had one.'

McGuire frowned. 'And what if he did?' The penny suddenly dropped. 'Connie might have had a motive for murder,' he said. 'Jealousy?'

'But an alibi would exclude all opportunity.' Pearl waited for the inspector's response.

His look told her all she wanted to know. 'She doesn't have one. At the time of Vinnie's death she said she was at home. Alone.'

Pearl persevered. 'And at the time of Stroud's death?'

'Out for a walk.'

'Witnesses?'

McGuire slowly shook his head.

'Okay, so we know Stroud arrived at Manston, and he probably hired a car . . .'

'The GPS system on the satnav showed he came straight here.'

'To the Continental?'

McGuire nodded.

'Do you know which room he checked into?'

The inspector took a notebook from his pocket and flipped through it. 'Number forty-two.'

'That's a suite,' Pearl said. 'With a sea view.' She chewed her lip in thought. 'Were there any sightings of him between the time of him leaving my office and my finding his body?'

'None at all.'

'Then that's what we have to work on.'

'We?'

'You're the one with access to Forensics. I can help with everything else – contacts, local knowledge.' Aware that McGuire was eyeing her suspiciously, Pearl added a coda. 'Look, I promise to share whatever I come up with.'

'Why would I trust you?'

'Because you know I'm a former police officer and you've now eliminated me as a suspect.'

McGuire stared at her.

'Oh come on,' she continued. 'I'm also a witness, remember? I can provide you with evidence, intelligence . . . in fact, I already have. So if it makes it any easier, just consider me a useful informant.'

She waited for McGuire's reaction but he simply posed another question. 'What did you call that "indescribable taste"?'

'Umami.'

McGuire slipped his notebook back into his jacket pocket. 'Sounds pretty fishy to me.'

'Tastes, Inspector, tastes. You hear with one sense but you taste with all five. Which reminds me, how are you enjoying that beer?'

McGuire glanced down at the glass in his hand. 'I'm guessing there are no oysters in it?'

'Correct. But if you'd ordered that in town two hundred years ago you'd have been served up as many salty oysters as you liked. All free of charge.' She leaned in to him. 'They'd have given you a thirst – so you'd have kept on buying more stout.' She grinned. 'Old-fashioned tapas. And a good combination. You should try it some time.' She drained her glass and got to her feet. Picking up her bag, she remembered to ask, 'Oh, and I nearly forgot – did you happen to find any binoculars in Stroud's luggage?'

McGuire looked blank. 'No – why?'

She smiled, a little too innocently for his liking. 'I'll be in touch.'

Pearl moved off quickly and McGuire watched her go, half-tempted to call her back, but in no time she had vanished into a crowd of noisy tourists and it was at that point that McGuire noticed that almost everyone else in the Hotel Continental was eating oysters on the half shell. He picked up a menu and scanned it. A waitress bustled across and McGuire finally made a decision.

'Same again,' he said, handing his empty bottle across. The waitress disappeared with it while McGuire sipped what was left in his glass. The oyster stout was rich, nutty and curiously distinct from any other beer he had ever tried. It was a taste that was definitely growing on him.

Pearl failed to return directly home but headed instead towards Tankerton Road, then straight past the Castle and up onto the Slopes. Once there she took out her mobile and dialled

Charlie. Sometimes it was impossible to get a mobile signal in the area due to poor reception, but she managed to leave a short text, thanking him for Tizzy's number and letting him know how grateful she was for the recipe. She was sure her last comment would intrigue Charlie.

Slipping the mobile back in her pocket, she moved towards the cannons, then halted as her attention was caught by the old telescope. She hadn't stared through its lens for many years so couldn't be sure whether it even still functioned, but if it did, she wondered if someone had made use of it recently. Perhaps they might even have observed Vinnie at work on *The Native*, sorting his catch at the culling table.

Pearl pushed a twenty-pence piece in the slot and a circle of daylight appeared in the lens. Shifting the telescope, she gained a good view as far as the Red Sands fort. For almost a decade, a local charity had been making serious attempts to protect the rusting towers from further deterioration. Similar forts had suffered irreparable damage, but a new landing stage had been added to the gun tower of Red Sands and it was now clearly visible through the telescope. Access to the tower itself was by two steel ladders stretching some thirty feet up from the stage into the base of the tower. It was an impressive feat of engineering and Pearl was just wondering whether the fort might even be fully restored in time when something suddenly flew across her view. She realised she was looking at a kite surfer, one of several performing somersaults at sea in front of a crowd gathered on the beach. Pearl was about to abandon the telescope when she recognised a face among the spectators. However, Ruby wasn't following the progress of the kite surfers but was smiling instead at the person standing beside her.

Curious, Pearl shifted the telescope to identify her waitress's companion but her view was suddenly eclipsed as a figure moved in the way. The telescope lens then faded to black, leaving Pearl to search fruitlessly in her pockets for more coins, rifling through her bag where she managed to find a single twenty-pence piece. She pushed it into the slot and re-focused, but this time there was no sign of Ruby. The girl had vanished from the beach.

Pearl lowered the telescope, aware that time had run out on her before it had been possible to identify Ruby's companion. Nevertheless, she was certain of one thing: the expression she had just seen on the face of her young waitress had been the look of – love.

Chapter Eleven

'That's not a bad photo of you, Pearl.' Billy Crouch was leaning on his bait shovel, studying the front page of the morning's local newspaper before he handed it back to her.

'Thanks, Billy.' Pearl didn't explain that it was, in fact, an old shot, and one which the local *Courier* had drummed up from its own records. Taken a few years back, it had accompanied a restaurant review and showed Pearl outside the oyster bar, proudly indicating her menu. Under any other circumstances she would have welcomed more publicity but for the photo's cliched headline: DOUBLE DEATH FIND FOR WHITSTABLE'S PEARL, which gave the impression that the two fatalities had possibly resulted from eating her food.

It was early morning out at Seasalter Beach and Pearl was suitably dressed in wellies and an anorak, having followed Billy out onto the mudflats at low tide. He was digging for lugworm which he sold as bait to the fishing-tackle shops in Whitstable, and he smiled as he dropped a fine specimen into his bucket. Although semi-retired, Billy still fished for pleasure, casting off from the beach or from the Street, where he had once boasted of landing a bass weighing more than nine pounds. He nodded to the newspaper article. 'Did they pay you much for that?'

Pearl shook her head. 'I didn't give an interview and I doubt they'd have paid me if I had.'

Instead, a keen young journalist by the name of Richard Cross had left a bunch of messages on Pearl's answerphone, to which she had failed to respond. Cross had then woven a front-page story from the facts available to him, concluding with a request for anyone with information to contact Detective Chief Inspector McGuire at Canterbury's Incident Room.

Billy gave a disappointed sniff. 'So you don't reckon I'll have the press knocking on my door?'

Pearl grinned. 'I shouldn't think so, Billy.' She gave up trying to focus on the small print of the newspaper and gazed out instead across the muddy flats. Although Seasalter lay only two miles west of Whitstable and boasted a fine Michelin-starred restaurant in an old coastal pub, it always seemed to Pearl to be an isolated spot. The railway line sped past, taking passengers to Ramsgate at one end of the line and to London at the other, but there was no station, just a few bus stops, a limited stretch of mainly bungalow housing, some caravan parks and a shore that backed onto open marshland. The 'flats' stretched out a good mile at low tide, offering an underwhelming view of the Isle of Sheppey, home to caravan parks and three prisons.

More interesting to Pearl was the fact that the area, part of the estuary of the River Swale, had once formed a vast prison camp to house captured French soldiers in rotting hulks during the Napoleonic Wars. During the same period, the empty marshes had become useful to the smuggling trade, which had burgeoned following the increase in customs duties to fund the war. The notorious 'Seasalter Company', as it had come to be known, stage-managed the landing of illegal consignments of tobacco, brandy and perfume, with the woods at Blean offering cover for the goods' eventual transportation to London. Decoy systems and elaborate signals involving lanterns in windows and broom-heads up chimneys had allowed the smugglers to play a cat-and-mouse game with the local coastguard, although sometimes the authorities had won. In 1780, a seventeen-year-old smugglers' accomplice was executed and his body hung in chains on a gibbet at Borstal Hill.

Thinking on this, Pearl felt a shiver run through her in spite of the early-morning sun. She took a flask of sweet tea from her backpack and offered a mug to Billy but he declined, choosing instead to continue sifting with a long fork through the thick mud. Pearl now decided to do some sifting herself, not for lugworm, but for information. 'So when was the last time you actually saw Vinnie?' she asked.

Billy shrugged. 'Like I said, about a week ago he was out here. That was the last time we talked properly, though I'd see him around the harbour most days.' He straightened up for a moment. 'It must have been a couple of days before he died. He was up on the quay and I would have gone over, only I saw he was chatting to Marty.'

'Marty Smith?'

Billy gave a nod.

'What were they talking about?'

'I dunno – I didn't go over. Didn't want to interrupt. Wish I had now.' He allowed a moment's silence before continuing. 'Before that, I saw him out here, like I say, about a week ago.' He looked at Pearl. 'Stood where you're standing right now.'

'Just a social visit?'

Billy placed a hand against the small of his aching back and stretched. 'I reckon so,' he decided. 'Some days he'd lend me a hand. Other times he'd be after relaxing. He used to come down a lot around October time. Liked to watch the Brent geese flying in for the winter.' Billy scanned the empty sky. 'They come for the eelgrass.'

Pearl nodded. 'And what did you talk about?'

'Not much. We never did. Never felt the need to.'

'How about on that last occasion?'

This time Billy heaved a long sigh. 'We made the usual noises about what had happened here with the cultivation.' He glanced down at the mix of mussel and oyster shells at his feet. 'If you ask me, this is all a crying shame.'

Pearl understood what Billy referred to: sacks of farmed oysters washed up regularly on Seasalter Beach, the remains of a method of cultivation in which the spats or seeds were bagged and sunk on racks at the estuary bottom. They were harvested not by dredging, but by simply raising the sacks from the water. One benefit of this method was a reduction in the loss to predators, but it had also led to the importation of the herpes virus which was said to have arrived in equipment from France.

Billy raised his head and stared unseeingly at the old, abandoned racks that lay like the bones of a rusting skeleton on the mud bed. 'To be honest, I think he just fancied a bit of company that day,' he told Pearl. 'He was in an odd sort of mood.'

'Why d'you say that?'

'I reckon he must've been thinking about Shane,' Billy said, ''cos once we'd filled the bucket with worm he got a look on his face and turned to me. "Why d'you think kids get mixed up with drugs, Bill?" he asked.' The old man broke off and looked at Pearl.

'And what did you say?'

'What *could* I say? No one knows that for sure, do they? Only the kid himself.'

Pearl recognised that Vinnie and Tina must surely have asked themselves that same question many times. 'Tina said something similar to me just the other day.'

Billy looked up.

'She's back,' said Pearl. 'Staying up in Margate.'

'Then she'd better stay there,' Billy warned. 'Or we'll be in for fireworks before the Regatta.'

Pearl peered down at the newspaper still in her hand and Billy watched her squinting, noting the effort she was making to read the copy. After a few moments he leaned in and offered a suggestion. 'Ever thought of getting yourself a pair of glasses?'

McGuire inched the receiver slowly away from his ear. He had been waiting for some time for a suitable gap in the stream of vocabulary that was flowing from his phone and now he chose his moment. 'Thanks. I'll do that, sir.' He ended the call and set the receiver down, half-expecting it to ring again, but instead it remained silent. McGuire exhaled. He had been calmly updating Welch on the progress of the investigation when the Superintendent had suddenly hijacked the conversation in the same way that Pearl seemed apt to do. McGuire hadn't told

Welch about Pearl. Not the whole story anyway. He was far from convinced that he should trust her, but as none of his officers had turned up much in the way of information, he saw no reason to prevent Pearl from digging around. She was, after all, a local, and as such might get lucky, perhaps even find a useful witness with a good recollection of events.

Time was always of the essence in any investigation, the first forty-eight hours being a crucial period in which forensic evidence might link a suspect to a crime. An early arrest usually made that easier but in this instance McGuire couldn't even be sure that a crime had actually been committed. If it had, he was well aware that Pearl had managed to contaminate the forensics at both scenes. Although she hadn't disturbed much at the beach hut, she had opened the door and turned over the body, and the latter would certainly have affected lividity – the pooling of blood within the body's tissues after the heart had stopped pumping. The police surgeon hadn't been overly concerned about that since McGuire had arrived shortly after Pearl's discovery, so the time of death had been pretty much fixed.

There seemed, on the face of it, no suspicious circumstances – other than the barred beach-hut door. Nonetheless, McGuire was uneasy about a second death, particularly since Stroud was linked to Vinnie Rowe by the debt. Pearl, in turn, was linked to both men, which presented McGuire with a dilemma. His staffing on both cases would soon be reduced and he didn't much like the idea of an 'informant'. In the past he had sometimes made use of them, but in general he was suspicious of their motives, especially the betrayed wives or girlfriends who volunteered their services while keen to even up a score. 'Hell hath no fury like a woman scorned' was about right, as far as McGuire's previous experience had gone, though he was aware of another kind of informant, more tricky and unpredictable, the kind who enjoyed wielding power from the possession of information.

McGuire knew that it was crucial to maintain control of a case. After all, you might choose to let a dog into your home, but not at the expense of having to live in its kennel. Strictly speaking, the use of any informant had to be registered by an officer so that the relationship between the two could be monitored, but since Pearl had volunteered her services without any need for payment, McGuire had recognised his loophole. He didn't much fancy the idea of Welch discovering he was using a rookie gumshoe – that was far too Mickey Mouse. But McGuire was sure he knew what he was doing. He would allow Pearl to believe she had been discounted as a suspect while, in reality, he would continue to keep an open mind. He rose to his feet, closed the file on his desk and plucked his jacket from the back of his chair. With or without Pearl, he resolved to keep on digging.

The restaurant had been closed for almost half an hour when Pearl switched off the lights in the oyster bar. She went into the kitchen, peering down at the notepaper in her hand. 'Ruby, does that say one ounce or . . .'

'Seven,' replied the young waitress.

Pearl could see now that Ruby was right. 'Of course,' she realised. 'It just threw me for a moment.'

'What did?'

'The seven has a line through its stem.' Pearl indicated the number on Tizzy's recipe and saw that Ruby was eyeing her. 'The light's not too good in here,' she continued.

Ruby looked around. 'The light's fine.'

Pearl frowned ruefully at Tizzy's recipe in her hand. She knew that it wasn't the light, nor the style of writing, nor the size of the print but her own eyesight that was at fault. She should have known better than to fight the truth. Dolly had relied on reading glasses for years and wore colourful frames which hung on jewelled chains around her neck. They had become a necessary part of her life and she now viewed them in the same way she viewed her clothes: as an extension of herself. Pearl, however, had difficulty viewing glasses as anything other than evidence of growing old.

Ruby began to chop a little faster, working her way through a pile of garlic cloves on her board. She had agreed to stay on a little later this evening to help with preparation of the new dish, but now she used it as a distraction from the delicate subject of Pearl's dodgy eyesight. 'So what's this going to be?' she asked brightly.

'*Caccuccio di Livorno*. That's fish stew to you and me.'

'Something for the restaurant menu?'

'Something I'm trying out for a client.'

Pearl took Ruby's chopping board and slid the garlic onto the onions she had already begun to sauté in a pan over the heat. Tizzy's recipe hadn't actually called for onions but Pearl couldn't stop herself from improvising. As the onions began to take on a translucency, she added some parsley and a hefty glug of white wine. Waiting for the wine to reduce, she gave the mixture a stir, assured by the knowledge that she had followed the recipe as far as the inclusion of bony fish. There was the conventional use of skate, John Dory and gurnard, but the chunks of meaty monkfish had been Pearl's own idea, along with some fresh grey mullet. Tizzy had noted that there should be as many varieties of fish as there were 'Cs' in *caccuccio*. Pearl's own mix included baby octopus, shrimp, mussels and clams.

'Is it a dinner party?' asked Ruby.

'A bit less formal. An early supper at home for the family who had lunch here with the Harcourts the other day. They're staying up at Beacon House.'

Ruby said nothing as she washed her hands, her back now turned to Pearl.

'How would you like to be my assistant for the evening?' Pearl asked.

At this, Ruby turned round. 'Cooking, you mean?'

'Giving me a little help with the kitchen prep and service?' When Pearl saw that Ruby was looking decidedly anxious, she added, 'It wouldn't be anything more difficult than you're doing right now. You'd like to learn a little more, wouldn't you?'

Ruby bit her lower lip, considered the proposition and gave a quick nod of her head.

'Good,' Pearl said. She was pleased. 'It's set to be a beautiful evening and the house is stunning with that view of the beach.'

'I bet,' said Ruby with a small sigh, before she began cleaning her chopping board.

Pearl chose her moment. 'Didn't I see you down there last night?' Ruby paused, allowing tapwater to run into the sink as though she was totally unaware of it. 'On the beach,' continued Pearl. 'I was up at the Slopes and thought I saw you watching the kite surfers.'

After a moment, Ruby switched off the tap and turned to Pearl, the chopping board still in her hand. 'It wasn't me.'

'Really?' asked Pearl, surprised.

Ruby nodded. 'I went straight home last night.' She offered a little smile. 'Maybe you do need glasses, Pearl.'

Before Pearl could protest, a ringtone sounded – a chirpy cartoon melody, at odds with the expression on Ruby's face as she noted the caller ID. She turned away to answer. 'Hello?'

Pearl's reduction continued to simmer noisily in the pan as the girl listened to the voice on the end of the line. A bright pink tassel swung backwards and forwards from the mobile in her hand and when Ruby finally turned back, Pearl instantly knew that something was wrong.

'No, I'll . . . come,' Ruby stammered, ending the call to stare down vacantly at her phone.

'What is it?' Pearl's voice seemed to bring the girl back to her senses.

'A nurse from the care home,' Ruby told her. 'She said Nan's upset and needs to see me.'

Pearl hesitated for only a moment. 'Then you must go.'

Ruby's face crumpled in frustration. 'But what about this?'

Pearl glanced around the kitchen, at the counter-top spread with ingredients for her untried dish and the wide-bottomed pan still bubbling away on the hob. She moved to switch off the heat and set a bowl of seafood into the fridge. Taking Ruby's jacket from a hook by the door she handed it to her. 'Come on. I'll give you a lift.'

The drive down into Canterbury was a clear one since most traffic was heading into Whitstable and not out of it. Mary Hill's care home was situated in an area known as Rough Common, but there was nothing 'rough' about it. Fairfax House was Georgian and set in well-kept grounds.

Pearl found a space in the car park, killed the engine and turned to Ruby. 'Shall I come in with you?'

Ruby looked pitifully grateful. Pearl took the girl's arm as they trod a York-stone path leading to the entrance. The hallway was imposing with Victorian portraits lining the walls, and while Ruby spoke to a receptionist, Pearl waited by a small antique stand, on which stood a large vase filled with lilies. At first sight it seemed a welcoming feature until Pearl noticed that small beads of water on the petals were slightly dusty: everything about the place was artificial, including the general air of cheerfulness.

'Nan's on the second floor,' said Ruby. 'They say we can go straight up.'

A lift stood vacant in the hall and Pearl and Ruby stepped into it before the doors slid silently shut. In the mirrored panels which lined the lift's walls Pearl saw the girl's innocent young face was clouded with concern.

'Are you okay?' she asked.

'Yes. The nurses are good and they can give Nan something to calm her down, but . . . sometimes I can do that just by being here.' Ruby gave Pearl an incongruous smile. 'Some days she'll play them up like a big kid. Other times I'll call, and I can tell straight away that something's wrong. "She's not herself today, Ruby," they say, and I know exactly what they mean. She really is like someone else. Not my Nan at all.' She paused. 'Every time I come to see her, there's a little bit less of her left.'

The thought stayed with Pearl as the lift stopped and its doors opened to release them into a corridor. Ruby took a few steps off to the right before stopping and looking back at Pearl. 'I'd better go in first, is that all right?'

'Of course.' Pearl gave her a reassuring smile, thinking

how very young Ruby looked as she opened the door to her grandmother's room.

Alone, Pearl found herself staring at the opposite wall of the hallway, noting that the small prints hanging there were of hunting scenes and studies of wildlife. It was natural, after all, for life to pass away, she thought, but it seemed especially hard on Ruby to have lost her mother at such a young age and now to be losing Mary, slowly, in bitter instalments.

A middle-aged couple passed by, making for the lift. The man nodded politely, acknowledging Pearl, while the woman forced back tears. She was clutching the handle of a canvas shopping bag. When the lift doors closed and ferried them away, for a moment Pearl couldn't help wondering if, one day, she might have to visit Dolly in a place like this. As a distraction she took out her mobile phone and quickly texted her mother, explaining where she was and what had happened, before switching off the phone and putting it away.

Just then, Ruby emerged from Mary's room, an empty jug in her hand. Pearl rose instantly. 'How is she?'

'Confused,' said Ruby. 'She didn't even recognise me at first.' She glanced down at the jug in her hand. 'I'm going to get her some water.'

'Let me,' offered Pearl, glad of something to do, but Ruby shook her head.

'I know where to go. Could you sit with her till I get back?' The girl gave a grateful smile and hurried off down the corridor.

Pearl braced herself as she entered Mary's room.

Mary Hill had always been a stout woman with a rod-straight back and a bosom like the prow of a ship. Now, seated in a chair beside the window, she looked to be a mere silhouette, frail and timid, diminished by the demons of her own dementia. The last of the day's sun shone past her, throwing a shadow upon the floor – a shadow of herself, thought Pearl, before she moved to sit beside the elderly woman. 'It's me, Mary,' she said softly. 'Pearl Nolan.'

Mary's eyes turned from the window and scrutinised Pearl's face. A smile played upon her tight lips and she nodded. 'Pearl . . .' she echoed, as if trying to convince herself. 'Dolly Nolan's daughter.'

Pearl smiled in return and took the old woman's hand in her own, glancing beyond her to the many photographs on the wall. They showed Ruby looking proud in her infant-school uniform, a Christmas scene at the Windsor House flat with Ruby dressing a tree, a couple outside a register office smiling as confetti flies, the man in a white tuxedo, the woman wearing a crisp white bolero jacket, her waist cinched above a full skirt layered with petticoats. Pearl found herself wondering whether this could possibly be Mary. Beside it, a later photo from perhaps twenty years ago or more showed what looked to be an older version of Ruby, a pretty young woman with dark hair cropped short at the sides in a style that made Pearl think of the Human League and their hit from the 1980s 'Don't You Want Me?' Another girl, other than Pearl, had been a fan of this record: Ruby's mother, Kathy Hill, the face smiling wistfully off into the distance from Mary's wall.

'He's dead, isn't he?' Mary's voice broke suddenly into Pearl's thoughts. 'The oysterman, Vinnie Rowe. *She* came to see me the other day and told me all about it.'

'Ruby?'

'No.' Mary shook her head. 'Sadie – Billy Crouch's wife. It's a terrible thing.' The old woman wiped a handkerchief beneath her nose before tucking it up into the sleeve of her cardigan, her face quickly taking on a stain of anxiety as she glanced around the room. 'Where's the lass gone?'

'To fetch some water for you, but she'll be back soon.'

In the next instant, a small embroidered cushion fell to the floor from Mary's chair. She looked around helplessly but Pearl picked it up and resettled it into the small of the old woman's back. Mary reached for Pearl's hand. 'You're a good girl. You're looking out for her, aren't you?' Before Pearl could respond, Mary's pale eyes darted to the photographs on the wall. 'I can't do it because she's too far away. But you can. You can take care of her for me because she needs someone. Especially now *he's* turned her head.'

Pearl wondered aloud: 'Who?'

'That boy,' replied Mary. 'He's no good for her, Pearl. I've seen the signs but there's nothing I can do. Not while I'm here.' Her fingers pressed tightly into the flesh of Pearl's hand while her eyes searched for reassurance.

'Mary, you're confused . . .'

'*No,*' the old woman insisted. 'I know what he'll do. So you've got to promise me. Promise me you'll look after my girl, 'cos if you don't, he'll be the death of her.' Mary paused to catch her breath and Pearl saw the fear in her eyes.

'I don't understand. Who'll be the death of her?'

Mary's parched lips opened to speak but her mouth gaped as if lost for an answer. Pearl realised her attention was now taken with something else. Ruby, at the door, said, 'It's all right, Nan. I'm here.' She crossed the room quickly, a jug of water in her hand. 'I've told you before, there's no need to worry. Mum's safe now, remember?' She poured water into her grandmother's glass and offered it to her.

'Safe?' Mary echoed.

'Yes,' said Ruby softly. 'Nothing, and no one, can hurt her any more.'

In the silence that followed, Mary looked slowly from Ruby to Pearl. 'Yes,' she murmured finally. 'You're right. No one can touch her any more.' Consoled by the thought, she took the glass from her granddaughter and began to sip from it.

'Maybe you should go,' Ruby whispered to Pearl. 'I've arranged to stay the night.'

'Are you sure?' breathed Pearl.

Ruby nodded and offered up a small smile while Mary, watching her, did exactly the same. Pearl got to her feet and moved slowly to the door but once there, she looked back to see that Ruby had already taken her place. Mary was quietened, looking much like a pacified child as her granddaughter's tiny hands stroked the old woman's hair. Without either of them noticing, Pearl slipped out of the door and closed it silently behind her.

Half an hour later, Pearl was standing at the front door of Seaspray Cottage. The phone was ringing inside. Opening the door as quickly as possible she made a grab for the receiver but the caller had given up. A moment later, Pearl's mobile sounded in her pocket. It was Dolly. 'How's the old girl?'

'Better for seeing Ruby.' Pearl threw off her jacket and slumped into an armchair. 'I didn't realise how bad she is – or how Ruby copes.'

On the end of the line Dolly reminded her, 'Kids are often more resilient than we give them credit for.'

Pearl knew that Dolly was right but before she could respond, her mother went on: 'Listen, I had a call from Sadie Crouch earlier. She's talked to the vicar who's been round to see Connie, and it seems you're right about the police refusing to release Vinnie's body. There'll be no funeral for a while but there's a plan to hold a gathering on Wednesday night.'

'A gathering?'

'A memorial of sorts,' Dolly said. 'As the festival's on they've decided it'll be at the Neptune.' She paused. 'I said we'd both be there.'

Pearl reflected on this for a moment.

'Pearl?'

'I'm still here,' she replied, listening abstractedly to the bells of St Alfred's ringing out into the night.

'Well, get some rest and we'll talk more tomorrow.'

Dolly's voice disappeared from the line and Pearl ended the call, putting the mobile back into her pocket to find something she had almost forgotten about. She pulled out the crumpled pages of Tizzy's recipe and read them through, troubled by several things but determined that at least one would be tackled successfully tomorrow morning.

Chapter Twelve

'Better or worse?'

Pearl focused on the line of letters in an illuminated box on the optician's wall, and though it pained her to say it, she had to admit that her vision was improved. Henry Blunkell, the High-Street optician who had taken care of Dolly's sight for the past twenty years, smiled kindly from behind his own heavy lenses. His test had taken less than twenty minutes to present Pearl with a truth she had been avoiding for far longer. She needed glasses.

'These will be for reading only,' Henry explained as he scribbled out a prescription. 'But you may find you need another pair for driving. Particularly at night.'

'Why?'

The optician glanced up as he completed his paperwork and saw that Pearl was frowning petulantly.

'I mean, why should all this be happening now when I've had perfect eyesight all my life?' she asked.

Henry gave a small shrug. 'Everything gets a little flabby with age.'

'Charming.'

'Including eye muscles,' he added quickly.

'So I'm now short-sighted?'

Henry scratched a greying temple and offered a more professional explanation. 'You have a fairly common condition known as presbyopia. It literally means "old person's sight".'

Pearl's jaw dropped open. 'I'm thirty-eight, not seventy-eight!'

'Thirty-nine in February,' Henry corrected. 'It's quite usual for this to begin at any time between the ages of forty and fifty. The lens becomes a little less flexible while the ciliary muscle has difficulty focusing.' Pearl looked dejectedly down at the prescription he had just handed to her while Henry peered at her across his own horn-rims. 'I'm afraid you can't fight time, my dear.'

Ten minutes later, Pearl had tried a variety of frames. Narrow ones made her face look large, wide frames swamped her features. She finally opted for the most invisible glasses she could find, but their clear frames made her look scholarly and serious – two things that Pearl was decidedly not. She checked the price tag, her eyes widening, but after paying for them and being informed that her new glasses would be ready for collection in two days' time, she left the premises feeling somehow that she had only lost out rather than gained anything from this appointment.

Outside on the pavement, tourists were shuffling in the heat, sporting shorts and sunburn in equal measure. Then Pearl caught sight of a smartly dressed group milling around on the other side of the street. She recognised the councillor, Peter Radcliffe, among them, a few members from the Chamber of Commerce, and the odd face she knew from the festival committee. Clipboards in hand, they were processing from shop to shop as part of the judging process for the show window displays.

As the group paused outside Cornucopia, Marty appeared from inside to greet them. Pearl could see, even from across the street, that his window was a riot of green netting interspersed with tropical flowers. Kitsch and colourful, it featured a desert island scene in which a treasure trove had washed ashore to spill oyster shells, pineapples and mangos in equal measure. Bananas hung from raffia palms on which a mechanical stuffed parrot swayed to and fro. Marty hadn't seen Pearl but remained intent on entertaining the judges, who made quick notes on their clipboards as he appeared to be explaining his tableau. Pearl observed him for a moment but felt guilty for doing so and moved instead to cross the busy High Street for the Horsebridge. That was when she noticed a familiar figure coming out of a white-stuccoed building.

Connie Hunter was alone and carrying what looked like a buff plastic folder. She checked a mobile phone and stared anxiously towards Harbour Street, just as an open-topped bus, chock-full of holidaymakers, was approaching the request stop. For a time, the vehicle obscured Pearl's view but once it had moved off it revealed Connie still standing on the pavement. A sleek black car drew up beside her and Connie smiled, and got in next to the driver. As the car indicated and pulled away into traffic, Pearl recognised the driver. It was Frank Matheson.

For a few moments, Pearl stood stock-still as she tried to make sense of what she had just seen. Holidaymakers were forced to step around her until she crossed the road and stared up at the building Connie had just left. Barrett & Collins was a long-established company of solicitors, but in recent years a few more partners had been added to their list. Pearl studied the names of the new associates on a polished brass plaque beside the door then rallied her thoughts and entered.

In a stuffy reception, a young woman with spiky black hair was giving her attention to a computer screen while she spoke into a telephone headset. Pearl waited for the call to end and stepped forward, appearing a little stressed.

'I've been held up in traffic,' she said, 'but I'm meant to be meeting a friend. Is she still here?'

As Pearl checked her watch, the receptionist frowned. 'What name?'

'Connie Hunter. I think her appointment was with Mr Barrett?'

The receptionist checked her computer. 'No,' she said eventually, looking up again. 'She was here to see Stephen Ross but she left a few minutes ago.' The young woman then paused, as if waiting for further instruction.

Pearl smiled pleasantly. 'Thanks for your help.'

That evening, after the restaurant had closed, Dolly shoved some potted Norfolk shrimp into the fridge and turned to Pearl, who was stirring the contents of a large saucepan that was bubbling on top of the stove.

'So he did her a favour and gave her a lift. So what?'

'Matheson doesn't do favours,' Pearl said grimly. 'Unless there's something in it for him.'

'You're jumping to conclusions.'

'I'm telling you what I saw.'

'Which was?'

'She came out of the solicitors with a folder of papers in one hand and a mobile phone in the other. She'd probably just called him.'

'How could you possibly know that?'

'Because he arrived straight after. Pulled up right in front of her.'

'He could have been passing by.'

'She was waiting for someone,' Pearl insisted. 'She could have got on the bus, but instead she was looking out for a car. *His* car.'

'Matheson hasn't been interested in a woman since he was jilted by Carrie Carpenter in 1981,' Dolly scoffed. 'Money he can handle, but women are a different thing.'

'Then maybe they're up to something else.'

Dolly looked sidelong at her daughter. 'The sooner you get those glasses, Pearl, the better.'

'I'm serious.'

'I know. But lighten up, will you? You're creeping around the town like some kind of—' She broke off at the sight of Pearl's expression.

'Some kind of what?'

Dolly braced herself. 'Like a stalker, poking around in other people's affairs.'

Pearl's jaw dropped open but Dolly was unrepentant. 'Anyone would think you had nothing else to do, but you've got a business here . . .'

'Two businesses,' Pearl reminded her.

'No,' countered Dolly. 'One restaurant and one time-wasting hobby.'

'Now you're sounding like McGuire,' Pearl said.

'So maybe the Flat Foot's right. Leave this to him.'

'I'm helping with information.'

'Helping – or competing?' challenged Dolly. 'Horses for courses. Stick to what you know.'

'Which is?'

'Running this place. That's your name over the door and no one else's. Be proud of it.'

Dolly held her daughter's gaze for a moment until Pearl turned away to carry on stirring. Sensing that she had gone too far, Dolly moved closer and adopted a gentler tone. 'What is it, love? All of a sudden this isn't enough?' She heaved a weary sigh at her daughter's silence. 'I miss Charlie too, but he's all grown. He's his own man.'

'He's barely twenty,' Pearl protested.

'And in love,' said Dolly. 'D'you remember how that feels?' In the silence that followed, she reached her own conclusion. 'No,' she decided. 'And maybe that's the problem.' Then she gave up and turned away, but Pearl spoke out suddenly.

'You're wrong. I'm happy for Charlie and I'm pleased he's found Tizzy. As a matter of fact, I invited her round for tea yesterday.'

Pearl expected some surprise from her mother but instead Dolly stared knowingly at the saucepan on the hob. 'To ask for the recipe?'

Pearl glanced at the steamy aromatic *caccuccio* and her hold tightened on the ladle in her hand. 'I . . . happened to think this would suit the Bertholds' party.'

'And that's the reason you've been struggling with it ever since?'

'I'm not struggling.'

'No, Pearl, once again you're competing. If it's not with

the Flat Foot, it's with Tizzy. Why not admit it? I probably would've felt the same if you'd been born a boy.'

Pearl cut in testily. 'What on earth are you talking about now?'

Dolly shrugged. 'They always say there's a special bond between mothers and sons.'

'As opposed to mothers and daughters, who simply argue all the time?' Pearl said pointedly.

The question remained unanswered as Dolly untied her apron, hung it up and walked over to the door. She paused before looking back. 'I'm sorry.'

'For what?'

'For touching a nerve?' Dolly cast another look towards the saucepan on the stove and put one arm into her jacket. 'I hope it goes well tonight.' The door closed after her.

As soon as Dolly had left, Pearl felt all the pride drain out of her. Staring back at the pan she turned off the heat, noting how the golden liquid, infused with oil and spices, had taken on a glow from the saffron she had used. Dipping the ladle into the broth, she apprehensively raised it to her lips. But the broth instantly scalded her palate. Flinching, she tossed the spoon towards the sink where it fell with an angry clatter. When the echo subsided, Pearl plucked Tizzy's recipe from her jacket pocket and recognised that she would have to do better if Dolly's 'hope' was to become reality.

Later that evening, Ruby arrived at 'The Whitstable Pearl' as arranged, wearing a crisp white blouse and black trousers, with her fair hair gathered into a tight ponytail. Pearl thought she noticed, perhaps for the very first time, that Ruby was also wearing some make-up in the form of mascara and a slick of pale pink lipstick. She looked pretty, but nervous, her small hands trembling as she tidied stray wisps of hair from her temples. 'Do I look okay?'

Pearl smiled. 'You look lovely.'

Together, and on Pearl's instructions, they loaded the restaurant van with all that was required: crockery, cutlery and the ingredients for the Bertholds' supper. Pearl's large catering saucepan was the last item to enter the vehicle. She slammed the van door shut on it, determined that she would pull off the meal to everyone's satisfaction. If Dolly was right and Pearl did feel the need to 'compete', it was surely because the presence of both Tizzy and McGuire in her life at this time was causing old insecurities to surface.

She thought of her guarded reaction to McGuire's question about why she had left the force. Her reluctance to explain hadn't been a reaction to him personally, for whenever she was asked about this Pearl usually skated over the subject with a well-rehearsed story, so neat and so pat that it left little room for further questions. But McGuire, as a detective, had a professional instinct for what was being withheld and would surely suspect that there was more to this story, certainly more than he was being told. Pearl now considered that perhaps the reason she felt unable to explain the simple facts to him was that the emotional truth behind them was more complex. The failure of her relationship with her first love and the abandoning of her career had affected her more than she had ever admitted, even to herself. But tonight seemed a milestone of sorts, a catalyst that might allow her to move forward in a different way.

Climbing into the driver's seat, she switched the ignition and looked at Ruby beside her. 'Let's go.'

*

Less than ten minutes later they hadn't gone far, since the van was stuck in a traffic queue heading east to Tankerton. The traffic lights had failed, causing cars to stack at the entrance to Gorrell Tank car park opposite the Harbour. The area known as the 'Tank' was actually a reservoir, formerly a backwater constructed by the railways to flush out silt at low tide. These days, water was still pumped out from it but a host of visiting cars now sat above. A bored young traffic policeman stood at the junction, directing traffic flow.

Pearl turned to Ruby. 'How's your gran?'

'I went to visit her earlier and she seemed a lot calmer.' The girl paused. 'But she's never going to get better, is she?'

Pearl searched for a suitable response. 'She's getting good care.'

'Yeah, I know.' Ruby stared idly out of the car window, her tiny hands still fidgeting as they rested on her lap.

'Are you worried?'

Ruby looked back at Pearl.

'About tonight?' Pearl explained. 'If you are, then don't be. It'll all be fine.'

'Course it will,' said Ruby, heartened by Pearl's smile.

She felt for the girl. 'You work so hard, Ruby, *and* you have your gran to care for too. It's important you take time out to relax. What do you do in your spare time? For fun, I mean.'

Ruby offered a small shrug. 'Not much. I go for walks.'

'On the beach?'

'No. To Victory Woods usually, or Duncan Down. I used to go there with Mum when I was little.' She asked Pearl: 'You didn't know her, did you?'

Pearl shook her head. 'Tell me about her. What was she like?'

'A free spirit, that's what Gran always says. She was a bit

173

of a hippy. Dad was too. When they first got together they travelled around the countryside in a gypsy caravan.'

'I didn't know that.'

'Yeah. They'd camp up with other travellers, go to rock festivals and stuff like that.'

'Before you were born?'

'Yes, but we lived like that right until I went to school. Gran thought I wouldn't remember so she gave me a whole load of photos.' Ruby paused. 'But I do remember. I remember the woods and Mum being happy then. One day I'll take *my* kids there. We'll pick bluebells, go mushrooming and have picnics.' She turned to Pearl and said, 'Like you do when you're a proper family.'

For a moment Pearl found herself lost in Ruby's innocent smile, then she noticed that the young policeman was waving her on, and so she stepped on the accelerator.

A parking space had been reserved for Pearl on the promenade right outside Beacon House. Ruby helped ferry everything inside and though it was well before dusk, fairy lights were already twinkling across the veranda as a young woman busily arranged flowers for the tables. Pearl recognised her as Nicki Dwyer. Tall, attractive and with a commotion of shoulder-length red hair, Nicki had arrived in town just a few months ago from London to set up a new shop on the High Street, specialising in fresh and dried flowers. Pearl realised not only how well Nicki must be doing to have got work with the Bertholds, but also that the bird of paradise blooms in Marty's shop window display had no doubt been provided by Nicki too.

'It looks beautiful,' remarked Pearl.

Ruby's hand hovered over an arrangement of gypsophila

on the central table. 'Baby's breath,' she said, almost to herself.

'That's right,' smiled Nicki. 'Mrs Berthold's upstairs but she said to go straight through.'

Pearl had catered enough functions to know that the secret was always to maintain a general sense of calm. Hosts and hostesses needed to be reassured that every possible hitch had been considered and taken care of. To that end, once everything had been unpacked, Pearl set to work on a fresh *caccuccio* while Ruby prepared starters of fresh figs and caviar. It wasn't long before Sarah Berthold swept into the kitchen.

'Have you got everything you need?'

Pearl turned to see Sarah securing the stud to one of the silver hooped earrings she was wearing for the occasion. Her beauty was almost unsettling. In spite of the sultry heat, she appeared ice cool in a long white dress, and statuesque in high sequinned espadrilles.

'Everything,' Pearl replied.

Sarah looked relieved. 'Good. Leo should be back in half an hour and the guests arrive at seven-thirty.' Before Pearl could respond further, Sarah's gaze shifted to the window as she noticed someone else on the veranda. 'And there's Alex at last. I thought he'd be late as usual. Will you excuse me?'

Sarah moved off quickly to greet her son on the deck. Pearl saw through the window that he was dressed in faded jeans, a white vest and surf shoes, his hand running agitatedly through his blond hair as he responded to his mother's instructions. His eyes met Pearl's before he came inside, his footsteps sounding on the creaking panelled staircase, his voice, slightly stressed, protesting, 'Okay, okay, I'm getting ready,' before a door closed somewhere upstairs.

At 7.30 sharp, Pearl looked through the same window to

see the Harcourts arriving, bearing an arrangement of flowers and an expensive bottle of Scotch. Robert in particular seemed to exude confidence, pumping Leo Berthold's hand as the latter greeted the Harcourts like old friends. Ruby moved off to ferry a tray of plump green olives to the garden tables while Pearl listened carefully, hearing only the Harcourts exchanging pleasantries on the deck before she noticed more guests arriving. A short, middle-aged man was climbing the steps to the veranda, arguing tetchily with the woman beside him. Seeing Pearl at the window, he fell silent and rang the doorbell.

'Who's that?' whispered Ruby as she came back into the kitchen.

'Peter Radcliffe,' murmured Pearl. 'And his wife Hilary.'

Ratty Radcliffe, as he was known locally, was a taciturn county councillor, familiar to Pearl since the time she had locked horns with him to oppose a one-way scheme for Whitstable's traffic system. Pearl's argument had been that other towns adopting such routes had lost all character, though Radcliffe had refused to consider her view. He wouldn't be shifted from a vanity project of creating a pedestrianised 'café society' in Harbour Street, with traffic circling around it. He had also positively supported the idea of an influx of chain stores to compete with Whitstable's independent shopkeepers, but this had proved to be his downfall. Shopkeepers had joined force with Pearl's campaign, compelling the one-way scheme to be shelved.

At the time, Pearl remembered clearly how Radcliffe's ill-fitting toupee had provided a welcome source of diversion at local council meetings, looking as it did like something that wild animals had fought over. But this evening 'Ratty' appeared to be sporting a miraculously healthy thatch of grey hair, presumably transplanted onto his scalp at great cost. It was an improvement on the toupee, but the shade failed to match his eyebrows, which hovered like two thick black caterpillars above his gimlet eyes. Pearl allowed herself a smile at his expense. It disappeared, however, when another figure took Radcliffe's place on the veranda. The new arrival was staring straight out to sea, his back turned to the window, but Pearl knew instantly from his stature who it was: Frank Matheson.

It was nearing dusk when Pearl brought the *caccuccio* to the table, and Ruby had long since collected the starter plates. The Bertholds were seated with their guests at the far end of the garden, enjoying glasses of a fine Touraine sauvignon as Pearl approached. 'Oh, I'm *so* pleased we introduced you to Pearl,' Phoebe Harcourt trilled. Peter Radcliffe's pinched expression showed that he failed to share her view.

Sarah smiled. 'I'm sure you've enjoyed Pearl's food, Councillor Radcliffe?'

'Oh yes,' he said with a sour smile. 'Though I hear she's juggling two jobs at the moment.' He sipped his wine, leaving his wife to explain.

'We heard you'd started up a detective agency, Pearl.'

'Really?' asked Sarah, startled by the news.

'That's right, isn't it?' sneered Radcliffe. 'A private detective with the spectacular misfortune to find not one but two dead bodies recently. You must have all seen the story in the newspaper. Front-page news, eh, Pearl?'

Sarah Berthold looked confused. '*You* found the bodies?'

'I'm afraid so,' confessed Pearl.

Sarah's brow creased into a frown. 'But we talked about this just the other day – the body in the beach hut. You didn't mention it at the time.'

Leo Berthold said diplomatically, 'I'd imagine it's not the kind of experience anyone would like to revisit.' He gestured to Pearl to begin serving the *caccuccio*. 'Even a detective.'

A short silence was soon filled by Phoebe's curiosity. She could not let the subject drop. 'Are the police any closer to discovering what happened?' All eyes were upon Pearl as the guests waited for her reply.

'I'm not sure,' she replied guardedly. 'The investigation is a police matter and nothing to do with me.'

Robert Harcourt refilled his glass. 'The poor fisherman's death was clearly an accident.'

'That fisherman worked for me,' Matheson announced. 'Once upon a time.'

'You mean . . . you actually knew him?' asked Sarah.

'Pearl knew him too,' said Matheson, successfully shifting attention away from himself.

'Oh, how dreadful!' exclaimed Sarah.

'Yes,' Pearl agreed. 'He had a partner and two young children. It's a terrible loss.'

'A senseless loss,' Matheson decided.

'And what about the other fellow?' asked Leo.

'Heart attack,' Radcliffe said succinctly.

'So the two deaths aren't connected in any way?'

Sarah looked to Pearl for an answer but it was her son who replied, tersely, as though irritated either with his mother or the topic of conversation. 'Why would they be?'

His mother seemed taken off guard by his tone. 'I don't know. One occurring so soon after the other, perhaps? Remember when we first found out about that fisherman? I said to you how very ironic it seemed that I'd been to Evensong on the actual night he had died and we'd sung "For Those in Peril on the Sea". Do you remember, Leo?'

'Yes,' he said rather wearily. His eyes met Pearl's. 'But can we please now change the subject? It's hardly a topic for the dinner table.'

The host had spoken and his guests' attention duly moved to the food that Pearl had served. Sarah picked up her spoon and was the first to taste the *caccuccio*. She said nothing for a moment then finally declared it to be 'divine'. Everyone followed, purring delight. Gratified, Pearl slipped off towards the house, but looking back from the door, she saw that one person still stared after her. It was Frank Matheson.

Later, as Ruby was stacking plates and cutlery from the dessert course into plastic crates, stilted laughter burst forth from the garden.

'What's going on?' asked Pearl. Ruby peered out of the window.

'That councillor bloke's told another bad joke and his wife's just kicked him under the table.' She grinned. 'Shall I take this lot out to the car?'

'Please.'

Once Ruby had left, Pearl moved to the rear window to study the guests at the foot of the garden. They seemed relaxed now, liqueur glasses in hand as tea-light flames flickered in the darkness. Choosing her moment, Pearl darted into the hall, then up the panelled stairway. On the landing, a door was ajar to what Pearl judged to be the main bedroom. Downstairs, Ruby was heading back into the kitchen. Pearl listened but could hear nothing more than Phoebe's tipsy voice carried on the night air from the garden. Moving silently across the landing, she opened the bedroom door more fully.

The room was dark but pierced with shafts of pale moonlight which flooded in through a window to fall directly on a tall object by the window. It was a large telescope, mounted on a tripod, and Pearl had just moved over to look at it when she heard a sudden sound from the promenade. Peering out, she saw Ruby ferrying more trays into the van. Alex then appeared behind the girl to exchange a brief few words before he began helping her with the load. Pearl positioned herself at the telescope.

Through its powerful lens she saw a freighter seemingly hovering on the horizon. Fishing trawlers were dotted out to the west at Seasalter, but the telescope held something more directly in its sights – the abandoned Red Sands fort. Laughter suddenly burst from outside and Pearl stepped quickly away from the telescope. She was on her way to the door when something caught her attention. Jewellery was lying on a dressing table – a gold chain and some dress rings – abandoned choices for the evening's occasion. Beside them, a decorative box lay open, inlaid with what looked like pieces of ivory – a priceless treasure from the Far East. It now housed further treasures – a string of pearls glowing in the moonlight, a necklace of rubies clustered like ripe berries, a stack of silver bangles coiled like a spring.

Pearl reached out towards the casket, fingers hovering before she pushed aside the rubies to expose a flash of blue. It was a single piece of turquoise, but nothing like the earring Connie had revealed on Reeves Beach. Instead, this gem formed part of a pendant hanging on a gold chain. As she dropped it back into the box, a sharp voice sounded.

'What are you doing?'

Pearl's heart raced as she turned to see Alex standing at the door. His fingers searched for the light switch and the room suddenly lost its glow of moonlight.

'I . . . seem to have lost my way,' Pearl lied. 'I was trying to find the bathroom.'

Alex's gaze shifted to the jewellery box on the dressing table and Pearl sensed that he was carefully weighing up the situation, trying to form the right decision. Finally he stepped away from the door.

'Then you should have turned right,' he said starkly. 'Straight across the landing.' He indicated back towards the hallway.

Pearl offered a smile before leaving the room. 'Thanks.'

At this, the boy seemed to relax. 'No problem,' he replied, watching her move off.

It was shortly after ten when Pearl dropped her young waitress back at Windsor House.

'Long day, Ruby.'

'Yeah, but I enjoyed it.' Ruby gave a tired smile, yawned and stepped out of the van. She was just setting off towards the tower block when she stopped in her tracks and called back: 'What you said earlier, about me learning more. Did you mean it?'

Pearl nodded. 'How about I sort you out a few books tomorrow?'

'Cool.' Ruby returned Pearl's smile and set off for Windsor House again with a spring in her step.

Back at her cottage, Pearl went straight to the kitchen to pour herself the glass of chilled white wine she had been looking forward to all evening. Taking a long sip, she opened the door to her garden and stepped outside. The night was still warm but there was a certain stillness to the air, a thick heady scent rising from the white jasmine that climbed up the window frames of Pearl's timber office. She unlocked the door and sat down at her desk. Switching on her computer, she brought up the website for the High-Street solicitors, Barrett & Collins. On her screen she saw photographs of the company partners, alongside short paragraphs detailing their services. Scrolling up, she reached the name Stephen Ross, and the face of an amiable man in his early forties smiled back at her. Beside his photograph was the information Pearl had expected to see: *Specialist in Wills, Trusts and Probate.*

Her mobile suddenly cut into the silence and startled her. Pearl quickly answered it and heard a woman's voice on the line. 'Sorry. It's late, but I got your text and you did say to call.'

'Thanks for getting back to me, Marion.' Pearl waited for the caller to continue.

'Well, the answer to your question is no. There's no telescope up at Beacon House and there never has been.'

Pearl considered this for a moment. 'Thanks,' she replied thoughtfully. 'Will I see you at the next Book Club meeting?'

'I'll be there,' came the reply. '*If* I can ever get through the vicar's choice.'

Pearl set down the phone, amused as she recalled that a hefty and sentimental misery memoir was next on the Book Club's reading list. She looked up and saw that the pale moon, rising in the sky, seemed to hang heavily as though encountering some resistance. But she knew it could be only an illusion. Everything in the heavens was surely following its prescribed path – as was Pearl with this new discovery.

Chapter Thirteen

McGuire's body sliced through the choppy water, arms powering against the incoming tide. His stroke was usually smooth and even, but he sensed that today he made a clumsy figure in the water, perhaps because he hadn't swum outside of a pool for some considerable time. He cast his mind back to the last time he had done so, during the long-weekend trip to Venice which had marked Donna's thirtieth birthday. McGuire realised that in just one month's time it would be five years since they had stayed at the old hotel overlooking the Rialto, but, for a moment he could still hear bells pealing from St Mark's Square and see the Grand Canal's muddy waters flowing again beneath the hotel balcony.

He closed his eyes and conjured up an image of Donna wearing a black swimsuit with a silver clasp at the cleavage. She was waist-high in the sea, one hand pinning up her long auburn hair while the other beckoned to him to join her in the welcoming blue water of the Lido. McGuire's stroke quickened as though he was swimming towards her, but it wasn't long before the freezing estuary waves took his breath away, slapping against his head as though reproaching him for this foolishness.

Treading water, he paused to catch his breath and noticed a few other morning swimmers at a distance. A woman's white bathing cap rose and fell beneath the waves with each powerful breast-stroke. A man with a bald pate appeared to be heading out to deeper waters as effortlessly as the two Labradors who flanked him. McGuire had barely reached the exposed limit of the timber groynes but was considering joining the other swimmers when he happened to glance back towards the beach and saw that someone was beckoning to him. The offshore breeze had caught the woman's hair, obscuring her face for a moment, but as she pinned her long curls high on her head, McGuire knew his mind wasn't playing tricks. It was Pearl who was waiting for him on the shore.

He came out of the water, stepping painfully over the pebbles while wishing he owned a pair of surf shoes. Reaching for the towel that was lying beside his clothes, he wrapped it round himself and asked, 'What are you doing here?'

'Don't worry, I'm not stalking you,' Pearl smiled. 'I saw your car parked by the Neptune.'

The old white clapboard pub stood on the beach itself – audaciously, some would say – since several times over the years the right, or maybe wrong, conditions of wind and wave had created seas to threaten the Old Neptune's existence. It had survived a great storm in 1883, after which it had offered itself as a temporary morgue for those who had lost their lives. But it had failed to escape a high tide of the 1897 winter, when a devastating surge had engulfed not only the pub but most of the town itself. That single event had swept away the entire building, leaving behind just a few planks in its wake, but with a spirit of indefatigability the old alehouse had risen again, this time re-fashioned from the timber reclaimed from its original construction.

The 'Neppy' as it was known locally, stood in defiance of the elements, immortalised in many paintings, its foundations shifting over the years to support a sloping floor on which customers could appear either giants or Lilliputians depending on which end of the bar they happened to stand. The old pub was an integral part of Whitstable's landscape.

'It's not open yet,' continued Pearl, 'so I knew you had to be out here somewhere.' She watched as McGuire rubbed the towel through his fair hair before wiping it across his wide, angular shoulders. A neat brown 'V' speared the paler skin of his chest, and his strong back was flecked with cinnamon freckles, so distinct from Pearl's dark colouring that it occurred to her that they had sprung from different tribes.

'Cold.'

McGuire looked over his shoulder at her.

'The water,' she explained. 'You should have gone further out to the other swimmers. Before high water, the incoming tide from Seasalter moves across the mudflats and warms the current as it sweeps across the bay. If you'd swum out another hundred yards, you would have caught it. It's eighty-five degrees on a good day.' She moved across to sit at a wooden bench outside the pub.

'Now you tell me!' McGuire said, staring out towards the white bathing cap still bobbing out at sea. He picked up his clothes and followed after her. As he approached, a speedboat roared past on the high tide, drowning out something she was trying to tell him – something about a telescope.

'It didn't come with the property,' he heard her say. 'So the Bertholds must have moved it into Beacon House.' She paused. 'What do you think they could find so interesting on this stretch of coastline?'

'You tell me,' McGuire invited.

Pearl gestured out to sea. 'The old Maunsell Forts,' she said. 'Named after the engineer who designed them.' She checked McGuire's expression, but it was blank. 'There were three originally,' she continued. 'Nore, Shivering Sands and Red Sands. The first was destroyed after a ship collision. Shivering Sands is still out further to the east and that's Red Sands you can see straight off this coast.' She gazed at the hazy silhouettes on the horizon but McGuire was looking only at Pearl. The loose silk blouse she was wearing exposed the tiny silver locket lying against her sun-kissed throat, and he found himself wondering whose photo might be inside.

'Maybe Leo Berthold's a bit of a navy enthusiast,' he said finally.

'They were built for the army,' Pearl informed him. 'And Berthold doesn't exactly strike me as an anorak. He's a businessman, which is, no doubt, why he had a local councillor to supper last night, along with Frank Matheson and the architect, Robert Harcourt.'

'How do you know that?'

'Because I fed them. Which reminds me, have you tried an oyster yet?'

McGuire ignored the question, keen to stick to the original subject. 'What else did you find out?'

'A retired fisherman who works part-time for Matheson told me he'd seen Vinnie a week before he died, and that he'd seemed preoccupied.'

'He was in debt.'

'But from what Billy Crouch had to say, I don't think that was uppermost in Vinnie's mind. He was coming up to a difficult anniversary. His son died during an Oyster Festival twelve years ago.'

McGuire frowned. 'How?'

'A motorbike accident,' Pearl explained. 'But Shane had taken some Ecstasy that day. He was twenty years old and nobody knew that he was into drugs, least of all Vinnie and Tina.'

McGuire was silent. He was thinking of two other twenty-year-olds, caught speeding one December night through the rainy streets of Peckham.

'Did you hear what I said?'

Pearl's words snapped him back to the warmth of the sun on his face.

'Parents are often the last to know,' he said quietly. 'They'll often turn a blind eye to the warning signs. Teenage angst covers a lot.'

'What sort of warning signs?' Pearl asked.

McGuire shrugged. 'Depends on the drug. With marijuana and heroin a kid usually becomes withdrawn. With uppers, like speed and crack, they'll be hyper, even more so with something like meth.'

'Meth?'

'Methamphetamine. Crystal meth. These days, there are any number of drugs to choose from but it's nothing new. Recreational drugs have been part of youth culture for nearly half a century. Twenty years ago it was Ecstasy. Now, old-fashioned coke's back in fashion.' He cleared his throat. 'Can we get back to the subject?'

But Pearl was still thinking about drugs. 'Cocaine, you mean?'

McGuire nodded. 'It's estimated that something like five per cent of sixteen to twenty-four year olds have tried it at some time, which might not seem like a lot, but . . .'

'How can kids possibly afford it?'

'Street price has dropped. The average buyer pays around ten pounds less per gram than they did ten years ago. With demand high there's more entering the country, and it's easily cut, so there are big profits available to dealers.'

Sensing she was hiding something, McGuire asked her: 'What's on your mind?'

'I'm thinking that university is a great place to learn about drugs.' She sighed. 'I have a son studying in Canterbury.'

McGuire considered this. 'Got his head screwed on?'

'I hope so.'

The inspector looked again at the locket at her throat. 'Maybe you and his father should have a word with him.'

'Charlie's father isn't around,' Pearl said quietly.

McGuire immediately framed another question, but decided not to ask it. Instead, he summoned a smile. 'Well, if it's any consolation, I think it'd be difficult to hide much from a mother like you.'

After a moment, Pearl returned his smile. 'I take that as a compliment.' She then asked: 'Are you any closer to knowing when Vinnie's body will be released?'

'The autopsy report could be through later today, though I'm not counting on it.' McGuire stretched his long legs beneath the wooden pub table, knowing that as soon as his shorts had dried he would get dressed and drive back to Canterbury. Nevertheless, sitting here with Pearl made him wish he could simply lie on the beach until the sun went down, like the holidaymakers who had just arrived, carrying folded chairs and windbreaks.

Pearl brought him out of his thoughts when she said, 'It might not be too out of place for you to come along here tonight.'

'Here?'

'To the Neppy. There's going to be a small get-together for Vinnie, in lieu of the funeral. Come by later and share some information with me for a change.' She got to her feet. 'That's if you're not too busy sunbathing?'

As McGuire looked up, he saw the locket was glinting in the sun.

'What time?'

Pearl smiled. 'About seven.'

As she headed off across the beach, Pearl knew McGuire's eyes were upon her. She passed a beach cottage, framed with scaffolding, and a group of bare-chested workmen called out from the upper level, offering her a wolf whistle.

McGuire's reaction took him by surprise: he felt protective but also a little possessive of Pearl. But as he watched her move on, proud and independent, he knew those reactions were misplaced. Pearl was her own woman and belonged to no one, least of all to Mike McGuire. As she rounded the corner into Neptune Alley, McGuire looked back towards the Red Sands fort, struck suddenly by something she had just told him.

*

'I think they suit you.' Charlie was sitting across the table from Pearl, a cup of coffee and the remains of some tiger prawns on the plate in front of him.

'You don't mean that,' his mother scoffed.

'I do. They make you look clever – but in a laid-back kind of way.'

Pearl eyed him. 'And what's *that* supposed to mean?'

Charlie sifted for another prawn among the shells on his plate. 'You could have gone for something a little more "out there", like Gran's, but those are . . .' he trailed off, searching for the right words. 'Kind of inconspicuous.'

At this, Pearl took off her spectacles and fiddled with them. She wasn't sure that she wanted to be 'inconspicuous', though she knew that might be required of a proper detective, someone who needed to blend into their surroundings while conducting surveillance work. The spectacles, however, hadn't been chosen as a component of some cunning disguise. Instead they would become part of Pearl's identity from now on. Recognising this, she laid them disappointedly down on the table.

'So how did the party go?' her son asked.

'Fine,' she smiled. 'The client was pleased – and Ruby did well.'

Charlie glanced across at Pearl's young waitress who was serving at a nearby table. Ruby shot him a brief smile before moving off to the kitchen. As she did so, Charlie noticed how many heads were turned towards Pearl. 'Is it me,' he asked, 'or are people looking at us?'

Customers were certainly peering over, hiding ineffectually behind menus as they exchanged furtive conversations.

Pearl sighed. 'It's been like this ever since the local paper came out. Someone even asked me to sign a menu.'

'Maybe they were impressed with your cooking.'

Pearl was about to respond when a man's voice said, 'Miss Nolan?'

They looked round to see a young man approaching. He wore a jacket, in spite of the heat, and a winning smile. 'Richard Cross from the *Courier*.' With hare-like speed, he slipped into the vacant seat beside Pearl. 'I wondered if you could spare me a few minutes.'

Pearl exchanged a glance with Charlie before offering her reply. 'Afraid not.'

'But I don't think you understand,' Cross persisted. 'There's a lot of interest in the story. Not one but *two* dead bodies – and during the festival? People really want to hear your side of events.' He looked hopeful.

'I'm sure they do,' Pearl said evenly. 'But I shan't be telling it.'

'But you don't understand,' the young man repeated.

'I understand perfectly,' said Pearl. 'I recognise you have a job to do, but so do I.' Feeling suddenly guilty at destroying Cross's headline, she asked, 'Have you had any lunch yet?' And when the young man shook his head, Pearl beckoned Ruby across. 'Get something for Richard here from the seafood bar, would you, Ruby? On the house.' Cross recognised that he had just landed the consolation prize and followed Ruby obediently to the seafood bar.

'Nice one,' grinned Charlie.

'I'm sure it'll be Ruby and not the food that takes his mind off the subject,' said Pearl.

Charlie suddenly asked, 'Look, Mum, is it okay if I bring Tizzy along to the Neptune?'

Taken off guard, Pearl looked back. 'Tonight?'

Charlie was slipping into the denim jacket that had been resting on the back of his chair. 'Yes. I'm picking her up from the Coastguard's Cottage. She's rehearsing there regularly with a drummer and a guitarist.'

'She mentioned that,' said Pearl, summoning a tight smile. 'Of course you can. Bring her along.' She picked up her coffee and drained the cup.

'You don't have a problem with this, do you?' Charlie was picking up on his mother's mood.

'With what?' asked Pearl.

'Tizzy.' Charlie had said it outright.

Pearl set down her cup, shocked by her son's candour. 'Why would you think I have a problem?'

'Well, maybe you don't like her,' he asked, honestly

'What's not to like?' asked Pearl. 'She's beautiful, talented and a brilliant cook. How could I possibly have a problem with you finding the perfect woman?' Her smile was still in place but Charlie failed to respond to it. 'Come on,' she said, 'that's your cue to say . . .'

'She's not the perfect woman but you are?'

'I was joking,' said Pearl.

'I know.'

Pearl felt uncomfortable under Charlie's gaze and heaved a sigh as she finally articulated, 'Maybe it's not Tizzy I have a problem with, but you, Charlie. You could have told me a little sooner, couldn't you?'

'Told you what?' he asked, confused.

'About Bruges, for instance. You said you were going alone.'

Charlie gave a small shrug. 'I was going to, but then I changed my mind. I didn't know how I really felt about her then.'

'And you do now?'

Her son grinned. 'I fancy her like mad.'

'Charlie . . .'

'Mum, I just want you to like her, that's all.'

Pearl recognised the look she saw in her son's eyes – the look she had given in to so many times throughout the years. She took another deep breath and admitted, in all honesty, 'I do.' At that moment, she reached into her bag for a small gift-wrapped parcel which she handed to Charlie.

'What's this?' He stared quizzically down at the pretty pink – wrapping paper dotted with silver butterflies.

'It's for Tizzy,' Pearl replied. 'From me to her – so just make sure she gets it.'

Charlie popped the last prawn into his mouth, savouring it for a moment before he leaned across the table to give his mother an unexpected peck on the cheek. He then got to his feet, saying, 'You really are the perfect woman,' before adding pointedly, 'almost.' He was still grinning as he headed to the door, where he raised his hand and waved goodbye.

As soon as her son had disappeared from the window, Pearl looked down at her despised spectacles and shoved them back into their case.

A couple of hours later, Pearl was sitting at her desk in the office in the garden. There had been no rain for weeks and none was forecast. Instead, the sky appeared like a taut blue canvas. Outside on the beach a loud voice suddenly boomed through a megaphone and she looked out to see two teams preparing for the annual festival tug of war. There were several faces she recognised: fishermen, a local builder, a few local athletes – and Marty. Pearl observed him from the window, feeling rather like a voyeur as she watched the muscles tighten on his bare chest, his face creasing with effort as both teams struggled to find a foothold in the foreshore mud. Crowds were egging them on, locals and tourists alike, reminding Pearl that the festival still continued in the background in spite of all. After a time, a final cry went up and Pearl saw Marty, arms raised in triumph as the opposing team fell defeated in the mud. For a moment it seemed he might be staring towards her, but she realised this was an illusion. Marty was simply lost in his moment of victory.

As he turned back to his teammates, Pearl returned to her computer and clicked on a local website address. She had recently paid for a small ad for her agency but had yet to receive a single inquiry. Perhaps Dolly was right, perhaps she was merely wasting her time, diverting energy that would have been better spent on the restaurant. It was possible that access to technology, in the form of computer search engines, now meant that people were better able to solve their own mysteries. But if that was so, why was Pearl unable to solve her own? Maybe, she conceded, there really was no mystery to solve and McGuire's post-mortem result might yet provide answers to all the questions in her mind concerning Vinnie's death.

Pearl stared at a word on the top left-hand corner of her computer screen. *Search*. Typing the name *Leo Berthold* into the empty box beside it, she paused for a moment before tapping another key. Links suddenly began to fill the screen, taking Pearl to newspaper stories, magazine articles, quotes from City analysts and opinions on business mergers. Among society-page entries were a variety of photographs: Leo and Sarah posed together at their wedding in Geneva and a notice of Alex's birth. A colour-supplement profile showed a more recent study and Pearl brought the image full screen, zooming close in on Leo's face.

In this photo, Leo Berthold looked much as he always looked: cool, confident but somehow mechanical rather than human. Beside him, Sarah's delicate beauty seemed a fragile counterbalance, but could her perfect smile be concealing family secrets? Standing slightly in front of them both was Alex, his father's hand clamped to his shoulder as though steadying him, commanding him in this single gesture to look towards the camera – and possibly the future.

It was the image of a perfect family but it led Pearl to wonder if people living so much in the public eye had any place in which to hide. Perhaps that was the reason Leo Berthold had chosen to spend one particular summer in a little bohemian backwater – or was it that the hotel project required his presence here? Sarah had confided that her husband rarely stood still and yet there was evidence of holiday homes in far more glamorous places than Whitstable.

A magazine image showed the Bertholds' summer home in Sardinia, the Villa Leoni, perched high on a cliff above the Mediterranean, while a photograph below revealed the family at a restaurant on the beach, looking like a pride of lions themselves. The caption below identified them. One section caught Pearl's attention: *Alexander Berthold, son of Leo, soon to be studying Economics at university in Milan.* So, thought Pearl, Alex was to follow his father's footsteps into business. But another image now fixed itself in her mind: it was of Alex, casually dressed in his signature Bermuda shorts and surf shoes, making it hard for Pearl to imagine him ever as successor to his father's empire. For a moment, Pearl felt sympathy for the boy, wondering if the health problems his mother had referred to might have been connected in any way to stress. Certainly his family would have high expectations of him, but he was young so there was still time for Alex to become his father's son, in the same way that Charlie was becoming increasingly like his own father.

Pearl took a slim folder from her desk drawer and opened it. Inside were some sketches separated by sheets of crumpled tissue. They showed West Beach at dusk, the old oyster racks at Seasalter, the Street viewed from the Slopes and a young girl, with long dark hair, seated on a breakwater as she stared out to sea.

Looking up from the last sketch, Pearl stared towards her window. Beyond it, the view was hardly changed but for the white sails of the wind turbines turning on the breeze. Looking back at the pad, Pearl's fingers trembled slightly as they hovered above the young girl's face. She knew for sure that Dolly was quite wrong: Pearl remembered only too well what it was like to be young and in love.

Chapter Fourteen

On the beach behind Island Wall, seagulls and turnstones scavenged among the ribbons of bladderwrack left stranded on the exposed coast at low tide. In the distance, hunched figures appeared to glide mysteriously across the muddy flats: parents and children searching for crabs and clams in the hazy sunshine, reminding Pearl of a time she had combed the same shore with her own father. A rebel by nature, Tommy Nolan had always instilled in his daughter the importance of questioning the status quo but, over the years, Pearl had come to observe for herself how fishermen nearly always found themselves in conflict with authorities of one kind or another. If nowadays they were protesting for better quotas, a few centuries back they might well have been seeking ways to circumvent a corrupt coastguard. As at Seasalter, Whitstable's own smuggling fraternity had been responsible for many illicit landings of alcohol, tobacco and lace while having also played a part in the illegal transportation of an extraordinary human cargo.

Three hundred years ago, Whitstable's oyster yawls had regularly smuggled escaped French prisoners of war from the hulks to an offshore mooring more commonly used by the deep-drafted vessels unable to come ashore at low-tide. It was said that from an old timber platform, the escapees had sought cover, losing themselves among the bustle of fishermen and sailors before alighting on this very beach. Perhaps they may even have heard an unfamiliar shanty like the one Pearl heard now, which sailed on the evening air outside the Old Neptune pub. Seated on a low stone wall, a group of young musicians were playing on a squeeze box, harmonica and fiddle, seemingly keeping the past in tune with the present until a brash voice rang out, shattering the moment.

'There you are!'

Pearl turned to see Dolly. Her mother was wrapped in her crimson shawl, with a glint in her eye and a man on her arm. The man was of a similar age and height as Dolly, although his straight back and flattened shoulders gave him the appearance of someone considerably younger. He was dark, with a stocky physique, not plump but strong, with short legs and broad shoulders that gave the impression that he might have been compressed, with some force, into a shape much like a box.

'Juan,' said Dolly. 'Let me introduce you to my daughter, Pearl. Pearl, this is Juan, our Flamenco teacher.'

As if on command, the man took a sudden step forward, offering a paw-like hand. Pearl noticed thick dark hairs sprouting from the back of his fingers.

'*Encantado*,' he purred.

'Charmed,' Dolly translated. 'But Juan does speak perfect English, don't you, my dear?'

'Indeed I do,' smiled Juan, exposing a great flash of white teeth while pumping Pearl's hand. Conscious of an awkward silence having fallen, he then proceeded to fill it. 'I shall wait for you, Dolores. Over there, by the music.' And with a graceful flourish of his hand, he made himself scarce.

'*Hasta pronto!*' called Dolly, waving rippling fingers after him.

Pearl looked back at her mother. 'Dolores?'

'Doris doesn't suit me.'

'Is that what he told you?'

'Juan recognises I have the "soul of an Espanola". He's helping me with my Spanish.'

'As well as your flamenco?'

At that moment, Juan blew a kiss towards Dolly before giving his attention to the musicians. Dolly glowered. 'No need for insinuations, Pearl. There are over a dozen of us in the class.'

'That's a lot of castanets. I hope he can keep up.'

Dolly pulled her shawl tight and made as though to move off.

'Why on earth would you invite him here?' asked Pearl, frustrated.

'Why wouldn't I invite him?' Dolly summoned up some of her own inimitable logic. 'Vinnie would have loved Juan!' Her gaze suddenly hardened. 'Though I doubt he'd have welcomed a Flat Foot.'

McGuire was nearing them on the beach, but halted as he became aware he was the subject of their conversation. Dolly offered her daughter a knowing look. 'I'll see you inside.'

Dolly left to join Juan, who was still waiting for her at the door to the pub, and McGuire took the opportunity to approach; he was respectfully dressed for the occasion in a dark suit and a pressed white shirt. His smart brogues were still in place, looking incongruous upon beach pebbles.

Pearl was just about to speak when a sudden ripple of applause could be heard. The musicians had finished their song and children were clapping from the steps of the pub outside. Among them were Vinnie's own daughters, making it seem for a moment as though it might have been any other summer's evening, but for the numerous guests filing into the pub to remember a dead fisherman.

McGuire sensed Pearl's mood. 'Are you sure this is a good idea?'

Pearl looked back at him and nodded. 'Come on.'

It was a measure of the town that so many people had gathered in the bar. On a table by the door stood a framed photograph of Vinnie, smiling against sunlight as he worked on the deck of *The Native*. A smell of old timber and ale hung in the air while trestles groaned with platters of sausage rolls and quiche. The publican, Darrell, a bluff fellow with a ruddy face, had set aside a free bar until 8 p.m. Pearl guessed that no one would take too much advantage of the gesture except perhaps Billy Crouch, who stood amongst a group of fishermen with a pint of stout in one hand and a whisky chaser in the other.

Across the room, Pearl caught Dolly's gaze as Juan handed her a glass of wine. Dolly raised her glass to Pearl then sipped from it before moving over to Connie, who was surrounded by well-wishers – mostly other young mothers grateful not to be young widows. Pearl studied Connie, noting that her hair was newly styled, her make-up highlighting her pretty features, her petite, curvy figure encased in a short black shift dress as she stood, backlit by the last of the sun streaming through the window behind her.

McGuire noted Pearl's interest. 'What is it?'

Pearl realised. 'I . . . don't think I've ever seen Connie Hunter look quite so beautiful.' As she spoke, she recognised a familiar figure approaching from the kitchen. It was Ruby. The girl stopped suddenly, casting a guilty look down at the tray of food in her hands.

'Pearl!' she gasped, as though having been caught out. 'You don't mind, do you?'

'Mind?'

'Me moonlighting.' Ruby's face was a picture of regret as a torrent of excuses tumbled forth. 'Except it's not moonlighting really, more a favour, because I bumped into Darrell and he happened to ask if I fancied doing a few hours. A one-off – that's all.' She waited anxiously for a reaction.

'What you do in your spare time is your own business, Ruby,' Pearl told the girl kindly.

Ruby's relief was obvious and she seemed suddenly to remember the tray she still carried, on which sat a selection of sandwiches, cut neatly into triangles and sprinkled with chopped parsley. 'Here. Have one of these,' she said. 'I made them all myself.' Her attention fell on McGuire. 'You're the detective, aren't you? I just saw your photo in the local paper.'

McGuire winked. 'Hope it didn't scare you too much.'

Ruby offered a smile before her eyes darted around the room. 'I didn't know the man who died,' she confessed in a low voice, 'but I reckon he must've been some nice fella to bring all these people together like this.'

'He was,' agreed Pearl, sadly, remembering her friend.

For a moment, Ruby seemed about to say something else, but instead she decided quickly, 'I'd better go,' and hurried away, offering her tray to other guests.

Pearl took a bite of her own sandwich and considered the filling. It was a long time since she had tried anything as unadventurous as corned beef and sweet pickle, but there was something vaguely comforting about the taste, reminding her of childhood picnics on the beach. She turned to McGuire. 'Any news on the post-mortem?'

The inspector gave a shrug. 'These things can take time.'

'Obviously.'

Pearl's clear disappointment made McGuire suddenly feel ineffectual. He looked down at the cheese and cucumber sandwich in his hand, searching for a distraction. 'So whose idea was all this?'

Pearl nodded towards a swarm of people around Connie. 'The vicar's.'

McGuire scanned the crowd for a suitable candidate. 'The tall guy in the black suit?'

'No, the short woman in the blue skirt.' Pearl eyed McGuire. 'Nice to know you don't think in stereotypes.'

Nettled, he was about to respond when a laugh went up suddenly in the hushed bar. 'Who's that?'

'Billy Crouch.'

McGuire stared across at the old man leaning on the bar, holding the attention of some fishermen with yet another anecdote. 'Looks a bit of a character.'

'He'd be even more of one if his wife didn't keep him in check.' Pearl's gaze shifted to a group of older women who were sampling Ruby's sandwiches. 'That's Sadie over there with the lilac rinse. She worked as a midwife at the local cottage hospital until she retired recently. Now she's everyone's Mrs Capable, running everything from the local Women's Institute to the knitting circle. She's the unofficial Town Crier, so if you want something kept secret, don't tell Sadie.'

As soon as the words were out, Pearl thought back to Mary in the nursing home, remembering that it had been Billy's wife who had told the old woman about Vinnie's death.

'Pearl?'

Turning, Pearl saw that someone was looking not at her but at McGuire.

'Marty. Hi.' Pearl offered a smile but Marty's fixed gaze failed to shift. 'You two have met before,' she continued. 'This is Inspector—'

'McGuire,' said Marty brusquely. 'I remember.'

An awkward pause followed, which McGuire decided to fill. 'If you'll excuse me, I'll get a drink.'

As he moved off to the bar, Marty's suspicious gaze followed. 'Is he bothering you?'

'Bothering?

'Harassing.'

'Of course not.'

Marty looked back at her. 'You told me he questioned you half the night.'

'On the night Vinnie died,' Pearl replied pointedly.

'And the other evening at the Conti'?'

'He's got a job to do.'

'And that's what he was doing with you on the beach the other day, was it?'

Pearl gaped. 'Were you spying on us?'

'No,' Marty said defensively. 'I was out in the kayak and saw you with him as I came ashore – not that you noticed.'

Pearl found it hard to meet his eyes. Instead, she caught sight of McGuire smiling at her from the bar, before turning to place his order.

Marty said accusingly, 'You two seem pretty chummy for strangers.'

'Look,' began Pearl, 'Canterbury has to manage this investigation because we've no CID here in Whitstable.'

'Only he's not Canterbury.'

'What do you mean?'

'One of my customers is ex-CID. I asked him about your friend over there and it turns out he's a DFL. Here on transfer. That usually means only one thing.'

Marty's sneer served to further irritate Pearl. 'What on earth are you talking about?'

'Think about it,' Marty said softly. 'Why would a city detective get moved to a backwater like this?' He moved closer to her. 'Because he messed up, that's why. Botched a case – that's why he's here. And I've got a good mind to ask him to leave.'

Marty had just started to move off when Pearl laid a hand on his arm. He stopped immediately, looking back down at her hand, but she let it fall as she explained, 'Inspector McGuire is here tonight because of me.'

'*You?*'

'I asked him to come,' she hissed.

Marty looked confounded as he watched McGuire, who was now paying Darrell at the bar. Pearl took advantage of the moment.

'What were you talking about to Vinnie the day before he died?'

Marty heard her but failed to reply.

'You were seen talking to him on the quay,' she prompted.

'So what?'

'So you didn't mention it.'

'Why should I?' Marty ran a hand quickly through his hair before jerking a thumb towards McGuire. 'Is *he* putting you up to this?'

'Of course not. I'm just asking a simple question.'

Marty thought about it for a moment then gave a small shrug. 'All right. If you must know, I was talking to Vinnie about shells – oyster shells. I wanted some for my window display.'

Pearl was left to consider this as she saw McGuire returning with two wine glasses. He offered one to Pearl, saying to Marty, 'Sorry – did you want something?'

Marty looked broodily between Pearl and McGuire before turning on his heels to stride off.

'Hope I didn't interrupt anything?' McGuire said crisply while Pearl stood, reflecting on what Marty had told her.

'I really think I should go and talk to Connie,' she told him.

McGuire nodded towards the window. 'Looks like *she's* about to talk to *us*.'

Connie had broken away from the other women and was now standing in the centre of the room. A hush went round the bar, silencing even Billy Crouch at the punchline of his story. Connie cleared her throat before beginning a speech in a hesitant voice.

'I won't talk for long. I . . . just want to say a big thank you, to you all, for turning out and . . . for being here tonight.' Her fingers toyed nervously with a handkerchief as she continued. 'Everyone's been so kind, with cards, messages and . . .' she broke off momentarily, 'letters of condolence.' She took a deep breath. 'At times like this, it's good to feel part of a community, and it's a tribute to Vinnie that so many of you have got in touch, wanting to know about the funeral. Wanting to be there.' She paused, shooting a sudden glance towards McGuire. 'But I still can't give an answer to that because there's an ongoing investigation into Vinnie's death.'

She looked away, back into the room, at the sea of faces trained upon her, as though lost for words, like an actor on stage having forgotten her lines. Pearl's instinct was to move forward and rescue her but Connie recovered as though returning from a kind of trance.

'I just want you to know how much I value your support,' she said, then paused again – and this time it appeared she was staring directly into space. 'I don't know what I would have done without you.'

The words seemed to hang in the air. Pearl turned to see what Connie was looking at. Frank Matheson stood at the door, like another actor waiting in the wings for his cue.

Connie gazed down at her hands, summoning more thoughts. 'Every one of you knows that Vinnie was a good man – hardworking, kind and . . .' she seemed to struggle with the next word '. . . honest.' She then picked up a glass of wine and raised it high so that it appeared to be spotlit by a shaft of setting sun.

'This is for you, Vinnie.'

As if choreographed, everyone in the room followed, but before a single drink had met anyone's lips, there followed the sound of a slow handclap. Heads turned to see that Tina Rowe had just entered. A murmur went around the room like a lit fuse. A weight of resentment lay in

Connie's look as she said, 'You're not welcome here.'

'Really?' Tina asked innocently. 'Now why doesn't that surprise me?' She ignored the warning look Pearl gave her and turned to address the whole room. 'Whatever you might think of me, I was still Vinnie's wife. And now I'm his widow. So I say I have *every* right to be here!'

It was clear to Pearl that Tina was seeking a response from the assembled guests but most looked away, either from embarrassment or guilt, Pearl couldn't be sure. Tina reached for a glass of wine but another hand wrenched it from her grasp. It was Connie, leaning in close, taking advantage of Tina's shock.

'I'll take you on and I'll win,' she said ominously.

The room was stilled until a murmur began, but McGuire had witnessed enough and he walked across to put himself between the two women.

'Did you hear that?' Tina asked, staring up at him. 'She just threatened me.'

'Yes,' continued Connie. 'I'll do what Vinnie should've done a long time ago. I'll—' She took a step closer but McGuire anticipated it and held the women apart.

Tina continued to protest. 'Are you going to let this bitch get away with that?'

Pearl stepped forward to help. 'Stop it, Tina,' she advised. 'You're only making things worse.'

'So it's all my fault, is it?' The woman looked at Connie but directed her next question to McGuire. 'Are you going to arrest her or not?'

McGuire shook his head. 'No. I'm going to see that you get home.' He gripped Tina's arm, taking full advantage of some confusion on her part to steer her quickly away. The assembled guests parted like a wave, allowing him access to the door. Once there, he glanced back at Pearl but said nothing.

Only when the door had closed after him, did sound and movement resume. Women instantly went across to comfort Connie, among them Sadie Crouch, fussing as she sat Connie down, saying, 'I can't believe she had the nerve to come here.'

'Who could have told her about this?' asked the vicar. At this, Pearl was sure she saw Sadie blanch.

When the pub door opened again, it was Charlie who entered. 'What's going on?' he enquired, pointing back to the door.

'Don't ask,' Pearl sighed, before registering that he was alone. 'Where's Tizzy?'

'Outside, making a call.'

At that moment, Pearl saw Ruby coming out of the kitchen; the girl's face lit up as she spotted Charlie. Taking off her apron with nervous fingers, she wiped a few strands of fair hair from her pale face and came quickly across. 'I didn't know you'd be here, Charlie.'

'Just stopping by on my way home.' Pearl saw Charlie smile, looking into Ruby's eyes, unaware that the pub door was swinging open behind them.

Tizzy looked around for a moment before she found Pearl and hurried over, then hung back politely as she saw Charlie engaged in conversation with Ruby. Charlie, sensing that she was there, turned instantly, slipping his arm around Tizzy's waist.

'I don't think you've met Ruby,' he said. 'She works for Mum at the restaurant.'

Tizzy summoned a warm smile. 'Pleased to meet you, Ruby.'

An embarrassing pause followed in which Ruby remained

trapped in Tizzy's beautiful gaze. To Pearl the moment seemed all the worse as Charlie was standing so close to his girlfriend it was as though he was experiencing a gravitational pull from her presence. Ruby finally came to her senses, eyelids flickering, as if waking from a dream.

'Me too,' she smiled. 'Sorry, I'd . . . better get back to the kitchen. I've got mountains of clearing up to do.'

She disappeared, leaving Pearl with the distinct impression that her waitress felt more for Charlie than Pearl had ever suspected. She was staring after Ruby, when another figure blocked her view.

'Miss Nolan?'

Richard Cross stood before her, a notebook and pencil grasped keenly in his hand. 'Could I ask what just happened back there?'

Pearl was momentarily caught off guard but the young journalist quickly clarified. 'The two women. I understand one of them was married to the dead fisherman?'

'Not now,' Pearl said firmly. She made an attempt to move off but Cross blocked her path.

'That was almost a cat fight,' he said keenly. 'Everyone saw it and there's bound to be talk. Wouldn't you like to put the record straight?'

'This isn't the time or the place,' Pearl said, firmly.

'Then how about tomorrow at your restaurant?' Cross was smiling winningly but it was Charlie who replied.

'You heard what she said.'

Cross looked from Charlie to Pearl, recognising that he was beaten.

As he dejectedly took his leave, Tizzy asked, 'Who was that?'

'Nosy journalist from the local paper,' explained Charlie. 'He was in the restaurant earlier, pestering Mum.'

'Doing his job,' Pearl corrected him. 'Or trying to.' She saw that Cross was still staring back at her hopefully before he finally left the gathering. 'So,' she said, changing the subject, 'how was the rehearsal?' She had directed her question at Tizzy but once again it was Charlie who replied.

'Great. The acoustics at the coastguard's station are amazing. Just wait until the concert . . .' He stopped as he saw that Tizzy was looking stressed. 'What is it?'

'My jacket. I've left it behind.'

'Then we'll go back and get it.'

'No,' the girl decided. 'We're here now. I'll call the caretaker and ask if he can put it somewhere safe until tomorrow.'

'Sure?' asked Charlie.

'Sure,' Tizzy promised, moving off across the room, exposing Dolly, standing with Juan at the bar.

'Who's that with Gran?' asked Charlie.

'Her flamenco teacher,' Pearl said archly. Charlie gave his mother a look but she shrugged and said fairly, 'Actually, he seems nice and I think she's quite smitten.'

Charlie noted Juan gazing intently at Dolly. 'I think the feeling's mutual.' He set down his empty glass and murmured, 'I'll just say hello and check him out.'

Pearl looked around for Tizzy and saw that she was still speaking into her mobile phone. Her expression was one of concentration, but on seeing Pearl she gave a small smile before ending her call.

Pearl headed over to her, saying, 'Well?'

'No problem. It'll be safe until tomorrow.' Tizzy then said warmly, 'I need to thank you for the present you gave to

Charlie for me. I recognised the waistcoat straight away. It's the one you wore in the photograph, isn't it?'

'Yes,' Pearl said. 'But please don't feel you have to wear it.'

'Oh, but I shall,' Tizzy insisted. 'It's beautiful and it fits perfectly. Thank you.' As she leaned in and kissed Pearl's cheek, something caught her eye across the room. Connie was still at the window, surrounded by well-wishers. 'Is that the dead man's wife?' she asked.

'His partner,' explained Pearl. 'He never got divorced, though his first marriage was long over.'

Tizzy glanced down at the photograph of Vinnie on the table by the door. '*Cosi triste*,' she whispered, almost to herself. 'A great shame.'

'Yes,' agreed Pearl, looking at Vinnie's smiling face while wishing, more than anything, that he was here to tell his story.

Less than an hour later, guests spilled out of the Neptune and on to the beach. Among them were Dolly and Pearl.

'Everyone's coming back to me for a nightcap,' announced Dolly. 'Fancy joining us?'

Pearl watched Juan, at a distance, offering his own jacket to Tizzy. Dolly noticed and said, 'There really is nothing going on between us, you know. It's strictly flamenco. But he does have a wonderful sense of rhythm.'

'And furry paws.'

Dolly caught Pearl's look and gave a knowing smile. Then she said: 'You're very observant, Pearl, and you normally see past the details to get the bigger picture. You should do that with Juan.'

'I'll try,' said Pearl, chided.

'Sure you won't come back with us?' asked Dolly.

Pearl considered changing her mind and joining the party but something prevented her from doing so. She told herself it wasn't the fear that she might feel like a gooseberry among two generations of couples, but rather more that she simply wanted to know how McGuire was coping with Tina. 'Not tonight,' she finally decided.

Dolly took Pearl's shoulders and kissed her daughter, wrapping her shawl tight around her before heading, a little unsteadily, along the pebbled shore. Pearl watched her go then noticed Darrell on the beach, staring around as though searching for someone. She recognised the familiar pink tassel attached to the mobile in his hand. 'Something wrong?'

'Ruby's only gone and left her phone behind.'

'She probably won't get far before she realises,' Pearl told him.

But Darrell shook his head. 'No, she's been gone for a while now. Got a call in the kitchen and said she had to shoot off to meet a friend. Could you give her this tomorrow?'

Pearl took the mobile from him. 'I'll do better than that, Darrell.'

A short while later, Pearl had passed under the old Oxford Street railway bridge and rounded the corner into Belmont Road. A poster outside the local Labour Club advertised *A Night with the Backroom Boys* and Pearl could hear the voice of Nigel Hobbins, a local musician, singing a contemporary folk song about the coming of spring bringing an end to war. It helped her to reflect on this evening's conflict. Connie's speech had seemed heartfelt but had nevertheless raised unanswered questions. How could she have spoken of Vinnie's honesty while suspecting that he had been seeing another woman – and why had it taken the appearance of Matheson to calm her nerves? Could he now have assumed the role of her protector, or might it be that, having long tired of Vinnie's debts and dreams, Connie was now pursuing Matheson?

The truth had surely been there tonight amongst all that Pearl had witnessed, but perhaps, as Dolly suggested, for some reason, Pearl was not seeing beyond the things she observed. Even Marty's jealousy of McGuire had been another shocking element to the evening, causing Pearl to wonder whether, if he had spied upon her unnoticed on the beach, might he have done so on other occasions?

In spite of the warm evening air, a shiver ran through her as she tried to order her thoughts.

The arrival of Tina had been a focus for long-standing grievances but it was possible that the whole altercation between the two women had simply served as a distraction. Connie had talked openly to Pearl about an insurance policy – had been sure, in spite of other financial lapses, that Vinnie had maintained all payments. But what if the sum was substantial? Could it be sufficient reason for murder? Pearl knew this was something she should discuss with McGuire, though she imagined that, at this very moment, he was stuck with Tina in the bar of the Walpole Bay Hotel, forking out for drinks while having to listen to her side of the story. Tina was adept at playing the innocent victim, thought Pearl, and yet she had been smart enough to effect the loan from Stroud to Vinnie. Could she now be manipulating the situation for her own ends? If so, Pearl couldn't yet see a proper motive. In fact, she couldn't really see further than Matheson.

If someone had wanted Vinnie dead, Matheson was the one person to whom Pearl kept returning. It was true that she disliked the man but not without reason. Matheson was ambitious and consumed with his own importance; moreover, Pearl was sure he was capable of vengeance for Vinnie's desertion. Perhaps he had decided on a lesson for his former employee? If he wasn't physically capable of murder himself, he was certainly well accustomed to paying others to do his work for him. In the bar that evening there had been plenty of men, eking out a living from the sea, who would surely have been tempted by the offer of Matheson's money to give a warning to Vinnie. A sudden thought came to Pearl: might Billy Crouch be one of them? Billy may even have considered he was doing Vinnie a favour, but what if things had got out of hand?

Pearl filled her lungs with night air, hoping that McGuire's post-mortem report brought answers soon, not just for her own peace of mind but in order to lay to rest a man who, from now on, would remain part of Whitstable's community in memory only.

As she walked across the lawn towards Windsor House, the music from the Labour Club faded into the distance. The tower block's lift arrived obediently and Pearl stepped in to ride it to Ruby's floor. When the doors opened, a vague smell of cabbage seemed to fill the hallway, not wholly unpleasant but a reminder that Pearl hadn't eaten more than a few triangles of Ruby's sandwiches since lunchtime.

At the front door, a light shone dimly through a panel of frosted glass. Pearl rang the bell and it sounded clearly but there was no response. Trying again, Pearl waited restlessly before tapping against the glass panel. Finally, she opened the letterbox and peered inside.

Another smell met Pearl's nostrils, not cabbage but the sulphur-like aroma of cooked eggs. An old hallstand was visible, standing against a riot of floral wallpaper. A red patterned carpet led to the living-room door. Pearl rang the doorbell one last time – but again there was no response.

Taking a step back towards the lift, Pearl suddenly remembered that she still had Ruby's mobile in her pocket. Knowing how much the girl relied on it, she decided she would post it through the letterbox, but turning back to the door, she saw that a shadow was approaching from inside. At first small, it grew larger against the glass until the door suddenly opened to reveal Ruby, clinging tightly to it. Her brow was glistening with sweat as she struggled for breath. Taking a clumsy step forward, she managed only two words.

'Help me . . .' she gasped, before falling unconscious into Pearl's waiting arms.

Chapter Fifteen

The waiting room for the hospital ward was cramped, airless and lit with the kind of neon that lent a ghostly pallor to everything on which it fell. It bleached the colours of *Swans Upon the Stour*, the rural study which hung crookedly on the wall and, for want of something to do, Pearl straightened the painting, noting that the silver plate on its frame was *In Loving Memory* of a stranger long dead. On a low table lay dog-eared magazines and a basket of dried flowers beside a box of tissues. It was clear that countless people had been given bad news in this room and as the door opened, Pearl hoped she wouldn't have to deal with the same.

She rose to her feet, expecting to see a member of the hospital staff, but instead came face-to-face with McGuire. He was bathed in sweat and struggling to unfasten a button at his shirt collar as he slumped into the empty chair beside her. 'Why are these places always so damned hot?'

Pearl had hoped that his presence might provide some comfort, but the inspector's bad mood put paid to that. 'Did they tell you anything on the way in?' she asked.

McGuire shook his head. 'The nurses were dealing with an emergency.'

He had raced here on receiving her call, grateful for an excuse to leave Tina Rowe behind in her Margate hotel, unprepared for the effect a hospital might have upon him, but even the smell of disinfectant had in fact taken him straight back to St Thomas's Hospital in London – to a night, two years ago, when he had been told that there was no hope. On that occasion he had walked straight out onto Westminster Embankment, had found a bench by the Thames and waited for the news of Donna's death to sink into his soul, like silt settling after a fast-flowing tide.

Looking now at Pearl, he felt suddenly exposed and sought cover in procedure. 'Have the parents been informed?'

'There are no parents,' said Pearl. 'Just an elderly grand-mother, suffering from Alzheimer's, languishing in a care home.'

McGuire had barely had time to absorb this when a tired young registrar entered the room, his shirt sleeves rolled up at the elbow. 'You're here for Ruby?'

Pearl nodded quickly and the registrar answered her unspoken question. 'She's stable.'

Pearl found herself breathing once more. 'Can I see her?'

'Not yet. We'd like to keep her in overnight for observation.'

'What happened?' asked McGuire.

'It was a reaction to something she ate,' the doctor said.

'An allergy?' asked McGuire.

'A fungal toxin,' replied the doctor. 'Clitocybe Dealbata. It looks like a mushroom but is actually a poisonous toadstool. Luckily, she didn't ingest too much. With larger doses there can be severe abdominal pain and nausea.' He looked at Pearl. 'You found her just in time. There's an antidote but we haven't had to use it. She's over the worst.'

Pearl slumped into a chair as though overcome with relief.

'Can I talk to her?' McGuire asked.

'Not tonight. She's sleeping and needs to rest so let's see how she is in the morning.' The doctor gave a weary smile and turned for the door. In the silence that followed his exit, Pearl glanced at the painting on the wall and the box of tissues lying unused on the table. McGuire knew exactly what she was thinking.

'Come on,' he said softly. 'I'll drive you home.'

The Blean roads were clear on the way back to Whitstable, allowing McGuire to speed around sharp country bends. Pearl glanced up from the mobile in her hand at his strong hands clenched on the wheel.

'So what have you got?' he asked.

Pearl read aloud the information from her phone screen. 'Dealbata. First described in 1799 as *Agaricus Dealbatus*, from the Latin verb *dealbare* "to whitewash". Known as the "sweating mushroom" due to of one of the symptoms of the poisoning. A small white or buff-coloured mushroom with white gills. One of a number of poisonous species.'

As she fell silent, McGuire glanced over at her. 'What is it?'

'Ruby goes mushrooming. She told me she's done so ever since she was a child. She and her mother used to visit Victory Woods not far from here.'

'So maybe that's where she picked the stuff that poisoned her,' McGuire suggested as he drew up at traffic lights.

'Maybe,' said Pearl thoughtfully. 'But why after all these years would she make a mistake like this?'

McGuire saw the lights change to green. 'Let's find out,' he said, making a quick decision to take a sudden right turn at the foot of Borstal Hill.

A few moments later, the car was parked outside Windsor House as Pearl and McGuire stood at Ruby's front door.

'You need a warrant for this,' Pearl reminded him, but McGuire chose to ignore her as he took a credit card from his wallet and slipped it into the narrow gap between the door and its frame. The front door opened soundlessly under his hand.

Once inside, McGuire quickly leafed through circulars scattered on the hallstand, before moving on down the hallway to where the odour of eggs still lingered, becoming stronger as they entered the kitchen. Pearl looked around, noticing Ruby's attempts to update Mary's style. A poster of One Direction hung on the wall and an orchid in a white ceramic cube sat upon the window ledge, but a teapot and knitted cosy still occupied Mary's old dresser beside a tea towel that advertised the amusement arcade at Margate Pleasure Beach.

'What are we looking for?' asked Pearl, uncomfortable about invading Ruby's world.

'I'm not sure,' said McGuire, continuing with his search as he checked out the draining board on which lay a single plate. 'I just want to see how this all adds up.'

Pearl peeked inside the pedal bin and noted the fresh liner inside. Opening the fridge door, she said to McGuire, 'The smell of eggs was really noticeable when I came by earlier. There are three in the fridge but no shells anywhere, so she must have cooked and then emptied her rubbish into the chute at the end of the common hallway. Can you make a search of it?'

'For what?' scoffed McGuire. 'Eggshells?'

'For mushrooms – toadstools – whatever it was that poisoned her. Hang on – how many plates are on the draining board?'

'Just the one,' said McGuire, picking it up, along with a single knife and fork lying beside it. 'Why?'

Pearl stood thinking for a moment. 'Darrell told me that Ruby took a call when she was in the pub kitchen. That's the reason she left – because she was meeting someone.' She suddenly remembered something. 'Her mobile!' Taking it out, she checked the phone's log. 'The last call is from me. Yesterday afternoon.'

McGuire shrugged. 'So the barman's mistaken. Or she deleted the call from the friend. Maybe she just used it as an excuse to leave.'

Pearl set the phone down on the worktop, her eyes now drawn to something else. Picking up a small notebook with a floral cover, she began to flip through it.

McGuire moved closer. 'What is it?'

'Recipes,' said Pearl softly. 'She's written everything down in here – how I prepare every dish I serve in the restaurant.'

McGuire watched her flip through the book, clearly moved by the poignancy of Ruby's efforts. 'You're fond of her, aren't you?'

Pearl nodded slowly. 'She's all alone.'

McGuire said nothing, recognising that this was true of himself too. He reached out to take the book from Pearl and set it gently back down on the counter. He smiled. 'She still has you.'

*

It was past 3 a.m. when McGuire's car finally turned the corner from Nelson Road on to Island Wall, the first faint streak of light appearing in the sky as he pulled up outside Seaspray Cottage. Stunned by fatigue, neither had spoken on the way back.

McGuire got out of the car first to go round and open the passenger door for Pearl. As she stepped onto the pavement, Pearl's bag tumbled from her lap. She caught it, but not before her keys had fallen onto the ground between them. Pearl made a move to pick them up but the detective was quicker, and as he handed them over, his eyes locked with hers. For a brief moment their fingertips connected, and whether through a sense of loss or longing, the touch seemed to linger like the effects of an electric shock.

It was Pearl who broke away. She took a step towards her front door then turned back, realising in that instant that the ground between them had been levelled by the night's events. In spite of her doubts, she heard herself voice the question that was dominating her mind at that moment: 'Do you want to come in?'

McGuire held her look, aware that daylight was spreading like fire across the sky. He thought again of Donna, of how she had been snatched from his life, and of all the empty nights he had spent alone since her passing. Strangely, it seemed as if they had been compressed into this single moment. He opened his mouth to speak, unsure of his reply, but at that moment, and as though choreographed, a murmuration of starlings took off suddenly from the beach, swarming and swaying, splitting and reforming before heading like an arrow towards the morning sky.

Witnessing the scene gave McGuire sufficient pause for thought. He looked back slowly at Pearl, saying merely, 'You'd better get some rest.'

Pearl watched McGuire get back into his car and start up the engine. He drove away and rounded the corner without once looking back. Pearl looked down at the keys in her hand then turned to open the cottage door. She was feeling unsettled, not by McGuire's rejection but by the silence and emptiness of her home – two things she usually cherished. It was then that she noticed the light flashing on her answerphone. For one moment she thought it might be the hospital having called with bad news about Ruby, but on hitting the play button she heard a familiar voice issuing from the machine.

'Do not be alarmed, Pearl,' began Juan. 'Your mother is fine but . . .' he paused as if searching for words before ending simply: 'She's going to need your help in the morning.'

Chapter Sixteen

'Look, I realise you'll be stretched with Ruby in hospital, but I can't trust my guests to anyone else but you.'

Dolly was lying on her daybed in the conservatory, propped on chenille cushions with her tabby cat, Mojo, secured to her lap with a heavy hand. The garden doors were open but the room was still uncomfortably warm from the early-morning sun. Pearl could see that the cat's eyes were fixed upon the lavender bushes outside as though plotting his escape.

'It's not just the cleaning,' Dolly went on. 'It's the meeting and greeting that's so important. The guests need a friendly face – someone totally reliable.'

Pearl bit back a rude comment. 'It'll be fine,' she promised, baffled as to why Dolly couldn't delegate the care of her guests to an agency, as most holiday landladies did in town. 'I'll take care of it all until you're back on your feet.'

At this, Dolly visibly relaxed. 'Good. The French leave at

three and the Austrians arrive at five. It's the only changeover you need worry about because I'll be right as rain after a few hours' rest and a bag of peas.'

'Peas?' queried Juan. He had just come in from the kitchen, carrying a cup of tea with two garibaldi biscuits in the saucer. He raised his eyebrows in some confusion.

'Frozen peas. For my back,' Dolly explained. 'The cold's good for the muscle.'

'Are you sure about that?' he asked. 'Wouldn't heat be better?'

'Or a visit to the chiropractor?' suggested Pearl.

Dolly shook her head. 'Peas.'

Pearl shared a look with Juan before he gave a small exhalation of breath and moved to the door where he placed a straw hat on his head. He addressed both women. 'Then I will return,' he announced. 'With peas.'

Dolly waited for the front door to sound after him before smiling wistfully. 'He is such a kind soul.'

'And probably worried that you're going to sue him.'

'I didn't do this when dancing flamenco,' Dolly protested. 'If you must know, I was showing him my *asanas*.' As Pearl's eyes widened, Dolly quickly clarified: 'My yoga positions. I've never had a problem getting into the plough before, but this time . . .'

Pearl had said nothing but her silence spoke volumes.

'I know what you're thinking,' Dolly told her, 'but what would you prefer I do? Join Sadie Crouch and the Jam and Jerusalem brigade? Or become a Saga Lout and traipse around some stately homes?'

She winced suddenly from a painful twinge and Pearl rushed forward to help, saying, 'I'll call the doctor.'

'You'll do no such thing! All he'll do is fill me up with painkillers. I've some arnica somewhere. Take a look in my remedy box.'

Pearl decided against arguing and fetched instead a large mirrored box that stood on a shelf by the window. It was a familiar object from her childhood, containing as it did a variety of potions, pills and essential oils. Dolly wasn't one for trusting pharmaceuticals but instead relied on a dilettante's knowledge of alternative medicine – herbs grown from her own garden, used with tried and trusted remedies handed down from a grandmother who most believed had been gifted with healing, if not psychic, abilities. Pearl handed the box to Dolly and waited for her mother to slip on her spectacles before sifting through the numerous plastic packets inside.

'Have the hospital said when Ruby can come home?' Dolly asked.

'No. I called this morning but they wouldn't let me talk to her. The consultant needs to see her again but I'll go and visit later. I'm sure she'll be fine once she comes home and rests.'

'In that depressing little flat?' tutted Dolly. 'Find her some light duties at the restaurant. She'll be much happier around you.' She peered across her glasses to see Pearl was frowning. 'Well, surely you know?'

'Know what?'

'How much she thinks of you. It's obvious to anyone – she adores you.'

Pearl felt suddenly conflicted by this. She was fond of Ruby, and wanted to protect her, but had no wish to use the girl to fill a space in her own empty nest. She began to help Dolly search amongst her remedies. 'Here – arnica. D'you need some water with it?'

'Of course not,' her mother said tetchily. 'It's homeopathic. Just fetch me a small spoon.'

As Pearl turned to do so Dolly saw that her daughter really had caught the sun in these last hot days of summer. Her limbs were dark, like Tommy's had always been, and her long hair tumbled down her back as it had done when she had been a teenager. The passage of two decades made Dolly reflect for a moment.

'You could've gone with him,' she said softly.

'Juan?' asked Pearl, surprised by this non sequitur.

Dolly shook her head. 'Don't you ever wonder what life would have been like if you'd done that? If you'd followed your heart?'

Pearl recognised the look in her mother's eyes. It was the same one that always accompanied rhetorical questions such as this. Questions about the past.

Pearl felt herself closing down. 'I did,' she replied finally. 'My heart is here.' She held out the spoon to Dolly. At that very moment Mojo chose his opportunity for escape, leaping from Dolly's lap to the conservatory door before disappearing into the lavender bushes in the garden.

'Ungrateful little . . .' she called after him, as arnica pills spilled all over the floor.

A door opened behind them and Juan reappeared, catching his breath and holding a plastic bag aloft, which he offered like a trophy to Dolly.

'Peas!' he beamed, fully satisfied with a successful mission. Dolly's expression melted with gratitude – while Pearl, like Mojo, took the opportunity to escape.

Two hours later, Pearl walked through the white Art Deco

entrance to Kent and Canterbury Hospital and headed along a busy corridor which at times resembled a shopping mall, with its chains of stylish eateries offering panini and skinny latte. She queued at one to buy overpriced fruit, chiding herself for not stopping off at Cornucopia after leaving Dolly's. The fruit made her think of Marty and his injured pride at seeing her again with McGuire. Perhaps his comment at the Neptune had been merely sour grapes? But there was still a chance he was right about the reason McGuire was stationed on the north Kent coast.

Leaving the hospital shop, Pearl soon became lost. Confronting a confusing maze of walkways, it appeared that, as with the investigation, she was being presented with any number of wrong turnings. Trying to put McGuire firmly out of her mind she continued on her way, finally picking up a trail which led her to the swing doors of the correct ward.

Opening them, she saw the unnerving image of Ruby's empty bed. The linen had been stripped and the bedside table cleared. No evidence remained that Ruby had ever been here – and that single thought sent a chill through Pearl's heart, reminding her of entering another ward, at another time, to find her father's bed empty, Dolly seated in a chair, head in hands before she looked up at Pearl to explain that Tommy was gone. A heart attack had taken him at forty-two years of age, a shock as sudden and unexpected as finding Vinnie's dead body anchored in the cold sea. Just then, Pearl sensed that someone was standing behind her.

It was Ruby: dressed in last night's clothes, her fair hair scraped back from her forehead, her skin as pale as alabaster. She raised a smile. 'You look like you've just seen a ghost, Pearl.'

Pearl held out her arms and pulled the girl close, breathing in the bitter scent of hospital soap. 'Are you really okay?' she asked, stepping back to study Ruby's features.

'Sure,' Ruby smiled. 'They actually discharged me a couple of hours ago but I had to wait for this paperwork.' She held up a brown envelope. 'A letter to give to my GP in case I get ill again.'

Pearl returned Ruby's smile and grasped her tiny cold hands, trying to warm them in her own. 'Come on, let's get out of here.'

In the hospital car park, Ruby took her place in the passenger seat of the car.

'I'm sorry if I worried you,' she said. 'I was going to call you this morning but I couldn't find my mobile.'

'You left it at the pub.'

Ruby flinched.

'I was trying to drop it off to you last night,' explained Pearl. 'That's how I found you.'

Ruby sat thinking, as though trying to compute something. 'So . . . my phone's at home now?'

The traffic lights at the old level crossing at St Dunstan's had suddenly turned to red and Pearl braked before the gates came down. In that instant, she decided against disclosing the details of her visit to the flat with McGuire.

'Yes. I left it on the kitchen table.'

At this, Ruby seemed satisfied, and a train passed by at speed before the gates to the crossing rose again. Pearl stepped on the accelerator, heading out on the Blean road, but as she passed the turning for the university campus, she wondered whether Charlie might be nearby, in the library – having coffee, perhaps with Tizzy. Almost as a distraction from that thought, she found herself asking, 'What happened?'

Ruby gave a sickly smile. 'I ate the wrong kind of mushrooms – but don't worry, I won't do it again.'

'I didn't see any mushrooms.'

Ruby looked at Pearl.

'Last night at the flat. There were none in the fridge or in the rubbish, so . . .'

'I ate them all,' Ruby cut in hurriedly. 'I made myself an omelette when I got home. Then I washed up, put the rubbish out and . . . I was just getting ready for bed when I started to feel ill.'

Pearl kept her eyes on the road ahead. 'Didn't you have to meet someone?'

'What d'you mean?' the girl asked, defensively.

'Darrell thought you got a call from a friend?'

'Then he thought wrong,' Ruby said crossly. Pearl could see the girl's hands were trembling.

'Ruby, I'm just trying to work out what happened, that's all.'

'Like a copper, you mean?' Her tone was now suddenly, and shockingly, abrupt. 'Has that detective asked you to spy on me? Is that why you're here?'

'No, of course not. Look . . .' Pearl reached for Ruby's quivering hand but it was like trying to contain a frightened bird.

'Let me out. Stop the car!'

Pearl hit the brakes and swerved the car into the kerb. It took a moment for both women to catch their breath. 'What is it? What did I say to upset you?'

But Ruby wasn't listening. 'I just need to get out and see my nan before she hears about any of this from someone else,' she said feverishly.

'Why should she?' Pearl could see that Ruby was staring

through the windscreen towards Fairfax House a few hundred metres away.

'Oh, she will,' Ruby said bitterly. 'You know what Whitstable's like. If you've told even one person about this it'll be halfway round town by now, and the next thing Sadie Crouch'll be visiting, filling Nan with gossip, making her worry about me. Can't you see how Nan gets the past confused with everything that's going on now?' Her breaths were quickening. 'I don't want her to know I've been in hospital, okay? It'll only remind her of Mum.'

Ruby's anxiety seemed to be tipping over into paranoia. Pearl found herself agreeing. 'Okay.'

At this, the girl's breathing steadied and she opened the car door, stepping out on to the pavement, ready to head off towards Fairfax House. Pearl stayed in the car, observing her. Once through the gates, Ruby hurried across the gravel path to the entrance, where her tiny frame seemed dwarfed by the portico. Before entering the nursing home, she finally turned and offered a brief smile and a wave before disappearing from view, leaving Pearl unsure if the smile had, in fact, been one of gratitude, or relief to have escaped more of Pearl's questions.

Chapter Seventeen

After recruiting some help for the afternoon shift at the restaurant, Pearl made her way to Dolly's Attic to prepare for the incoming guests. She had assumed that an hour and a half would be plenty of time – but on opening the door, she quickly revised that idea. The Soulets had left Dolly's little apartment looking as though it had been ransacked. Magazines were scattered on the floor, together with picnic plates and cups. The sink was piled with washing-up and pillows smeared with what Pearl hoped was chocolate. The panic of an unmet deadline began to rise in her chest, only to fall again when a call came through from Herr Breit, terse and efficient on the line, explaining that the family was delayed at the airport – not at punctual Linz in Austria but at 'incompetent' Stansted in Essex. Nevertheless, Pearl recognised that she had a challenge on her hands. The attic flat was stiflingly hot and smelled of nappies, so the first thing to be dealt with was the rubbish. She wrestled it from the pedal bin and was halfway downstairs when the doorbell rang. A familiar figure stood on the threshold.

'Tizzy!'

'How long until the guests arrive?'

Pearl's mouth gaped before she glanced quickly at her watch. 'Not long enough.'

'Don't worry,' Tizzy smiled. 'There are two of us now.' With that, she plucked the bag of rubbish from Pearl's hand, tossed it into the bin, then moved quickly past Pearl and headed upstairs.

Pearl followed her into the living room, where Tizzy was taking off her denim jacket. Beneath it she wore a loose white shirt which Pearl instantly recognised as one of Charlie's.

'I had a rehearsal this morning,' the girl explained. 'So I popped in to see Dolly and she told me what had happened.' Tizzy paused, brought up short as she surveyed the midden of Dolly's holiday rental. 'You need help. Why don't I take the kitchen, you take the living room and we'll finish the bedroom together?'

Pearl suddenly felt all the stress draining out of her. 'You're on.'

During the next hour, Tizzy worked quickly and diligently in Dolly's little kitchenette, while Pearl struggled around the flat with an ancient, noisy vacuum cleaner. It precluded all conversation but when she had finally switched it off, she heard Tizzy humming to herself in the bedroom. As the tune came to an abrupt end, Pearl went inside to see Tizzy studying a driftwood painting on the wall. 'This is really beautiful,' the girl remarked.

'It's one of my mother's from last year,' Pearl said.

'Ah, so it's from Dolly that Charlie gets his love of art?'

Pearl hesitated, unwilling to say more about Carl, his artist father. 'Perhaps.' She looked up at the many pieces of artwork around the room. 'They were always painting together when he was little. I'd come home from the restaurant to find them creating some masterpiece or another.'

'But now he studies the work of others,' said Tizzy. She looked at Pearl. 'He doesn't paint any more. Why?'

Pearl felt uncomfortable under Tizzy's scrutiny. 'Maybe you should ask him.'

'I have. He thinks he doesn't have much talent.'

'That isn't true.'

'Then maybe he doesn't have anything to prove.'

Pearl turned to her. 'What do you mean?'

'Artists are usually troubled, aren't they? Trying to work through things? But Charlie is together. Complete. Perhaps he just doesn't have anything to say.' Tizzy paused. 'Yet.'

'Possibly,' admitted Pearl. She considered the tidy room and picked up a fresh duvet cover. 'You've been a great help.'

'No problem,' Tizzy replied brightly. 'I've enjoyed this today. It reminds me of when I was a chalet girl for a season. Up in the Alps at Claviere.'

'Italy?' asked Pearl.

'Yes.' Tizzy reached out for two corners of the duvet cover in Pearl's hands. 'They say Hannibal crossed over the Alps there – with elephants. Can you imagine that?' She gave a shrug. 'It's a popular resort now. The work was hard but the skiing was fun.'

Standing opposite one another across the double bed the two women stuffed a light summer duvet inside the cover and shook it, watching it fall, like a white cloud, upon clean sheets.

'And how is your waitress – Rosie, is it?' Dolly said that she was taken ill.'

'Her name's Ruby,' Pearl said. 'And she's fine now, thanks.'

'Good.' Tizzy smoothed the *broderie anglaise* cover with her slender hands until she was finally satisfied. 'Now everything's done.'

'Amazingly,' Pearl said ruefully.

Tizzy made a move for the door but Pearl stopped her. 'Tizzy?' She gestured around the orderly apartment. 'I really couldn't have done this without you. Thank you so much.' Then she crossed the room and embraced the girl, breathing in a young, sweet perfume, meaning every word she had just said.

It was after 7 p.m. when the Breits finally arrived at the Attic. Relieved to be off the busy road and with Dolly's roof over their heads at last, they seemed happy with their accommodation in spite of some debate as to whether the summer duvet might be warm enough despite the stifling heat.

Pearl reported back to Dolly that the new guests were safely ensconced and, an hour later, she walked home along the beach, realising that she had missed the Blessing of the Waters – another ritual component of the Oyster Festival. This took the form of a service and procession of clergy and choristers – a ceremony to appease the sea and give thanks for its bounty – but the crowds that had gathered for it had long since dispersed and the beach was almost empty. When her mobile rang, the voice on the line sounded hesitant and a little guilty. 'Pearl?'

'How are you, Ruby?'

'I'm fine, thank you. But I'm sorry about what happened earlier.'

Pearl sat down on the upturned hull of her boat and listened as the girl muttered, 'Everything got on top of me.'

'I understand. You've not been well, have you.'

'But that's no excuse,' Ruby said. 'I am grateful, Pearl. For everything you've done. Giving me the job and taking me to Gran the other night.'

'How is she?'

'The same. But I feel better now I've seen her.' For a moment there was just the hypnotic sound of waves lapping up onto the shore before Ruby spoke again.

'Can I come back to work tomorrow?'

'As long as you feel up to it.'

'Thanks, Pearl.'

As the mobile went dead in her hand, Pearl switched it off and looked out to sea. The sun had already set and Reeves Beach was deserted, apart from a few brightly coloured towels that had been left there by swimmers. She got to her feet and decided to take her thoughts out onto the evening's high tide.

A sign outside the Yacht Club always gave notice of wind speed and weather conditions but Pearl didn't stop to check, relying instead on her own sailor instincts. The day had been so busy she hadn't thought about McGuire but now she considered calling him, wondering if the results of the post-mortem were through. But if so, it was clear he was keeping them to himself, still playing his cards close to his chest.

After launching the boat, Pearl pulled away from the beach, thinking back to her conversation with Dolly that morning. Twenty years ago, Pearl had been given the chance to start a new life – a life unlived, since she had chosen instead to stay in Whitstable on the stretch of coastline that she loved. Her inner voice had told her to give up on her police work and take up fully her role as Charlie's mother – but she sometimes thought of that parallel life, the one she might have lived if she had chosen another path. It was true that some of her antipathy towards McGuire, and perhaps part of his fascination, stemmed from the fact that he held the position she had always wanted for herself – and yet, last night she had felt a connection with him. Had this been prompted only by her vulnerability in that moment, her sense of helplessness, coupled with relief at Ruby's recovery?

She reassessed what she had felt in that hospital waiting room: her first fear having been that Ruby's life had been put in danger by someone – until the young doctor had made it clear that the girl had simply committed a basic error in choosing to eat the wrong mushrooms. An innocent mistake. Explicable. Pearl then allowed herself to consider the possibility that her own instincts had guided her wrongly too – about everything, including Vinnie's death.

A star fell against the darkening sky and Pearl touched the collar of her jacket, a mark of respect for a dream unrealised, a hope dashed, as her father had always taught her. Perhaps her own dreams would fail, as had Vinnie's, but nevertheless life would move on like the greater pattern of stars shifting in the night sky above.

A cool wind blew up suddenly, scattering the tops of the waves. The lights on the wind farm were now visible, red and white against the night sky. Others were spread across the sea: navigation lights from some fishing boats and a cruiser disappearing below the line of the horizon. Waves lapped against the hull of Pearl's own dinghy, reminding her that she was drifting. It was time to go back.

At that moment, something caught her attention. A red

port light was growing brighter at sea and Pearl rested on her oars to observe it. The craft appeared to be heading straight towards her but she knew this could only be an illusion. As a starboard light became visible Pearl saw that the vessel was actually turned away and making for the shingled Street. She reached for her binoculars, recognising now that she was looking at a RIB, bouncing at speed on the waves. It had set a direct course away from the Red Sands fort and was passing by at a distance of only metres.

In the fading light, three figures stared silently towards the coast ahead. Pearl lowered the binoculars as the boat passed by, having instantly recognised Leo Berthold, sitting alongside Robert Harcourt, as Billy Crouch steered them towards the shore.

Chapter Eighteen

Peering through the window of a small café on Beach Walk, Pearl saw that most of the tables were occupied by families. Only when a few workmen moved away from the counter was she able to catch sight of the person she had been looking for. A young man sat alone, hunched over a laptop. Pearl hurried inside and took a seat opposite Richard Cross. Without taking his eyes from his computer screen Cross picked up his cup of coffee and had pressed it to his lips before he finally noticed her.

'Miss Nolan!'

'Pearl,' she corrected him. 'We need to talk.'

Cross glanced back at his laptop screen. 'What – right now?'

'Yes – now,' Pearl said decisively.

She got to her feet and Cross closed his laptop, draining his coffee cup before hastening after her to the door.

Once outside, they wove past the many tourists who were heading to the Hotel Continental. On the beach Pearl finally turned to face the young journalist and stated: 'I want to give you a story.' The young man's face lit up. 'An exclusive.'

'Great!'

'In return for some information.' She reached into her pocket and handed him a piece of notepaper.

As the young man began to read it, his face clouded with confusion. 'I don't understand. Who's Audrey Stone?'

'A secretary at the Town Hall.' Pearl passed him a sealed envelope. 'There's enough money there for you to take her out to lunch in Canterbury. Make sure you get all the answers to those questions.'

'But I—'

'No buts, Richard. You'll find a way. Any journalist worth his salt makes good contacts at the local council, and this one will stand you in good stead. Besides,' she added, 'Audrey's very cute.'

'Really?' Cross brightened.

'Timid, but industrious. In fact, she reminds me of something out of Beatrix Potter.' When Cross looked bemused, Pearl explained with a wicked grin, 'She's sixty if she's a day and coming up to retirement. She's been working far too long for a man called Peter Radcliffe.'

'The councillor?'

Pearl nodded. 'So Audrey could definitely do with a treat,' she said. 'You, Richard, are that treat.' She gestured to the sheet of paper in his hands. 'Now get to work.'

Pearl made to go, but Cross protested, 'Wait! Look. I'll do what I can, but I've got an urgent piece to file on the Blessing of the Waters.'

'Audrey first,' Pearl said heartlessly. 'Or there's no exclusive.'

The young man sighed deeply, then conceded defeat. 'Okay.'

*

Pearl's car nosed its way through the traffic on Borstal Hill. As she headed down the country road from Blean a few hours after seeing Cross, a heat haze was shrouding the spires of Canterbury Cathedral that rose above the pillars of Westgate. She found a space in Pound Lane car park and took her chances among the sea of shoppers and tourists heading along St Peter's Street. She wondered where McGuire might be, whether he was working at his desk at the station or out somewhere having lunch.

At St Peter's, Canterbury appeared much like any other historic regional city with its central thoroughfare studded with national chain stores. The River Stour provided seasonal work for the local students who were guiding visitors aboard boat trips at the bridge. From here they would be rowed to a small Franciscan island on which a thirteenth-century chapel spanned the riverbanks before voyaging on to a Cromwellian forge and various Dominican priories, ending up in Solly's Orchard, the site of the old Abbot's Mill in the city.

Most visitors, however, were making a beeline for the Cathedral. The old marketplace in front of it had long since lost its former name of the Bullstake – a reminder of a more brutal time when cattle had been routinely tethered and baited with dogs to tenderise the meat before slaughter. Now, the Butter Market provided a more innocuous title for an area that comprised a tourist information centre and several American coffee bars, one of which sat shoulder to shoulder with the Cathedral entrance itself – jostling, it seemed, for equal attention.

The blatant city consumerism contrasted sharply with small-town Whitstable, where a predominance of independent shops formed a front-line resistance to any advance from supermarket chains or burger bars. Nevertheless, once off the main drag of the city, Canterbury's satellite paths of Palace Street, Sun Street and Burgate were filled with idiosyncratic junk shops, *crêperies* and tattoo parlours, together with seventeenth-century porticos which advertised only the news of a previous stay by Elizabeth I. These were the streets that had once been filled with a different kind of 'pilgrim', and the thought reminded Pearl of a few lines of Chaucer that she had learned in school – not from the Canterbury Tales but from Chaucer's poem *Troilus and Criseyde* in which the heroine speaks of being her own mistress and determined never to allow any man to trump her by saying 'checkmate'. But 'checkmate' was effectively what McGuire had said to Pearl regarding this case. He had managed to have the final word. But, after what she had witnessed at sea last night, Pearl was now more convinced than ever that she should pursue the investigation – with or without McGuire.

The tiny jeweller's shop she sought was close to the Crooked House – a well-known landmark in Palace Street with its entrance leaning at a precarious angle. As a teenager, Pearl had come here with her father one cold February day to find a present for her sixteenth birthday. She had set her heart on a ring, but choosing one from the array of semi-precious stones on the jeweller's black velvet tray had proved as challenging as selecting a single star from the night sky. It had fallen therefore to the jeweller's wife to make a suggestion that an amethyst might be a fitting choice as the birthstone of an Aquarian. Instead, Pearl had opted for the small silver locket, which had become her favourite piece of jewellery. More than two decades later, the old man and his wife had long gone, but a daughter had taken over the shop, running it in the same businesslike manner as her parents.

Seeing Pearl at her counter, she managed only the briefest

of smiles while Pearl, in turn, fished for an item in her pocket.

'I've been meaning to bring this in,' she began. 'I wondered if you could tell me something about it?'

Pearl passed her the item and the jeweller picked up a precision eyeglass through which she scrutinised the piece. For some time the woman remained silent before offering up an opinion. 'The stone is turquoise and very high quality.' She reached beneath the counter for two small bottles, dabbing tiny amounts of liquid onto the metal before observing the reaction. 'Silver,' she concluded. 'But unmarked.' She handed it back to Pearl. 'An exceptionally nice design.'

'Have you any idea where it might have been made?'

'It's almost certainly Navajo,' came the reply. 'There's a lot of turquoise to be found in California, but nowadays the internet has opened up the market. You'd be looking to pay upwards of a few hundred pounds for something as lovely as that.'

'For a pair, you mean?'

'No – for a single piece. Many Navajo earrings were made to be worn as single items. That could well be what you have there. They're known as "cuffs".'

A bell sounded suddenly in the shop and the owner looked up to see that new customers had entered. A young couple were heading directly to a display of engagement rings. Pearl looked down at the turquoise earring in her palm and slipped out of the shop before anyone had even noticed she was gone.

On the road back to Whitstable, Pearl was delayed by temporary traffic lights. Minor roadworks had now begun close to the spot where Ruby had demanded to be let out of the car less than twenty-four hours ago. Thinking back to the incident, Ruby's reaction had seemed all the more shocking to Pearl for being so out of character. Superficially, Ruby was an uncomplicated and easygoing teenager who appeared always bright and cheerful – but considering the insecurities of her childhood and the pressures of coping with Mary's illness, Pearl now saw how this might be only a mask the girl wore to conceal deeper, darker emotions. Continuing to reflect on this, Pearl noticed the traffic lights had changed and drove on, not to Whitstable, but towards the elegant grounds of Fairfax House.

Pearl was relieved to find Mary much improved since her last visit. The old woman sat in the same seat by the window, but the sunlight pouring in cast an altogether more positive glow on both the patient and her environment. Mary's silver hair had been combed neatly back and secured by one of Ruby's hair grips which was studded with tiny pink stones. Light glinted from them, casting dancing reflections against the wall as Mary recognised her visitor and exclaimed, 'Pearl!'

'I was just passing and thought I'd look in to see how you are.'

Mary took a handkerchief from the sleeve of her cardigan and wiped it gently beneath her nose. 'I'm well,' she beamed, patting a seat beside her. 'Come and sit down.'

Mary's smile remained fixed in place as Pearl sat down beside her.

'I'm very lucky to have so many visitors,' the old lady said. 'You've just missed Sadie. She comes regular.'

'So I heard,' said Pearl.

Mary leaned closer and spoke softly. 'I know there's some who'd say she's a nosy old mare, but she's a good soul at heart.'

'And a pillar of the community.'

'Not that she's much else to do,' Mary commented.

'Now that she's retired, you mean?'

'Yes. She expected to spend more time with Billy, but she grumbles he's never home. Always out, fishing and baiting, and . . .'

'Working for Matheson?'

'Billy'll never retire,' scoffed Mary, 'not while Matheson needs him. There are some that lead and some that follow, and we know who's who, don't we?' She squeezed Pearl's hand, noting that her visitor was looking beyond her, to the photographs on the wall. She said, 'You didn't know my girl, did you?'

'No,' replied Pearl, her eyes still fixed on a timeless image. 'I wish I had, but we didn't even go to the same school.' She paused. 'Tell me about her. What was she like?'

Mary said fondly, 'Quiet and a bit shy. Other girls chattered and gossiped about nothing in particular, bubbling away like noisy little streams, but my Kathy . . . she was like a beautiful lake. I never knew how deep she really was.' Mary stopped there, her expression hardening while her lips seemed to mumble a soundless phrase.

'Mary?'

Finally the old lady summoned up the words. 'Like bind-weed growing around a rose.'

'What?' asked Pearl, confused.

'That's what Davy was to her,' Mary said bitterly.

'Ruby's father, you mean?'

Mary nodded slowly. 'Kathy knew it too, which is why she broke free – but it was never long before she'd go back and let him take hold all over again. He was a dark soul. It was him that got her on to it all. She didn't know anything about drugs until he came along. That's what killed her.'

'I know,' said Pearl sadly.

'But you don't know all of it,' Mary countered. 'They said at the inquest it was suicide but it wasn't. I knew my girl. She'd been doing all right without Davy but then he came back that summer and everything went wrong again. He ran out on her and she got so low. That's what put her back on it again.' She wiped her eyes.

'An overdose,' Pearl murmured.

'Yes, but she didn't take it on purpose!' Mary said vehemently. 'The drugs killed her because she'd been off 'em for so long. Her body just couldn't cope.'

Pearl focused on the young girl's face in the photo on the wall, acutely aware of the waste of Kathy Hill's life – for her mother, for Ruby and for all those who could have loved her if only she had remained alive. And yet it was clear that she still lived on vividly in Mary's memory. Perhaps, thought Pearl, she might even be the last person to do so.

'And how's that boyfriend of yours?' Pearl saw that Mary was now looking directly at her, an incongruous smile playing upon her lips. 'The one I see you with on the beach. He's handsome, ain't he. You make a good-looking pair.'

Pearl realised that Mary had now travelled back in time. The past was eliding once more with the present, not just for the old lady, but for herself too. Twenty summers had passed since Pearl had sat on the beach with Charlie's father, Carl, but the truth of that season's events, prompted by Mary's question, remained as sweet and as painful as ever.

'Do we?' asked Pearl softly.

Mary registered some sadness in Pearl's reply. 'What's wrong? Dolly likes him, don't she? She told me herself – and mothers always know.'

'Yes,' Pearl sighed. 'She likes him.'

'Then what is it?'

Pearl fell silent. It had been so long since she had related her story but she knew it would remain safe with Mary. 'Carl's Australian,' she explained finally. 'He's just passing through, working in the bar at the Bear and Key until he's saved enough money to head off to the Far East. He's an artist. He doesn't want to be tied down.'

'Can't you go with him, girl?' Mary urged. 'You're young. You can do what you want.'

Pearl shook her head. 'I've got a job and a training course ahead of me. I can't leave. Not now.'

The old woman looked away, as if trying hard to make sense of this. 'Then you have yourselves a problem,' she decided finally. Her face came alive as she remembered something. 'You know, my old mother used to say, "if you love something, then set it free. If it comes back it's yours".'

'If it doesn't,' murmured Pearl. 'It never was.'

Closing her eyes, Mary Hills began humming a tune, leaving Pearl with the impression of someone smiling through great pain. In a few seconds, she was fast asleep, not waking even when a text arrived on Pearl's mobile. She looked down at the short message but couldn't quite make it out. Searching for her despised spectacles, she put them on and read five brief words on her screen.

I have what you want.

Ten minutes later, Pearl had tiptoed out of Mary Hill's room and was speaking on the same mobile to Richard Cross as she approached her car in the grounds of Fairfax House.

'Are you absolutely sure about this?'

'Certain.' Cross waited for a reply but Pearl was thinking

instead about McGuire and how he would react to the new evidence that Cross had just uncovered. 'So when do I get my story?' he asked eagerly.

Pearl unlocked her car and got inside. Once behind the wheel she finally replied: 'You have it, Richard. That *was* your exclusive.'

'What?' Cross sounded confused as Pearl started up the engine. 'Wait a minute. Ms Nolan? Pearl!' But the phone had been switched off and tossed on to the passenger seat as Pearl accelerated away.

Before reaching home, Pearl made three separate calls to McGuire. Infuriatingly, each time she encountered only the same voicemail message, informing her that her call would be returned as soon as possible. In spite of her discovery, arriving at Island Wall she felt cheated – until she saw that McGuire's car was parked outside her home. He was standing on the beach, close to the shore, and turned instantly as though aware of her presence, looking anxious for a split second until a brief smile dispelled all tension. Pearl wondered how he could have got here so quickly.

A few moments later, he followed her into the living room of Seaspray Cottage where Pearl opened a window, allowing a cool breeze to push against a white muslin curtain. When she turned again, McGuire saw she was handing him a turquoise earring.

'What's this?'

'The reason Connie suspected Vinnie might be having an affair. She found it on his boat several weeks ago.' Pearl waited for McGuire's reaction but he was merely looking at her, unconvinced. She took the earring back from him. 'I didn't believe it either,' she said. 'I was sure she was wrong, that Vinnie wasn't the type for an affair.' She paused. 'But maybe Connie is.'

'What are you saying?'

'Perhaps Connie's seeing Matheson, and perhaps she's been doing so for some time.' She held McGuire's look. 'She was heartbroken about Vinnie's death, but she was angry too. What seemed to console her was confirmation that an insurance policy was still in place and that Vinnie had made all the payments.'

'So?'

'So I happened to see her leaving a solicitor's office a few days ago. She was there about the money.'

'You know that for a fact?'

'No, but – look, she must have gone to see him about the will because ...' McGuire had turned away but Pearl persisted. 'Whatever you think, things are falling into place.'

Voices sounded suddenly from outside and Pearl saw a shuttlecock sailing past on the breeze to land in her garden. As a young boy climbed over the sea wall to retrieve it, McGuire finally turned back to face her.

'I talked to the solicitor she saw – the solicitor you failed to tell me about?' He was looking at her accusingly but Pearl remained unruffled.

'So I'm right? she said. 'She *was* there about the will.'

'A will from which she was never going to benefit.'

Pearl was taken aback. 'What do you mean?'

Children's voices receded outside as McGuire explained. 'Twenty years ago, Vinnie Rowe made a will leaving everything to his wife.'

'To Tina.'

'Yes. But for some reason, he chose not to update it.'

Pearl found this news hard to absorb. 'Why?' she asked. 'Why wouldn't he have updated it when he had a new partner and two children to provide for?'

'Perhaps he felt death was a long way off.' McGuire gave a shrug. 'He was making plans for the future – a fit man with no health problems.'

'And no money,' added Pearl quickly.

McGuire considered this. 'If there was nothing to leave, why update the will?'

'But the insurance policy . . .' she thought aloud. 'It could involve a considerable sum.'

'It does.'

'So that's where Matheson comes in. Money,' Pearl said contemptuously. 'I told you, it's his motive for everything. The day Connie left the solicitor's office I saw her get into his car—'

'Something else you failed to tell me,' broke in McGuire. 'But I interviewed Matheson and he told me that Connie confided her problems to him about the will. He offered to pay for some legal advice.'

'Which was?'

'To challenge Tina Rowe in the courts.'

Pearl turned away to face the window and saw a wasp buzzing angrily against the pane. 'Can she do that?'

'As the mother of Vinnie's children, yes, but it'll take time.'

'So that's what she meant, that night in the Neptune. It was about taking Tina on.' Pearl watched the wasp climbing the pane, only to fall back down again. She told McGuire, 'This still doesn't alter what I learned today. I got someone to do some digging around. Berthold may be publicising the development of the Canterbury hotel, but the real reason he's here is because of this.' She reached into her bag and handed a large white envelope to McGuire. 'Take a look,' she said triumphantly. 'A planning application's been submitted for development of the Red Sands Fort. It's eight miles offshore so Berthold can ignore a whole host of regulations.'

'I know,' said McGuire starkly. Those two words severed all Pearl's expectations. 'That day on the beach, after you told me about the forts, I went to talk to the charity that's been trying to preserve them,' he went on. 'It seems they have their spies too.'

He felt no pride in dashing Pearl's hopes, and offered up the ghost of a smile which she failed to return. 'So much for sharing information,' she said heavily.

'I have no obligation to share anything with you, Pearl. I'm a police officer.'

'All right,' she conceded impatiently, 'but don't tell me this isn't important, because it explains the whole relationship between Berthold and Harcourt, not to mention—'

'Councillor Radcliffe?' McGuire said. 'You're right. Maybe it is the reason there's a telescope at the house, why Berthold is staying there with his wife and son rather than wallowing in a luxury destination in some far-flung part of the world. But . . . there is *nothing* in any of that to connect to Vinnie Rowe's death.'

In the silence that followed, Pearl became aware of the wasp still dancing against the windowpane. She made a sudden realisation.

'And what about Ruby? If you'd only shared this with me sooner, I could have given my attention to . . . .' She halted.

'To what?'

'Well, Ruby said something to me only yesterday about protecting her grandmother. It set me thinking about history repeating itself.' She glanced down at the family photographs she had discussed with Tizzy only days ago. 'Ruby's mother died of an overdose. But everyone believed it was suicide due to heartbreak over losing her boyfriend, Davy. They'd been travelling around in a caravan, living a gypsy lifestyle, even after Ruby was born.' She paused. 'It was you who told me about drugs being part of our culture, that day on the beach. And you were right. Davy was a drug-user.' She looked up at McGuire. 'What if he'd been a dealer too? The person who supplied Shane Rowe?'

'Pearl . . .'

'Hear me out,' she said. 'Kathy Hill split up with Davy but he was back again in Whitstable that summer. Perhaps the guilt of knowing that Davy was responsible for Shane's death set Kathy back on the stuff one last time.'

McGuire slowly shook his head. 'This is all speculation.'

'I just came from seeing Mary and she talks of nothing else. She's locked in the past with her daughter.'

'She has Alzheimers.'

'And periods of lucidity.'

'Listen to yourself. None of this adds up to a single hard fact. No solid connection to Vinnie Rowe's death or Stroud's.'

'But it has to be there,' Pearl insisted. 'Somewhere, amongst all these events, we just need to find the catalyst that brings them all together.'

She saw McGuire glance quickly over to the door, anxious to escape, like the wasp that still buzzed against the window-pane. She was wondering if she bored him when another idea occurred to her.

'I phoned you,' she said, 'several times on my way back – but you were already here on the beach when I arrived. You didn't pick up those messages, did you? So why were you waiting for me?'

McGuire took some paperwork from his inside pocket and handed it to her.

'The post-mortem result?'

He nodded slowly.

'So what did they find?' Pearl began leafing through the pages but it was McGuire who explained.

'Contusions,' he began. 'Trauma to the head consistent with having been dragged across the side of the boat by a heavy anchor.'

'*No!*' Pearl exclaimed. 'Those injuries could just as well have been delivered another way. You know that, but if you're just looking for evidence that fits with an accident, then go right ahead and ignore everything else.'

'Facts, Pearl,' snapped McGuire. 'This isn't some dish you're concocting. It's life and death, and you know as well as I do that there are procedures to follow.'

'And you're following them, are you?' she asked pointedly – then caught her breath, brought up short as she made a further realisation. 'You're not going to pursue this, are you? *That's* why you were waiting for me tonight. To tell me you're closing the case.'

The inspector faced her and she recognised the look in his eyes, the same look she had given Marty so many times – the look that closed down all opportunity, the look that said, 'No.' 'It's not my decision.' He took the report back from her and headed towards the door.

'Wait!' Pearl implored. 'If this was the death of somebody you knew, would you be satisfied?'

She was staring up at him and McGuire could think only of another time, another decision, another case dropped – and Donna. He wished things could be different, that there might be another way: a form of recompense, of righting past wrongs – but finally he gave his answer.

'It's out of my hands.'

*

'McGuire?'

He was almost at his car when she caught up with him. 'You're right,' she said. 'Maybe I don't have enough evidence, but I know it's there, somewhere. More than that, I was the one who found Vinnie's body and my instinct still tells me this is all wrong. Okay, I should have been more open with you,' she conceded. 'But from now on we could work together – just a little longer. Please?'

'I can't, Pearl,' he said flatly. 'I won't be here. I asked for a transfer and it's been agreed. That's also why I was here tonight. To say goodbye.'

Pearl tried to make sense of what she had just heard.

'A transfer?'

'Back to London.'

'But I don't understand!'

'And you don't need to. I'm here because . . .' he wanted to explain, to tell her everything – even about Donna – but knew he would never find the right words to do so. 'I . . . just needed to get away for a while.'

Pearl felt as though she had been set adrift, but as she continued to stare up at him, McGuire thought only how easy it would be to kiss her – but not to kiss her goodbye. Instead he turned away and got into his car.

Pearl listened to it receding into the distance before she moved and went back into the cottage. Closing the front door behind her, she walked over to the French windows to find that the wasp was no longer fighting against the pane. Somehow it had made its escape. Pearl picked up her glasses from the coffee table and for the very first time accepted that she had been wrong – about everything – including McGuire. She just couldn't see straight any more.

Chapter Nineteen

'So the detective's leaving?' Charlie was at Pearl's kitchen table, toying with his coffee spoon as he waited for her reply.

'He says there's no case to answer.'

Charlie reflected on this. 'Well, it's good that they've reached a decision – that it was an accident, I mean. It'll give everyone closure.'

Pearl could tell from Charlie's look that he was referring to her too. She took a sip of coffee and observed her son for a moment. His hair was newly cut in a much shorter style and she wondered if this had been Tizzy's idea.

'You're still on for later, aren't you?' he asked suddenly.

'Of course. But I don't think your gran will make the concert. She's still laid up with her back.'

'Why doesn't she just see a doctor?' he asked, exasperated.

'You know why. Because she's stubborn and sees all establishment figures as part of a great conspiracy.'

'Yeah, but . . . doctors?'

'She's been like that about them ever since she read *One Flew Over the Cuckoo's Nest.*'

'One Flew Over what?'

'It's a novel,' explained Pearl. 'An old one – and a brilliant movie too.' Charlie still looked blank.

'Well,' he continued, 'maybe that Spanish boyfriend of hers can carry her down to the beach later, because I was hoping we could have a barbecue afterwards.'

'Nice idea,' said his mother. 'But there's talk that the weather might break.'

'It won't,' maintained Charlie optimistically. 'If we stay positive, it'll be fine.'

Pearl recognised that this was just the sort of 'Pollyanna' remark that Dolly might have given. She saw so much of her own mother in Charlie and, lately, much more of his father's physical characteristics – as though his parents' genes were vying for supremacy. No doubt one day, there would be more answers required by Charlie about his absent parent, but for now all he knew about Carl seemed to suffice. Either that, or he wasn't owning up to more curiosity.

'I've got a bit of a surprise planned for Tizzy later,' he went on. 'Something I want to give her.'

For a moment, Pearl wondered if Charlie was planning to present her with a ring. He seemed to read her thoughts.

'Don't worry, I'm not going to propose or anything. It's just a present. Something I've been making, but I haven't quite finished yet.'

'Finished what?'

Charlie stirred his coffee a little too quickly as if to hide some embarrassment. 'She's always going on about me getting back to doing some art, so I started a collage. I thought I'd drop it off here before the concert tonight and give it to her later at the barbecue, if that's okay?'

'Of course it is.'

'It's no masterpiece. It's just . . . made up mainly of photos. Everything to do with this summer. I thought it'd be something to remember.'

He picked up his cup and swallowed down the rest of his coffee as Pearl's thoughts drifted to a sketch-pad, sitting in a drawer in her office, containing drawings and watercolours created almost two decades ago. Something to remember.

'Not too corny?' asked Charlie, suddenly unsure.

'No,' replied Pearl softly. 'Not corny at all.' She saw that her son was ready to leave but found herself asking another question. 'Charlie, are you happy with the choices I made for you?'

His face creased in sudden confusion. 'What kind of a question is that?'

'I don't know,' Pearl said, honestly. 'I keep wondering lately how things would have worked out for all of us, if I'd made different decisions.'

'That's true of everyone,' Charlie said sensibly. He leaned towards her. 'But you and Gran have done everything for me. What could I possibly have missed out on?' He smiled, but Pearl's thoughts were drifting back to Carl, knowing the one thing that Charlie *had* missed out on was a father. He planted a small kiss on her cheek. 'I really have to go,' he said. 'See you later at the Harbour, Mum?'

'Tell Tizzy I'm looking forward to it.'

In an instant he was gone. Pearl checked the time on her watch and saw she'd have to get a move on if she wasn't to be late for her next appointment.

*

The Walpole Bay Hotel in Cliftonville, Margate had been built before the First World War, changing hands over eighty years later when an extraordinary project had begun to restore it to its Edwardian glory. It had continued, undaunted by a lack of finance, but driven on by the passion of its new owners, a family called the Bishops. Now, an original trellis-gate lift formed the centrepiece of a 'Living History Museum' in the reception, which comprised a collection of eccentric memorabilia. A variety of fossils were on display, examples of what could be found in Thanet's eighty-million-year-old chalk beds, and it was possible to hop into the lift to wander round all five floors, taking in the ballroom, with its sprung maple dance floor, and the original maids' sculleries with their ancient call systems and copper stills. Hotel uniforms were exhibited alongside flappers' dresses from the 1920s, when a dumb waiter had serviced all five floors, twenty-four hours a day.

Stepping into the Walpole remained a treasured experience for Pearl, like coming home. Here she always felt protected and valued, as though she might have been part of the Living Museum herself. Whenever she had time she would drive out to sit on the flower-decked veranda and 'take tea', choosing crust-less white triangles of sandwich piled high on china stands that had long since been rescued from oblivion. Today, however, she walked on past the marble steps of the hotel's frontage to take the elegant Art Deco lift down to the bay.

The sense of space on Margate's coastline contrasted with the shore at Whitstable, which was broken up by its many timber groynes. Here, on the eastern esplanade in Walpole Bay, the only containment of the sea was a vast sea pool, built for swimmers in 1900, which emptied and replenished itself with every changing tide. The pool captured not only the tide but an abundance of marine life which remained largely trapped within its walls. From time to time, the structure was drained for maintenance checks and the opportunity was then taken, by coastal wardens and biologists, to survey its contents.

Oysters existed even here. Sheltered from the extremes of weather and predators, they grew large, embedding themselves alongside many varieties of sponge. Blood-red beadlet anemones lined the pool walls while velvet swimmer crabs used the mud-filled cracks as refuge from the harsh winters. At low tide, pollack and wrasse could be seen, darting against strawberry anemone on the seabed, waiting for the incoming tide to escape. Some were lucky, some remained and some would ultimately perish, but the existence of the tide pool allowed the sea and its many inhabitants to be brought into sharp focus, if only for a brief period of time.

The pool was a microcosm of a greater whole, and in that sense shared something in common with Whitstable. Today it seemed clear to Pearl that Carl had chosen to be a small fish in a big sea while she herself had remained like the creatures trapped here at low tide, unable to leave, unable to glimpse much of the greater world beyond these walls.

A cool wind blew up from the shore, and as she turned away from it, Pearl saw a figure approaching from the direction of the hotel. Tina Rowe wore a light camel-coloured coat and, uncharacteristically for her, a pair of flat shoes. It wasn't just her height that seemed diminished. Tina's features were almost devoid of make-up and, in place of her usual brash exterior, she wore a timid smile.

'I wasn't sure if you'd come,' she began. 'I wouldn't blame you for not wanting to see me again. To be honest, you're the only person in Whitstable who's even given me the time of day.'

'How have you been?' asked Pearl, sensing a new humility about Tina.

'Sober, for the most part. I haven't had a drink now for days. My friend at the hotel says I should go to meetings. If I can sort myself out, she said she'll even try and get me some work.'

'Doing what?'

Tina shrugged. 'Waitress? Chambermaid? Beggars can't be choosers, but I'll have to find something.' She paused, voice hardening with her next question. 'You've heard about the will, I suppose?'

As Pearl nodded, Tina said, 'Connie'll get the money. She's got Vinnie's kids, right?'

Pearl recognised that the question was purely rhetorical as Tina gestured up at the high chalk cliffs above them. 'You know, I've been thinking back to when I used to come here with Vinnie. We were just kids, and sometimes on a sunny day we'd bunk off school and walk along the cliffs up there.' She squinted against the light. 'We used to stare across at the old Walpole and say, "One day, we'll stay there". And you know what? We did. When we got married, we booked in there for our honeymoon.'

'I didn't know that,' said Pearl.

Tina nodded. 'Year after year we came back. Used to bring Shane when he was little and take him to the amusement park in Margate.'

'Dreamland?'

'Yes. I'd say to Vinnie, "Let's go somewhere else next summer. Abroad. To the Continent". She looked back at Pearl. 'And we could have afforded it by then. But no, this was enough for Vinnie. Happy in Dreamland, that was him.' She took a deep breath. 'It was me who wanted to see the world. And I did. After our Shane . . . I needed to get away.' She thrust her hands deep inside her pockets. 'I went all over the Med, you know. Saw all the places I could only ever dream about. But in spite of all that, every new day was just . . . another empty day in paradise.' She fell silent for a moment. Then: 'But I'm not going to run any more, Pearl. I've got nowhere else to go, so I'm staying right here. And I'm going to stop thinking about the past.'

Pearl recognised Tina's determination but knew how difficult this would be for her – for anyone.

'It was that detective who said it,' Tina revealed.

'Said what?' asked Pearl, looking up quickly.

'That night he brought me back from the Neptune, I told him I drank because I was lonely. And he said that I was lonely because of what had happened.' She paused before continuing. 'Because I'd lost my Shane.' She looked at Pearl. 'He said that sometimes you need a bit of space in your heart to let it heal. And that maybe drinking was my way of keeping people from getting too close.'

Pearl thought about this, recognising that McGuire was right, wondering perhaps if he had noticed that she, too, had her own way of keeping people at bay.

A sudden gust of wind blew up and though it was warm, Tina pulled her coat tighter to her body as if for comfort. She gestured up at the cliffs. 'Will you come back with me?'

'I can't,' said Pearl. 'It's the last day of the Oyster Festival and I've too much to do.' Confronted with the reality that life had been going on without her, Tina took a step away before saying brokenly, 'It's not too late for me, is it, Pearl?'

Pearl shook her head. 'No, Tina. It's not too late for any of us.' And as the other woman moved off slowly towards the Walpole, Pearl held fast to that thought.

Pearl had returned to Harbour Street and was juggling a bunch of flowers and a bag of shopping when she spied somebody coming out of Dolly's front door. The woman beetled along Harbour Street. Her lilac rinse was unmistakable.

'Sadie?'

Sadie Crouch turned, her face crumpling into an expression of vague disappointment when she saw who it was. She cocked a thumb back towards Dolly's door. 'I just popped in to see your mother. She said you were off in Margate.'

A smile stiffened on Pearl's lips. Sadie had a way of making it seem as though Pearl was always skiving at Dolly's expense. 'Well, I'm back now.'

'And out later at the concert?'

Before Pearl could defend herself, Sadie continued self-righteously, 'I thought, in the circumstances, that *someone* should call in and see how your mother was.'

'I was just about to do that.'

Sadie saw the key in Pearl's hand. 'Good,' she sniffed, before staring back at Dolly's front door. 'I've left her much improved. I know more than most that the sick are often better for a bit of company.' She gave a constipated smile and began to move off.

'She's not sick,' countered Pearl. 'It's just an old back problem.'

Sadie turned. 'When you're Dolly's age, you'll realise . . .'

'Realise what?' asked Pearl. 'Sadie, look . . .' but she trailed off, reluctant to share with this busybody the fact that Dolly's original back trauma had resulted from a *Saturday Night Fever* disco move in 1974 on the dance floor of the old Bear and Key pub. 'It's hereditary,' she finished lamely.

Sadie remained unimpressed. 'Can't stay here talking. I've got to get back.'

'To Billy?' asked Pearl, a little archly. 'I'd imagine he could probably do with a bit of rest too, lately.'

'What do you mean?' asked Sadie with some suspicion.

'Working all hours for Matheson.'

Sadie shook her head, 'Part-time, nine till two, that's all.'

'And no overtime?'

'Billy never works late. Not unless he's baiting.'

'I see.' Pearl gave a knowing smile as Sadie scurried off amongst a sea of shoppers.

After opening Dolly's front door, Pearl found her mother sitting up on the daybed in the conservatory.

'Thank God you're here,' wailed Dolly. 'I've just had a visit from Sadie, God Bothering and Do Gooding Crouch. I thought it was Juan or I'd never have let her in. He's due back from the mobility centre any moment.'

'The what?'

'Well, I realise I won't make it to the concert but I would like to come to Charlie's barbecue. If I could just get along the prom . . .'

'In a wheelchair?'

'Of course not.' Dolly tossed Pearl a brochure. 'Take a look at the nippy little number on page four. It does almost ten miles an hour.'

As Pearl found herself staring down at a selection of mobility scooters for hire, her heart sank at the idea of a Dollymobile mowing down DFLs on the prom.

Dolly read her daughter's thoughts. 'Don't worry. It comes with insurance.'

'Good,' said Pearl, emptying grapes into a bowl.

'Have you heard about Marty?' Dolly asked.

'Don't tell me,' said Pearl. 'He's won best window display?'

Dolly tutted. 'Of course not. The result won't be announced until tomorrow.' She paused. 'But he does seem to have won someone's heart. Sadie reckons he's taken up with that new florist. The tall girl with the red hair?'

'Nicki Dwyer?'

'That's her. Seems he got talking to her at the Neptune the other night. One thing led to another and . . .'

'I'm very happy for them,' interrupted Pearl, not wishing to hear the details.

'Yes,' her mother agreed. 'They seem suited. Have similar interests.'

'Like?' asked Pearl.

'Horticulture, making money . . .'

'Maybe even kayaking,' thought Pearl, aloud.

Dolly gave her a knowing look. 'Have you talked to him lately?'

'Marty?'

'The Flat Foot.'

'Why on earth should I?'

'To say goodbye, of course.' Dolly sighed. 'But you're not very good at that, are you?'

Pearl looked down at the bunch of sweet peas wilting in her hand. She had just bought them from a pretty assistant in Marty's shop while wondering where he might be. Now perhaps she knew. Marty had moved on finally. 'I'll put these upstairs for your guests,' she said.

'Hold on!'

Pearl turned back to see Dolly plucking grapes from the fruit bowl in her lap. 'He really wasn't so bad, you know.'

'Who – Marty?'

'The Flat Foot.' Dolly tossed a single grape in the air and caught it expertly in her mouth. Pearl left the room, reflecting outside the door how her mother was almost always right.

At 6 p.m. McGuire looked up at the screen of a bookie's monitor which showed the 'card' for the late-night summer races at Kempton Park. A horse called New Horizons had captured, rather unusually, his interest in the last race. 'Unusually' because McGuire always studied some form, checked out the going and compared the runners in general but, in this instance, his attention had kept returning to the Irish mare even though she had little to attract him but an outsider's odds.

He glanced around the bookie's, wishing the room was still full of smoke. Since the ban had come into force there was no escaping the fact that these places attracted either overly sad or overly anxious men. He had never once seen a woman within these walls apart from the cashier whose job it was to take the money. She was in her early forties with a figure that had spread from what McGuire assumed had been a lifetime of sitting on stools behind counters. She was neither friendly nor unwelcoming but, like Switzerland, remained forever neutral. It seemed she was there only for the money, as were most of the punters, though regarding the latter, McGuire now knew differently.

To a gambler, money was only secondary. There were plenty of reasons for retreating into a world so dependent on chance. Some were attracted to an opportunity to even up the odds of a rough life, while for others the thrill of an unknown outcome was clearly addictive. There were those who sought sanctuary amongst their own kind, while others still saw it as the only way out of a desperate existence. For McGuire, gambling also represented an escape – from the past – which was why the two words staring back at him from the race card appeared so tempting at this point in time. *New Horizons*. The simple phrase seemed to suggest to McGuire the distinct possibility of moving forward with his life, as long as the transfer turned out not to be simply a move back – to old horizons.

He made a decision, quickly scribbled out his betting slip and handed it to the cashier along with a fifty-pound note. In spite of her detached manner, she reacted with a double-take on registering McGuire's choice, but he held fast: despite all the previous losses, he had never given up on the hope that one day, things might change. There were laws of probability, and no one's luck remained out forever. Like the tide it had to turn.

McGuire took the slip that the cashier handed to him and decided to return to the station. In a few more hours he could finish his shift and head back to this smokeless room to watch the race.

At 7.30 exactly, Pearl arrived at Whitstable Harbour to find that the oyster-eating challenge had just ended. The raised table at which this year's contestants had gorged their fill of Pacific rock oysters was being cleared, and the crowds had now moved on to the large south-facing deck at Dead Man's Corner which was fulfilling its new purpose as a stage, and milled around it, waiting for the concert to begin. There was a cross-section of ages, but nearer the front, the crowd was much younger – mainly local kids, many of whom Pearl recognised, flashing beer cans and attitude in equal measure. The atmosphere was one of contained excitement, teenaged girls giggling together in tight groups while youths wrestled and dead-legged one another. At festival events, the local kids usually took over, asserting their territorial rights. It had been that way for as long as Pearl could remember, though in her teenage years, Whitstable had been largely undiscovered by the city-dwellers who now flocked here in the summer months.

On such a night, Shane Rowe had died after a small gig at an open-air concert near the Castle. Pearl knew that McGuire was right – no one could be certain who had caused the young man's death, but perhaps no one had learned from it either. Surely here, at this very moment, there were kids, both local and visiting, on pills or powder, trying out substances for the very first time or using them from habit. As McGuire had stated with professional confidence, drugs were now an integral part of youth culture. The alarming thing to Pearl was that there seemed to be no sure way of knowing who was on them until somebody fell victim. There had been no previous signs of drug-taking by Shane Rowe, and the whole tragic experience appeared to have been a fatal one-off. Teenagers for the most part seemed dominated by moods, appearing garrulous, sulky, silent and excitable: it was surely impossible to tell if the reason for that was down to drug-taking. Mood swings were a natural part of being young, as was curiosity itself, a need for new experiences and short cuts to confidence and 'cool'.

Moving through the crowd, Pearl asked herself if any of the teenagers surrounding the stage area could have taken something this evening. She recalled her own teenage experiences of trying spliffs down on the beach, though the substance she'd smoked had looked and smelled much like henna, while inducing only the kind of vertiginous 'swirling pits' sensation that she had experienced after too much red wine. Youth always searched for its own way of looking at the world and Pearl had been grateful that Charlie's only 'bad influence' had been a boy called Bobby Pascoe who did wheelies on a mountain bike up and down Harbour Street. Bobby had chased girls and terrified pensioners, and had to be avoided at all costs on Bonfire Nights for his profligate use of pyrotechnic 'bangers'. But youth never lasts forever and Bobby was now an apprenticed scaffolder and the devoted father of an adored baby.

In a sea of young faces Pearl found herself wondering whether Marty might be here with Nicki Dwyer. She wasn't sure how she felt about this new pairing: part of her felt rejected, but she knew this was illogical as she couldn't blame Marty for recognising he had wasted enough time pursuing her. Marty had held a candle for her for so long, his fingers had finally burned. Perhaps it had been McGuire's presence that had finally clarified Marty's position, or perhaps something in the way Pearl had reacted to the detective on the day Marty had seen them together on the beach.

Pearl was still concerned about how many other times Marty had secretly observed her, perhaps even on the night she had rowed out to Vinnie's boat for the final time. Could Marty have been on the beach, or in his kayak on the lowering tide, spying on her from afar? If so, she would never know now, nor ever be sure if the last conversation he had been seen to have with Vinnie in the harbour had really been about oyster shells. Marty had moved on – something Pearl was finding hard to do since she caught herself wondering where McGuire might be and what he might be up to at that very moment. If she were to see him here tonight, might she use the encounter as an opportunity to say a proper goodbye? She wasn't sure, but as she scanned the crowd for him she knew that Dolly was right: she wasn't good with goodbyes.

Pearl suddenly felt a warm hand upon the small of her back and turned to see, not McGuire, but Charlie.

'I left the collage at home and put some beers in the fridge,' he smiled.

'I'll bring it all along later with the food,' replied Pearl. 'How's Tizzy?'

'Getting ready. There's an old marquee behind the gabion wall that they're imaginatively calling a Backstage Area. I tried to get her to come out for a drink as I thought it might settle her nerves, but she swears she doesn't have any.' He looked up at the blue sky dotted with scudding white cloud. 'Looks like the weather might hold. Is Gran going to make it to the barbecue?'

'Just try and stop her,' joked Pearl. At that moment, a sequence of lights blazed on above the stage, and there was a collective buzz of anticipation. 'It's a real shame Tizzy's parents can't be here to see this,' she said.

Before Charlie could comment, a DJ took to the stage and the audience gave out a sudden roar. Charlie tried to speak but was silenced by the noise. Finally he called out, 'I'm going backstage. Want to come?'

Pearl shook her head. 'I'll watch from here. See you straight after.'

In no time Charlie had disappeared among the kids who were bouncing around in anticipation. The speaker volume was deafening, so Pearl eased herself further back in the crowd, seeking a better position from which to watch the show. It was then she noticed Matheson moving off the balcony of the Crab and Winkle restaurant, ushering in front of him a female companion. Pearl craned above the heads of the crowd but it wasn't possible to identify the woman. Nevertheless, she felt sure she knew who she was and threaded her way nearer to the restaurant, keeping an eye on the door which led straight out onto the harbour. Food stalls and drinks vendors were now lining the quay and Pearl used them as cover as she approached the restaurant.

The door suddenly opened but a group of young DFLs burst forth, brandishing a bottle of champagne. Before the door swung closed after them, it opened fully once more. This time, Pearl saw Connie in its frame with Matheson behind her. The two began to walk off, not towards Matheson's office but instead towards the packed car park. Dipped headlights went on before they reached Matheson's car, and Pearl watched as he opened a rear passenger door for Connie, then rounded the vehicle and got in the other side. The car slowly set off, leaving Pearl unsurprised to note that the driver was none other than Billy Crouch.

Dance music pounded as Pearl reflected on what she had just seen. She looked back towards the harbour where, less than a week ago, Vinnie's boat had been tethered to the quay. Now it had disappeared and the newly designed public space was filled with revellers celebrating the end of yet another Oyster Festival. Time had already moved on.

The crowd erupted at the end of a song and the DJ once more took the microphone. Expectant faces waited for the next piece of entertainment. And suddenly, there was Tizzy, lit by a single spotlight, as a drummer and guitarist took up their places beside her onstage. Tizzy smiled and introduced herself as 'Firenze'. Her eyes seemed to search the crowd and Pearl raised her arm instinctively, feeling that Tizzy was looking for her. As their eyes met, Pearl saw that Tizzy was wearing the lilac silk waistcoat Pearl had gifted her. Pearl hadn't worn it herself for nearly twenty years, but now it had been given new life by the beautiful young woman on stage.

Tizzy waved, then grabbed the microphone, pushing her long hair back from her beautiful face as she waited for a drumbeat to sound. The guitarist struck a few slow chords and she nodded her head in time before she finally began to sing. Powerful and yet haunting, her voice seemed almost to break, stretched taut on the high notes of a song of loss and melancholy, commanding attention, silencing even the noisiest teenager in the crowd. In an instrumental passage, she swayed to the music, her eyes closed. Then a single note sailed clear on the evening air, in a seemingly timeless moment – until her beautiful eyes opened at the end of the song and applause rang out from Dead Man's Corner. Pearl recognised the smile that Tizzy always reserved for Charlie, and though he was still standing in the wings Pearl caught the look he gave her in return, a look full of pride and respect for the beautiful young woman who had conveyed such magic to her audience.

Pearl found herself applauding madly, along with every-one else, until the drummer set up a faster tempo. Tizzy encouraged the crowd to clap along to a reggae beat. Followed by the spotlight, she strutted the stage, owning it, and the audience, as they joined in with the chorus. Charlie clapped in the wings while sections of the audience began dancing, kids throwing moves. Pearl clapped too, losing herself in the whole performance until her gaze fell upon someone standing stock still in the crowd.

At first, Pearl assumed that Ruby was watching Tizzy until she realised that the girl was, in fact, staring directly towards Charlie. Pearl called out to her but at that very moment, Tizzy took up her song once more and Pearl's own voice was lost in the music. Pearl fought her way through the dancing teenagers but the music came to a sudden end and the crowd roared its approval, arms held high, baying for more, forcing Pearl to remain where she stood. Only as the applause died down was Pearl able to see that Ruby was leaving. The boy who had been standing beside her remained, just for a moment, before he wiped a hand through his tousled blond hair and headed off quickly after her. As he did so, Pearl saw that it was Alex Berthold.

At that moment, the DJ resumed his place on the stage and Pearl once more found her path blocked as the flow of spectators drifted from the stage area back towards the bar. When most of the crowd had passed, neither Ruby nor Alex were visible. Pearl looked back to the queues forming at the open bar, then once more towards the East Quay. Still there seemed no sign of the pair on the main route which passed beside the old bowling alley. Instead Pearl headed west of Deadman's Corner and found a group of swaggering youths in her path. She was just about to ask if they had seen anyone pass by when the group dispersed, allowing her to see that the gate leading to the most direct path towards the East Quay had been left unlocked.

Ignoring a *No Entry* sign, Pearl quickly passed through the gate and hastened on, beyond the old aggregates company with its steel tower dwarfing the masts of fishing boats in the harbour. The company was closed for the holiday but gravel was strewn across the path, crunching beneath Pearl's feet as the sound of music and laughter receded behind her. Unseen by the crowds that were still milling at the bar, she soon found herself on the East Quay, at the rear of a bar that bore its name.

Behind an old shed known locally as the Barrel Store, a battered campervan had been abandoned, adding to the general desolation of the spot. And then Pearl heard voices. Stopping in her tracks, she pressed her back close to the wall of the shed as a conversation continued around the corner, too faint to register, prompting Pearl to edge closer, until she realised that in the reflection of the van's wing mirror, she could see Alex remonstrating with Ruby.

'Tell me what's wrong,' he pleaded.

Ruby said nothing but in the next moment, she moved out of the frame of the mirror and it was left to Alex to appeal to her again. 'Come on, just chill out.'

'*No!*' the girl argued. 'Can't you see this isn't enough for me? I want more.' She stepped back into Pearl's field of vision and stared up at Alex for a response. In the mirror's reflection, Ruby looked like a stranger to Pearl as she stood before Alex, trembling with a quiet rage. 'You promised me.'

'I know. But you're never satisfied.'

'What am I going to do when you leave?'

Pearl felt suddenly stung by Ruby's desperation.

'I told you,' Alex explained, summoning reserves of calm. 'I'm not leaving.'

'So you say,' cried Ruby bitterly. 'But they'll take you with them. You have to go to university.'

'I know,' he conceded. 'But I'll come back.'

'When?'

Pearl could see Ruby, paler than ever, staring down at her

trembling hands. Then she blurted out: 'I'll be alone again. With memories.' She tried to move off, but Alex reached out and held her close.

'I've told you before,' Pearl heard him say. 'I'll have memories too, but can't we just leave the past behind and make the most of now?' His hands moved to frame Ruby's face before he whispered urgently, 'Please?'

As he bent his head to kiss her, Pearl closed her eyes, partly to protect the lovers' privacy, but mostly because, yet again, the kiss itself seemed to represent the collision of two worlds – past and present. In that instant, Pearl became aware only of the warm breeze upon her upturned face and another soft kiss, never to be forgotten. When she finally opened her eyes, there was no one to be seen in the mirror's reflection.

Inching forward, Pearl saw only the surf rolling in on the shore – no sign of Alex or Ruby. The moment was broken by the ringtone of her mobile phone.

'Where are you, Mum?'

At the sound of Charlie's voice, Pearl felt as though she was awakening from a dream. 'Not far,' she said softly. 'Please tell Tizzy she was amazing.'

'You can tell her yourself,' Charlie said. 'She's right here.'

A moment's silence followed before Tizzy's voice sounded on the line.

Pearl smiled. 'You were fantastic, Tizzy. You could have sung all night.'

'Thanks,' the girl replied. 'Will you come backstage? It's crowded but you could have a drink here with us?'

Pearl checked her watch: there were only two hours before sunset. 'Thanks, but I'd better go home and fetch what we need for the barbecue,' she said. 'Tell Charlie we'll meet in the usual place and to bring plenty of firewood. We'll talk then. In fact, you might even like to sing.'

Tizzy gave a laugh. 'Maybe.'

Pearl expected a further response but Tizzy had left the line; the phone was dead in her hand. She moved forward but stopped as she caught sight of her own reflection in the mirror of the campervan. Her smile faded as she thought of Alex and Ruby, before deciding to head home as quickly as possible.

Chapter Twenty

Arriving at Seaspray Cottage, Pearl found it unnaturally quiet: the silence punctuated only by the sound of waves lapping against the shore. It was always noisier when the tide was out and voices carried straight across the mudflats. The air would then feel closer, stuffier but somehow cleansed with the returning high tide.

Pearl's ears were still ringing from the noise of the concert but she found herself thinking, not of Tizzy's performance, but of everything else she had witnessed. The evening's surprise had not so much to do with seeing Connie with Matheson but in recognising the depth of the relationship between Ruby and Alex. Pearl thought back to another night when she had been certain that she had seen Ruby watching kite-surfers at Tankerton Slopes. The girl had denied ever being there, leading Pearl to doubt herself though it was clear now that Ruby had lied. This was difficult for Pearl to understand

– unless the girl was simply too embarrassed to admit that she found a boy attractive. But Alex wasn't just any boy – he was Leo Berthold's son, and yet he had chosen to use his charming smile on Ruby on the very first day Pearl had met him at the restaurant.

Alex was self-possessed, but to Pearl he also seemed strangely disconnected from his parents, preferring, as his mother had commented, to spend all his time on the beach. Now it seemed possible that there could have been times during this summer period when Alex might have seen Vinnie at sea. Pearl cursed herself for not having questioned the boy when she had had the chance. Might there still be time to do so – but if so, to what end? The case was closed and McGuire was leaving town.

Pearl had failed, not only with Stroud's mission for her, but in coming up with any real evidence that Vinnie's death had been anything other than an accident. Dolly had spoken: it was all best left alone and, as ever, Pearl knew that her mother was almost always right.

Pearl packed an icebox with Charlie's beers and worked quickly to prepare food for the barbecue, skilfully filleting several sea bass with her father's old knife, still sharp as a razor, his instructions burned into her memory. However, she worked automatically, constantly returning to what she had witnessed that evening, acknowledging that innocent young Ruby had not only lied to her, but had done so without her even realising it. Pearl knew she could tackle Ruby about her relationship with Alex – but would she ever get the truth? 'Make the most of now,' Alex had told Ruby. Not a bad idea, thought Pearl, as she looked down at the sea-bass fillets which still required her attention.

Pearl doused the fish in a marinade of sherry vinegar, rosemary, thyme and fresh ginger, remembering to include some samphire, but still she remained troubled, not only by the fact that Ruby had kept secrets so successfully, but by the demands Pearl had heard the girl make of Alex. 'What will I do when you leave?' The question seemed to resonate for Pearl, together with the inevitability of Alex's desertion. 'But I'll come back,' he had said: the same words Carl had told Pearl, the night of their own parting. Pearl sensed that her judgement was being clouded by her own experience – by memories she had held on to for far too long. Perhaps it was time for her to leave the past behind, as Alex had suggested to Ruby. But still something rankled for Pearl – had she really been witnessing the sad conclusion of a summer romance, or something far more significant?

Searching for a corkscrew, she opened the drawer in which it was usually kept, but found only cocktail sticks and Halloween serviettes. The chaos of Pearl's home kitchen seemed almost an act of rebellion against the sense of order she maintained at the restaurant. Pulling serviettes from the drawer she saw that, with them, came a piece of paper and, as it fell to the floor, she recognised it as a page of Tizzy's recipe for the *Caccuccio di Livorno*. It seemed an age ago that she had first tasted the dish at Charlie's flat, another event during this extraordinary festival and summer, and that single thought reminded her of Charlie's collage, still propped against the sofa in the living room.

Pearl went to investigate and found it wrapped loosely in brown paper and secured with string. For a moment, she wondered whether she would be able to carry it to the beach along with everything else she had to take, but on picking it up, she found it was strangely light.

Overcome with curiosity, Pearl untied the string and let the brown paper fall away to expose Charlie's work. A 'distressed' wooden frame surrounded a collage comprising cinema and theatre tickets, strands of dried seaweed and corn and various photographic images. It was a touching piece of contained memorabilia, like the Living Museum at the Walpole Bay Hotel. Pearl remembered her conversation with Charlie that morning and for the first time in a long while, she allowed herself to consider that she hadn't done too badly as a single mother. It was a sweet moment, and one to overcome the bitter truth of Charlie growing up and away from her.

The images in the collage provided evidence of that since they showed Charlie, happy with the girl he loved, posed against a variety of backdrops: the Street with its bank of exposed shingle piercing the incoming tide like a golden arrow, a terrace of bright beach huts at Tankerton Slopes, the sun falling into the sea at West Beach. These images of Whitstable would remain, even though the people against the landscape changed: Pearl with Carl, Ruby with Alex, Charlie with Tizzy. After a moment, Pearl found her vision clouding. Unable to take in further detail in the fading light, she reached for a small case in her handbag and plucked from it her glasses, accepting, once and for all, that she would have to rely upon them from now on.

Slipping on her glasses, she reviewed Charlie's work, finding everything to be now in sharp focus: Tizzy at the beach, captured in a moment in time as Pearl, too, had once been captured in the sketches and watercolours created more than two decades ago by Charlie's father. But now, another girl was seated on the timber groyne, her face turned towards the sun. Tizzy was smiling for the camera, beautiful, serene, vaguely mysterious like a young Mona Lisa as Pearl's own smile began to fade, along with every other image within the frame.

A single feature was becoming dominant, brought closer and closer to Pearl's attention like the subject of a zoom lens, until all she could see was a familiar triangle of silver, a flash of turquoise blue at its core, in the earring Tizzy wore.

Chapter Twenty-One

It was nearing 8.50 p.m. when McGuire finished his reports. He despised 'box ticking' but Superintendent Welch set great store by it. As a well-earned reward, McGuire considered that a cold beer might be in order before he sauntered back to the bookie's to watch the evening race. A little bar close to the station served his usual Mexican brand. Tables and chairs were spread outside so he didn't have to cope with the loud interior, its noise levels or the mock cacti and sombreros that decorated the place. Part of him, however, still hankered for the beach at the Neptune pub, to watch the sun sinking into the sea as he raised an oyster stout to his lips. He sat back in his office chair and closed his eyes, seeing Pearl seated in front of him once more, instructing him about something he knew nothing about: the Red Sands fort, a smuggling community, some pointless facts about small-town life.

Pointless. That's how he viewed this summer he had spent in Kent, punctuated as it had been by his numerous run-ins with Pearl. She had been, in turn, obstructive, critical, disrespectful of his methods and yet, paradoxically, her spirit and the brash, overbearing way in which she had tried to take over his case now seemed to be the only relevant part of it. She was a conundrum, like the case itself, a case that had now been dropped and, although something still rankled about it, McGuire knew there was nothing more to be done. Instead, he consoled himself with the possibility of a positive result for New Horizons and checked the betting slip in his pocket. With odds of 33-1, he stood to win over fifteen hundred pounds if the filly managed to cross the line first. That kind of money would certainly help with the move back to London.

McGuire slipped on his jacket and was almost at the door when his mobile rang. His first thought was that it was probably Welch so he left the phone in his pocket. Six rings and it would go straight to voicemail but curiosity got the better of him. On the fifth ring, he took out his mobile and checked the caller ID.

'I need your help.'

The words came fast, the voice sounding strained. McGuire looked up at the clock on his office wall and saw that there was less than half an hour until New Horizons was set to run. His desk was clear and so was his conscience, but still he heard himself reply: 'What is it, Pearl?'

Crowds were gathered outside the Hotel Continental. Raucous laughter, like the shriek of gulls, went up suddenly from a group of tipsy girls at the bar. The hotel balconies were filled with guests, drinks in hand, faces turned towards the incoming tide. A previously clear sky was now streaked with cloud and there was a heaviness to the air. A single stripe of nimbus speared the lowering sun. From an open window, the bassline of some dance music was pounding like the beat of Pearl's own heart as she headed down to the foot of the Slopes. There, she saw a figure standing at the water's edge. On hearing Pearl's footfall on the shingle behind her, Tizzy turned and said, 'Charlie's gone to fetch wood, but he shouldn't be long.' She tossed some seaweed towards a pile by the groyne and raised her eyes to the sky. 'Do you think it might rain?'

When she looked back again, Tizzy saw that Pearl was reaching a hand out towards her. In her palm lay the turquoise earring.

Music still rang out in the background, carried on the warm air from the East Quay bar as Pearl braced herself and spoke. 'You were wearing this in a photograph of Charlie's. You must have lost it.'

Tizzy moved closer to inspect the earring. 'Yes,' she frowned, 'but where did you—' she stepped back in shock as Pearl's hand closed tightly on the earring.

'It was found on Vinnie Rowe's boat.'

Tizzy's expression instantly clouded, her eyes narrowing in confusion. 'The fisherman?' She began to shake her head slowly. 'But how did it get there?'

Pearl held her gaze. 'Perhaps you lost it on the quay. The boat was often moored there. It could have fallen.'

'Yes,' said Tizzy uncertainly. 'That's possible.'

'But that isn't what happened,' said Pearl. 'Is it?'

Tizzy looked up.

'Do you remember telling me about the ways in which people reveal themselves? A look, an anecdote . . .' Pearl opened her hand slowly and glanced down again at the earring in her palm. 'The clues we leave behind? You were right, Tizzy. The recipe you gave me – I read and reread it, not the ingredients nor the method, but because the words on the page seemed to be saying much more.'

Tizzy shook her head. 'I don't understand.'

'You told us all the story of your father's accident, that very first night we met.'

In the far distance, lights had just blinked on at the wind farm. Tizzy looked towards them but remained silent, motionless, her eyes glassy, like a beautiful waxwork.

'You didn't have to do that,' said Pearl softly, 'but you did.' She paused, moving closer. 'But the man on the boat wasn't your father, was he? His name was Paulo Ragnelli. I checked with the authorities in Livorno. He was your stepfather. And the accident you told us about was fatal.'

Tizzy blinked finally, her eyes seeming to well with tears, but when she spoke, it was without emotion.

'You're right,' she admitted. 'Paolo was my stepfather, but . . . it really was an accident, Pearl.' Her beautiful features creased with pain. 'I told him to stop drinking, out on the boat that day, but he wouldn't listen, Pearl. It was his own fault.' The words seemed to sit on the evening air. 'Did the authorities tell you how old I was when my mother married him?'

Pearl shook her head.

'I was twelve years old and I really thought that he liked me. Why wouldn't I? He always found so much time for me.' She stopped, composing herself for just a moment before continuing. 'It wasn't long before I realised why.'

The look she delivered to Pearl was like a blow. She went and sat down on the timber groyne. 'I couldn't tell my mother the things he used to say. He said if I ever did, she would never believe me, because the truth was so much worse.' She paused, this time to raise the palms of her hands to her face, as though washing it clean. 'After he died, I thought everything might go back to how it had been before he ever came into our lives. He left us money and I told my mother we could go away. We could get over what had happened. But she wouldn't listen. She cried all the time. Grieving – the same way she had done when my father had died. But he didn't deserve that.' She looked back at Pearl.

'So you told her.'

Tizzy nodded. 'Of course. She needed to know what he was really like. But even from the grave, Paolo was right. She wouldn't believe me.'

As Tizzy fell silent, Pearl moved closer. 'What happened?'

The girl sighed and got to her feet. 'She sent me away, said it would be good for me.'

'Here?'

Tizzy spread her arms wide in an expansive gesture. 'No. To a *gran palazzo* in Sardinia. A cookery school. For a whole year I was away from Livorno, learning the art of *cucina italiana*.'

Pearl felt something biting into her palm and realised how tightly she held the earring.

'Suddenly I had a new role,' the girl went on, 'and I enjoyed it. I liked to cook. I'm good at it – though not as good as you, Pearl.' A bitter smile passed fleetingly over her lips. 'I went to help out in the kitchen of a villa and I met a boy. Not a romance,' she clarified hastily. 'We were just two bored teenagers looking for ways to feel better about ourselves. But in the winter, I followed him to Claviere.'

'The ski resort,' said Pearl. 'Where you worked as a chalet girl.'

'That's right.' Tizzy summoned her thoughts. 'There was a club we all went to. It was always fun. Everyone was always happy. I soon found out why.' She stared at Pearl. 'The first time I took a line of cocaine I felt like I was shining, like I was clean again – like snow beneath the stars. I saw everything so clearly, who I was, what I wanted to do. There was no past, only that moment, and I realised how things could be. Up there in the mountains. On top of the world.' The life suddenly went out of her and she fell silent.

'What happened?' prompted Pearl.

'It didn't last. The boy's mother found some cocaine in his pocket and his parents took him away. The club was closed down.'

'And you?'

'My mother didn't find out. She was proud of me, and of my year away. I was ready for some study, she said. So I enrolled in university. England has a great theatrical tradition, don't you think?' Tizzy offered an incongruous smile and at the same moment, some children skateboarded past on the prom, their laughter reminding Pearl that life was going on elsewhere. As they vanished from sight, Tizzy went on: 'I was never addicted, but I knew I had to find something to take its place.'

Pearl closed her eyes, thinking of Charlie. Tizzy seemed to read her thoughts.

'That first evening we met at the Gulbenkian, Charlie was so charming, so funny, so . . . normal. We began to see each other but at Easter he had his project to complete and he asked me to go with him to Bruges. We had a great time, Pearl. But on our last day, we returned to the Groeninge Museum to spend the afternoon there and, just as we were leaving . . .'

Pearl broke in and completed her sentence. 'You came face-to-face with your past.'

Tizzy looked astonished as Pearl filled in the gaps. 'The boy you had known in Italy. It was Alex Berthold.'

Tizzy gasped, 'How do you know?'

'His mother, Sarah, told me all about a family trip to Holland and Belgium. She mentioned summers in Sardinia.'

Tizzy looked away, absorbing this.

'What happened then?' Pearl asked desperately. 'What did you say to Charlie?'

'Nothing,' Tizzy faltered. 'I . . . couldn't even be sure I'd really seen him. Charlie and I left the museum, and when I looked back, Alex wasn't there so I told myself I'd imagined it.' She paused. 'The next morning we were due to return home. Charlie got up first but I stayed in our room to pack my bag, and when I came down for breakfast, Charlie was waiting for me at a table, but . . . he wasn't alone.'

'Alex?'

Tizzy's speech began to quicken. 'He must have found out where we were staying – perhaps he followed us from the museum? I didn't know what he wanted or what he might have said to Charlie.' She shivered. 'I didn't say a word, Pearl. It was only when I saw Charlie smile that I knew Alex hadn't told him about us.'

Pearl studied the girl. 'But you didn't explain to Charlie either?'

'I didn't have time,' Tizzy explained. 'Alex saw my reaction and he just took over. He let Charlie introduce us as if we'd never met.' She looked urgently back at Pearl. 'If you asked Charlie now, I'm sure he wouldn't even remember. Two strangers in a hotel? Alex had asked if he could borrow our map, that's all. And then he was gone.' She said bitterly, 'I'd hoped never to see him again. But he knew I was here because Charlie must have told him we were studying in Canterbury. That's where he found me – at the University.' She appealed to Pearl. 'I didn't want anything to do with him, I swear, and I tried to tell him – but he said it was fate. His father was here on business and this had given him an idea.' She wiped her dry mouth with the back of her hand.

'Go on,' Pearl said quietly.

'He . . . took down the mirror from the wall in my room and emptied a tiny pile of white powder onto it.'

Pearl breathed in sharply as Tizzy continued: 'Suddenly it was as though I was back in Claviere. Alex took a blade from his pocket and began tapping – chopping the coke, telling me . . .' she took a step towards the waves lapping up onto the shore '. . . that he had a friend in Amsterdam who could bring cocaine from Zeebrugge.' She fell silent as she looked far out to sea. 'Alex said he knew just the right place for it to be dropped off.'

Pearl followed her gaze. 'The Red Sands fort.'

Tizzy nodded slowly. 'Alex knew all about it from his father, how no one ever goes there. But there's a platform in place, so all he had to do was go out there, pick up the bags and bring them back to shore when we were ready.'

'I don't understand,' Pearl said. 'Why would a boy like Alex feel the need to do this? He has everything.'

'But not enough,' said Tizzy quickly. 'He'll never be his father, and he knows it. He's already failed his parents but he thinks he can succeed in his own way. He didn't need to put out too much for this but the return would have been more than a quarter of a million pounds. He wouldn't even have needed to cut it with anything harmful.'

'But he needed you.'

'Yes. To help him sell it – at the University, and here in Whitstable.' She sighed. 'Pearl, you've seen how many people are here for this festival.'

Pearl took a moment to think as music still pounded from the Continental. She said fiercely to Tizzy: 'You didn't have to do this.'

'I tried to say no,' the girl argued. 'I told Alex all about me and Charlie, how I wanted to leave the past behind. I told him to do the same, but he wouldn't listen. He said that whatever happened, he was going ahead – with or without me. Then he scratched out two long white lines on the mirror and handed it to me. "Go on", he said. "Walk away if you want to".' Tizzy looked down, ashamed, unable to meet Pearl's gaze.

'And you couldn't,' Pearl said softly. She took a step closer, wanting to comfort the girl, but aware that she had heard only half the story. 'And Ruby?' she asked. 'I saw her one night on the beach. She was with Alex but I couldn't be sure at the time.'

Tizzy said dully, 'It was up at the beach hut. The consignment had just arrived and Alex took the first load there. He wanted to cut it straight away. It was getting dark and we'd almost finished when we suddenly realised that your waitress had been spying on us.' She looked back at Pearl. 'Ruby was always down at the beach in the evening, looking out for Alex. She's not as innocent as you think. She knew what she was seeing.'

'Because her mother had been an addict.'

Tizzy recoiled. 'I . . . didn't know.'

'So you had to do something about her?' Pearl prompted.

Tizzy nodded guiltily. 'Alex knew that she fancied him so he flirted with her, then he gave her a line. After that, she was his.'

Pearl was remembering so many instances of Ruby's agitation, at work and at the nursing home, her pale features and tiny body, motivated by drugs, pure and simple.

'He gave her a little more each time, just to keep her quiet, but soon almost everything had gone to the local dealers. He wanted to leave the rest until the festival, but then he found out that his father was taking some people out to the fort and said we had to do something.' She became restless. 'We went out on the jet ski but he judged the tide wrongly. The sea was rough and by the time we made it to the platform, there was no way we could reach the ladder.'

Pearl looked out towards the free waters east of the Street, piecing together the events in her mind's eye. 'And Vinnie saw you.'

'That's right. He came and rescued us, took us on board his fishing boat and told us we were fools. He asked what we had been doing there and we lied, said that we'd heard that the place had been a radio station so we wanted to look around. We begged him to keep quiet, saying that Alex's father would be furious and would confiscate the jet skis. Your friend Vinnie was kind to us. He agreed not to say anything, as long as we never went there again. When he dropped us ashore, I even thanked him.'

Pearl looked down at the earring still in her hand. 'But you left this behind?'

Tizzy's breathing came faster as she pushed a hand through her long hair, 'I thought it had gone in the sea. And I hoped the fisherman would forget all about us. I told Alex we'd had a lucky escape and we should just leave the rest of it. He said that he would.'

'But he didn't.'

'No.' Tizzy shook her head. 'He went back alone. This time he made it and picked up the other packet, but as he headed back down the platform he saw the fisherman was there, threatening to call the coastguard if he didn't come aboard.' Her voice trembled. 'I got a crazy call from Alex, saying he was in trouble. He told me to come straight away, out to the boat to meet him.'

She stared out to sea. 'It was the night before the festival. Everyone seemed to be at the harbour so I went out on a jet ski, came aboard the *The Native* and saw . . .' She covered her face with her hands.

'What?' urged Pearl. 'What did you see?'

Tizzy's hands lowered and she blinked feverishly as though emerging from a dream. 'Your friend Vinnie was unconscious and the boat was drifting. Alex had struck him as he was getting ready to take *The Native* back ashore. I told him we should call the coastguard and get help but Alex wouldn't listen. He was panicking, going on and on about how angry his father would be. He was out of control and I'd heard enough, but I got as far as the radio when he grabbed hold of me. That's when I saw the fisherman. Vinnie was getting up – behind Alex. Not dead but struggling to his feet.' She forced back tears. 'He moved forward to pull Alex off me, but Alex struck out, almost like a reflex and the fisherman fell back onto the deck. He had hit his head against . . .' she struggled for the right word '*la gallocia*. The cleat,' she said finally. 'I wasn't sure he was going to get up this time.'

'He was dead?' When Tizzy said nothing, Pearl stepped closer and demanded, *'Was it Alex who killed Vinnie?'*

Tizzy said heavily, 'No. I reached down and felt the man's pulse. He was still alive. But Alex started crying, begging me to do something.'

'And you saw the anchor lying on the deck. You used it to fake the accident.'

Tizzy recoiled, shocked by Pearl's suggestion.

'No!' she insisted. 'I swear to you. The anchor was still on the deck when we got back on the jet skis. I told you, the boat was drifting.' She massaged her brow, as though to ease a headache. 'We got back just before dusk and there was no one around when we came ashore. We had just started heading up to the hut when out of nowhere, somebody spoke.' She trailed off for a moment. 'That's when I saw him – a fat man, sitting on the porch of the beach hut, fanning himself with his hat. It was like a dream, or a nightmare. I tried to ignore him, pretending he wasn't there, but then he spoke again, asking a question, wanting to know when Vinnie was coming ashore.' She looked at Pearl. 'I prayed I was imagining this, but the man pointed up to the telescope on the Slopes and said he'd seen us getting off *The Native*.' Music stopped playing at the Continental and Tizzy lowered her voice. 'I didn't know what Alex was going to do but he turned to the man and then he smiled, saying that Vinnie would be a little while longer.'

Waves lapped up on the shore. There was no music and no other voices but Tizzy's as she told her story.

'Alex asked the man if he could give us a hand with the jet skis. But the fat man laughed, said no way could he do that because he had a heart condition. As he got up from the step, he was panting. He had just put his hat on when Alex suddenly rushed at him and pushed him into the hut. I left the jet ski and ran up the steps. When I got there, the man was fighting for breath. "Don't hurt me!" he cried. But he was weak and . . . Alex didn't have to do a thing. A bottle of pills was lying there on the floor and the man reached down, but we just stood and watched as it rolled and rolled . . . and fell into a crack between the floorboards.' Tizzy whispered, 'I know we should have gone for help, but it was too late. The man had fallen forward. Suddenly, he wasn't gasping for breath any more.'

A warm breeze blew in across the waves but Pearl shivered as she felt only the merciless truth slice through her like a cold blade. 'Who put the bar across the door?'

'Alex,' Tizzy informed her. 'He said it could be days before the man was discovered. But Charlie told me next morning that you'd found a body.' She looked up at Pearl. 'It didn't seem possible. You, of all people? Alex told me to invite you over to see what you knew. He said all we could hope for was that the police would find no evidence and be unable to build a case.'

'But Ruby recognised you,' Pearl said. 'Much later, at the Neptune, she remembered she had seen you at the beach hut. I saw her reaction that night but I misunderstood it. She must have been confused to see you and Charlie together because you had been with Alex last time.'

'You're right,' admitted Tizzy. 'That night at the pub on the beach, I pretended I was speaking to the caretaker about my jacket but I'd called Alex to tell him we were in trouble.'

'And he then called Ruby on her mobile?'

Tizzy nodded slowly. 'She was upset. Said that you and

Charlie were like family to her and that she didn't want things to go any further.' Tizzy's voice took on a sudden note of desperation. 'I didn't know what Alex was going to do, I swear.'

'He cooked for her, didn't he?'

Pearl held the girl's look until Tizzy finally admitted, 'He used mushrooms he had picked in the woods. She'd shown them to him when they'd been walking one day, explained that they were poisonous, and Alex had kept some. He'd guessed he might have to scare her to keep her quiet.'

'And it worked,' Pearl said fatefully.

Tizzy agreed, accepting defeat. 'What we did was wrong, but I've told you everything. Now can you understand how things happened?' She looked imploringly at Pearl. 'I didn't hurt anyone. It was just . . . circumstances.'

'Circumstances?' echoed Pearl. 'Two men are dead!'

'And I wish I could bring them back,' cried Tizzy. 'But I can't. It's too late.'

Too late. The words seemed to echo back to Pearl as though McGuire was repeating them. But could it ever be too late for the truth?

Tizzy stood up and moved closer. 'We could make things right, Pearl, you and I.'

Pearl stared back at her, stunned with confusion.

'Forget I ever told you this. If not for me, then for Charlie.'

'Charlie?' Pearl challenged her. 'What has *he* to do with this?'

'Everything,' replied Tizzy simply. 'You love him. And so do I. That's why we understand one another – and why Charlie must never know.'

Pearl felt herself suddenly falling under Tizzy's spell and

closed her eyes. All she heard now were the waves upon the shore, insistent, reassuring, moving imperceptibly closer as surely as they had covered Vinnie's dead body on the eve of the Oyster Festival. Was it really possible for the truth to be ignored, covered up like sand on the beach with a rising tide, even for Charlie's sake?

Pearl thought of Vinnie, reminding herself that she had been the one to discover him, lying there beneath his own boat, close to the native oysters he had tended all year. She had been the one to bring him home.

A rocket whistled a sudden path up into the night sky and an explosion of light burst against the canvas of the heavens, vanishing just as quickly as Pearl felt the first drop of rain fall upon her face. She came to her senses only with the crunch of footsteps on the beach and turned, expecting for a moment to see Charlie – but instead it was Alex who stood before her. He offered an innocent smile before taking his phone from his pocket and explaining, 'I got a text.'

Pearl said nothing and so Alex's eyes moved to Tizzy.

'What text?' she frowned. Alex handed his mobile to her. Tizzy glanced quickly at the display before giving it back. 'That's not my number. It's Charlie's.'

'You said you were using Charlie's phone?'

Tizzy looked suspicious – and then her gaze shifted to Pearl. Alex's eyes followed. 'What's going on?'

'She knows,' said Tizzy. 'I just told her everything.'

Alex frowned but Tizzy repeated a single word so he could be in no doubt: '*Everything*.'

Alex stood stock-still. Then he turned his attention to Pearl and insisted, 'Whatever she told you, it's lies.'

'Alex!' Tizzy's voice rang out but he ignored her.

'It's true,' he went on. 'She's an actress, for God's sake!' He looked at Tizzy. '*She* did it.'

'She faked the accident, you mean?' asked Pearl.

'Yes,' Alex asserted. 'She said we couldn't leave the fisherman so she took the anchor line and wound it around his ankle . . .'

'That's not true!' Tizzy protested. 'He was alive when we left. Unconscious but alive.'

'Shut up!' cried Alex.

A wave crashed suddenly upon the shore. Pearl watched Tizzy's face creasing into a frown.

'Why are you saying this?' the girl asked Alex. 'Pearl isn't stupid. Don't you see? She sent you that text . . . just to get you here.' Tizzy looked across at Pearl as the truth slowly dawned for her. 'She's already worked everything out.'

Pearl saw that Alex's hands were trembling. His breathing came faster and there was panic in his eyes – the same panic Pearl knew he must have felt on the night Vinnie had died. The boy stepped forward, standing so close to her that Pearl could feel his warm breath on her face.

'Is it true?' he hissed. 'Why did you send me that message?'

Pearl stared into the boy's blue eyes and steadied her nerve. 'Because I needed to be sure,' she said calmly. 'And now I am.'

Before Alex could respond to this, Pearl grabbed her own mobile from her pocket, her eyes quickly scanning the short text that had just arrived. Looking up towards the Slopes, she saw two police cars suddenly speed from the road on to the wide grass verge, the door of the first flung open to release four officers. Seagulls flew up into the sky, scattering in the gathering clouds.

Alex looked around like a hunted animal as two uniformed police officers began to make their way quickly down the grassy slopes. 'What's happening?' he demanded. 'What's going on?'

McGuire leaped out of the second car and exhaled a sigh of relief when he saw that Pearl was safe. He slipped his own mobile into his pocket and moved away from the car, exposing a figure seated in the back with another officer.

Down on the beach, Pearl waited for Alex's reaction to this, watching the boy's eyes narrow as he recognised the man staring down towards him from the rear of the police car.

'Your father's just given a statement to the police,' she told him. 'A confession.'

'No. No!' the boy protested.

'He went back onto the boat that night,' Pearl continued, 'and he put Vinnie's unconscious body into the sea. He faked the accident. To protect you.'

Alex was still in denial but the tears welling in his eyes made it clear he was having to confront an awful truth.

'He was home when you got back that night,' Pearl went on softly. 'Your mother was at church, at Evensong, but your father must have known something had happened because of the state you were in. Perhaps he saw you coming ashore through the telescope in the bedroom? Maybe he even thought you were on drugs. Did you argue?'

Alex looked away for a moment and then said hoarsely, 'It wasn't his fault. He was trying to help me. He . . . said it would all be okay.'

Tizzy stepped forward to speak. 'You *told* him?' she asked in disbelief. 'How could you?'

'He's my father,' the boy said simply.

Alex Berthold looked around as if for further answers, but neither Pearl nor Tizzy had any for him. Footsteps followed, fast and heavy on the shingle, and police procedure took over as Pearl watched the two young people before her being handcuffed and read their rights. The sudden touch of McGuire's hand upon her shoulder felt reassuringly warm and she saw the look in his eyes, answering it only with a nod of her head, grateful for his presence.

Looking up once more towards the Slopes, Pearl's eyes met Leo Berthold's for just a second before he slowly turned his attention away, staring unflinchingly ahead through the windscreen, as unmoved and resolute as he had once appeared in an old family photo at the Villa Leoni, when he had looked towards a very different future.

Chapter Twenty-Two

Out on Reeves Beach just east of the Oyster Stores, there was a crispness to the air which made Pearl catch her breath. Lately, the sun had remained hidden within skies so laden with cloud that it was difficult to judge where the sea ended and the sky began, but now the estuary tide lay spread before her like a sheet of flat mercury on which pale rose and amethyst streaks shed a sudden opalescent glow, a reminder that even on a bad day these skies still deserved that description by the painter Turner of 'the loveliest in all of Europe'.

The weather had remained unstable since the last night of the Oyster Festival, days and weeks drifting by as the shift in light and weather seemed to reflect a change in Pearl's own perspective. It brought with it a sense of loss, of another summer gone, of life requiring to be viewed for what it was. Gone were the pleasure-craft from the water, no more jet skis or windsurfer sails, just the haunting spectre of the tall-masted

Greta – the historic Thames Sailing Barge – orbiting the forts that studded the dim horizon.

The shadow of a raincloud suddenly obliterated the glow of pale sunlight upon the water and Pearl heard the faint crunch of pebbles underfoot as someone neared her on the breakwater. McGuire sat down beside her but did not speak. It was left to Pearl to break the silence between them.

'There's a storm coming later.'

Pearl said this with certainty, but she remained less sure about many other things. She knew that the forthcoming trial would produce reports, evaluations and the final truth about a fisherman's death – but only one thing seemed guaranteed: Leo Berthold's money would not protect him, or his son, against the weight of the law.

'He could still retract his confession,' McGuire said, as if reading her thoughts.

Pearl shook her head. 'Not without implicating Alex. It's checkmate.' She looked at McGuire but thought suddenly of Sarah Berthold losing the two men in her life, and of Tizzy's mother, a woman who had been waiting for news of her daughter's progress at university when she had taken a call informing her instead of Tizzy's arrest. 'We may have discovered the truth,' Pearl continued, 'but I so wish the ending to this story had been different.'

McGuire knew she was thinking of Charlie. 'How is he?' he asked.

The question sat uncomfortably between them and Pearl wished she could be more confident in her response.

'I'm not sure,' she admitted honestly. 'He's made a decision about college, says he's not going back, but he *is* going to keep on the flat.' She frowned. 'He's talking about taking a year off, applying for art school and trying his hand at graphic design.' She suddenly recalled the business card that Charlie had designed for her, seemingly a lifetime ago. 'Perhaps that's what he should always have done.'

As soon as the words were out, another idea returned to Pearl about parallel lives, prompting her to wonder how Charlie's life might have progressed had he not taken up his place at university, had he not gone to see a play one night, had he never met a girl called Tizzy.

'He's been to visit her twice,' she said. 'Both times she refused to see him.' She looked now to McGuire for a response.

'Maybe you should thank her for that,' he said, sensing her dissatisfaction as she stared across to the forts. 'We're programmed for survival. Charlie's young. He'll get over this.'

'That's what my mother says.' She turned to him. 'That the young are adaptable.'

'And she's right,' confirmed McGuire.

Yes, thought Pearl. Dolly was nearly always right. 'All the same,' she reflected, 'you never forget your first love.'

McGuire looked down, recognising how true this was.

'And you,' Pearl said a little too brightly, 'Has your transfer finally come through?'

McGuire nodded, and in that moment Pearl felt a blow to her solar plexus, like the one she had felt many years ago, here on this same stretch of beach where she had felt her life begin, but also where she and Charlie's father had said goodbye. She had survived that parting, she thought sadly, and would survive this one too.

'I turned it down,' said McGuire unexpectedly. He looked at Pearl and found himself trapped in her gaze.

'Why?'

McGuire recognised that he could use this moment to explain several things: how a return to London promised little more than painful memories while an all too brief summer spent in a small, idiosyncratic coastal town had offered him a welcome escape. He might ask how a beer called Oyster Stout, bought from a pub that was slowly sinking into the beach, always seemed strangely intoxicating when he was looking into Pearl's pale grey eyes – as he was right now . . . but instead he merely said, 'Maybe I didn't give this place much of a chance. You know what they say about new horizons.'

As soon as the two words were out, McGuire suddenly remembered an old betting slip in his wallet. Other business had got in the way on the night of the race, and though McGuire had triumphed in one respect, he had lost in another as his 33-1 choice had fallen at the second bend.

Pearl gazed out towards the Street. 'Did I tell you that Billy Crouch is going to manage Vinnie's oyster beds?'

McGuire shook his head.

'He's signed an agreement with Connie,' Pearl told him. 'Matheson's tied in on the deal. Their relationship was strictly business.' She gave a wry smile. 'So I was wrong about that too.'

'But your instincts were right,' McGuire said. 'When you called me that night and asked me to check with the Livorno authorities, you told me you thought that the murderer could be Leo, covering up for his son's mistake.' He paused. 'How did you know?'

Pearl looked back at him and shrugged. 'I didn't. At least, I couldn't be sure. But everything you'd told me on the beach . . . about kids and drugs . . . stayed with me. I remembered Sarah telling me that Alex had been in bad health. She watched him too carefully, as though she couldn't trust him out of her sight. There had to be a reason for that. And I knew after the concert that there had been something going on between him and Ruby, but I hadn't fully understood what they had been talking about on the beach when I overheard them. I had watched them through the mirror of an old campervan – a reflection – and it hadn't given me the full picture. I began to realise that everything I'd learned from that conversation had been slightly skewed by my own faulty perspective. Ruby *was* attracted to Alex – but he was supplying her with drugs. That's what she had meant when she asked how she was going to cope when he left.

'Knowing that Ruby had lied to me made me think again,' Pearl went on, 'about everything. I remembered how Sarah had told us she had been at Evensong on the night Vinnie had died. She'd mentioned this at the dinner party – how the congregation had sung "For Those In Peril On the Sea" – but Leo immediately closed down all conversation on the subject. He was the only person who didn't want to discuss what had happened, and I realised that if he had been at home the night Vinnie died, then he certainly would have had the opportunity – but what about a motive? Sarah had told me how fiercely he protected his investments. "It's what motivates him", she said. I then began to wonder what greater investment could there be for a father than his own son.'

Pearl paused for breath. 'Knowing the earring belonged to Tizzy placed her on Vinnie's boat. Once I had confirmation from you that she had lied about her stepfather's death, I had to ask myself why she would have done so. For attention? No. It had to be something more. I wasn't to find out until she told me herself on the beach.'

'She could have been lying.'

'But I don't think she was. She made the mistake of thinking that drugs could help her to escape her past. Rather like Ruby. I sensed there was a connection between Tizzy and Alex that night in the Neptune when Ruby had reacted so strongly. Then I remembered that the Bertholds' holiday in Belgium and Holland had been at Easter, the same time as Tizzy had gone with Charlie to visit the Groeninge Museum there. Suddenly I had all the ingredients: it was just a case of putting everything together in the right way.'

'Clues,' corrected McGuire.

'Ingredients,' smiled Pearl. She felt herself staring for a little too long into McGuire's eyes and checked her watch for a distraction. 'And now I have to go.'

She got up quickly and McGuire followed. 'Where to?'

'A concert at the Dredgerman's Court. My mother will kill me if I'm late.'

As Pearl darted off, McGuire pursued her, edging his way around the shoppers milling at the stalls near Keam's Yard. The town's shops and markets were no longer populated by tourists seeking mementos, but by locals searching for bargains.

'Wait!' he called out. 'You haven't told me yet about Ruby.'

Pearl stopped as she reached a row of food stalls, but she failed to face McGuire.

'She's doing okay now – in fact, she's out tonight with a journalist called Richard Cross.' Pearl's back was still towards McGuire as she asked, 'Did I tell you he was promoted after the exclusive he wrote on the Red Sands development?'

As she turned finally, McGuire saw that she was holding a paper plate in her hand. It contained two Pacific rock oysters. She squeezed a slice of lemon across them and offered them to McGuire, and when he shook his head, she exclaimed: 'Oh come on. This is Whitstable! Don't tell me you still haven't tried them!'

'I'm allergic,' McGuire said suddenly.

'To oysters?'

He saw the shocked look on her face and shrugged. 'Seafood.'

Pearl reflected on this for a moment. Then: 'Are you sure?'

McGuire opened his mouth to explain but she interrupted: 'What I mean is, seafood allergies tend to fall within groups.'

'Pearl . . .'

'No, hear me out. Lots of people are allergic to only one kind of seafood.' McGuire was frowning but Pearl pressed on. 'Some react to crustaceans, like lobster and crab, but are fine with oysters and molluscs.' She looked into his eyes. 'Have you ever actually . . . tried an oyster?'

McGuire was no longer looking down at the paper plate; instead his eyes were now locking with Pearl's. He took the plate from her and set it down on the stall. 'Maybe I'll just hold out until there's an r in the month.'

Pearl gave a slow smile. 'For a native?' As she stared up at him, she noted his suntanned features, thinking that perhaps she and McGuire might be from the same tribe, after all. McGuire caught sight of the silver locket lying beneath the neckline of her blouse. As a gambling man he knew it was short odds that the locket contained a photograph of Charlie, but right now he wouldn't mind betting that there was room for someone else in Pearl's locket – and her heart.

McGuire leaned slowly forward, hesitating before kissing Pearl's cheek, but he was so close to her lips he could feel her soft sweet breath against his own. It was a kiss goodbye, but as they broke apart, something in Pearl's smile made McGuire feel, for the very first time in a very long while, that his luck might finally be changing.

'Was that McGuire?' asked Charlie as Pearl hurried to join him at the entrance to Dredgerman's Court. The detective was now heading down steps from the beach into Keam's Yard car park and Charlie saw that his mother was staring after him. 'Didn't you want to invite him?' he asked.

Pearl shook her head. Looking back at her son, she took his arm and held it close, aware that some families are torn apart by painful events while others grow stronger. Although the events of the summer would never be forgotten, she hoped that they would fade. Like a scar growing over an old wound, time would allow her family to be healed. And like grit in an oyster, perhaps even a pearl might result.

Together, mother and son turned towards the incongruous sound of Dolly's flamenco heels tapping on the wooden floorboards of the Dredgerman's Court, and Pearl smiled as she gave her answer.

'Next time.'

Acknowledgements

I would like to thank my husband, Kas, for urging me on to write The Whitstable Pearl Mystery, and my whole family for their love and continued encouragement.

I also sincerely thank my talented agents, Michelle Kass and Alex Holley, for their unstinting support and Mark Salisbury, Police Chief Superintendent (Retired), for his invaluable help regarding police procedure – which not only informed but inspired me.

Last, but by no means least, I will remain forever grateful to Krystyna Green of Constable & Robinson for bringing the Whitstable Pearl Mystery series to its readers.